### *Raja Rao*

Some of the best of Raja Rao's works ... a tribute to the writer and his quest for "modern" India.
— *The Pioneer*

The best tribute to one of the India's best writers in English ... Makarand Paranjape must be complimented for making this remarkable selection, the reading of which will expose the reader to the world of the author ... A must for any student of Indian English writing, and an admirer of Raja Rao.
— *The Hindu*

An acute case of Indian amnesia might be cured through Katha's endeavours to reclaim a lost legacy.
— *The Sunday Times of India*

A good initiation for readers and scholars concerned with a search for meaning in life.
— *The Asian Age*

A Katha Classic endeavour, a sincere and well-researched compilation ... A laudable effort.
— *The Statesman*

# OUR RECENT RELEASES

## Short Fiction

Katha Prize Stories 10
　　Ed. Geeta Dharmarajan
　　& Nandita Aggarwal
Hauntings: Bangla Ghost Stories
　　Edited and Translated by
　　Suchitra Samanta
Forsaking Paradise: Stories from
Ladakh, Edited and Translated by
　　Ravina Aggarwal
Ayoni and Other Stories
　　Edited and Translated by
　　Alladi Uma & M Sridhar
Home and Away
　　By Ramachandra Sharma
　　Translated by Padma and
　　Ramachandra Sharma
Vyasa and Vighneshwara
　　By Anand
　　Translated by Saji Mathew
Joginder Paul: Sleepwalkers
　　Translated by Sunil Trivedi and
　　Sukrita Paul Kumar

## ALT (Approaches to Literatures in Translation)

Ismat: Her Life, Her Times
　　Eds. Sukrita Paul Kumar &
　　Sadique
Translating Partition: Stories, Essays,
Criticism
　　Eds. Ravikant & Tarun K Saint
Vijay Tendulkar

## Trailblazers

Paul Zacharia: Two Novellas
　　Translated by Gita Krishnankutty
Ashokamitran: Water
　　Translated by Lakshmi Holmström
Bhupen Khakhar: Selected Works
　　Translated by Ganesh Devy,
　　Naushil Mehta and Bina Srinivasan

Indira Goswami: Pages Stained with
　　Blood, Translated by Pradip Acharya

## Katha Novels

Singarevva and the Palace
　　By Chandrasekhar Kambar
　　Translated by Laxmi
　　Chandrashekar
Padmavati
　　by A Madhaviah
　　Translated by Meenakshi
　　Tyagarajan

## YuvaKatha

Lukose's Church
Night of the Third Crescent
Bhiku's Diary
The Verdict
The Dragonfly
The Bell

## BalKatha

The Carpenter's Apperentice
The Nose Doctor
Grinny the Green Dinosaur
Battling Boats

## FORTHCOMING

Pudumaippittan: Fictions
　　Edited and Translated by
　　Lakshmi Holmström
Ai Ladki
　　By Krishna Sōbti
　　Translated by Shivnath
Daar se Bichchudi
　　By Krishna Sobti
　　Translated by Smita Bharti
Surajmukhi Andhere Ke
　　By Krishna Sobti
　　Translated by Pamela Manasi

# THE BEST OF
# RAJA RAO

**Selected and Edited by
Makarand Paranjape**

Katha Classics

## KATHA

First published by Katha in 1998

Copyright © Katha, 1998

Copyright © for the original stories
held by the author except
"Companions," "Indian — A Fable" and
"The Policeman and the Rose"
which are with OUP.

Copyright © for the Introduction
rests with Katha

KATHA
A3, Sarvodaya Enclave
Sri Aurobindo Marg, New Delhi 110 017
Phone: (91-11) 4141 6600, 4141 6610
Fax: (91-11) 2651 4373

E-mail: marketing@katha.org

Website: http://www.katha.org

KATHA is a registered nonprofit organization
devoted to enhancing the joy of reading.
KATHA VILASAM is its story research and resource centre.

Series Editor: Geeta Dharmarajan
In-house Editors: Chandana Dutta, Shernaz Cama
Original Cover Design: Taposhi Ghoshal
Illustrations: Vandana Bist

Cover Design: Geeta Dharmarajan
Cover Photograph: Mahesh Bhat
Courtesy: Art Today

Typeset in 10 on 13pt Baskerville by Suresh Sharma at Katha

Katha regularly plants trees to replace the wood used in the making of its books.

ISBN 978-81-85586-81-6

First Reprint 2016

Raja Rao, 1908 –

Mother
Gauramma.
Raja Rao
was four
years old
when she
passed
away.

Father
Prof H V
Krishnaswami,
and stepmother
Jayalakshmi,
with Raja Rao,
1918.

Raja Rao with a friend, visiting a 13th century monastery. Soissons, Northern France, 1963.

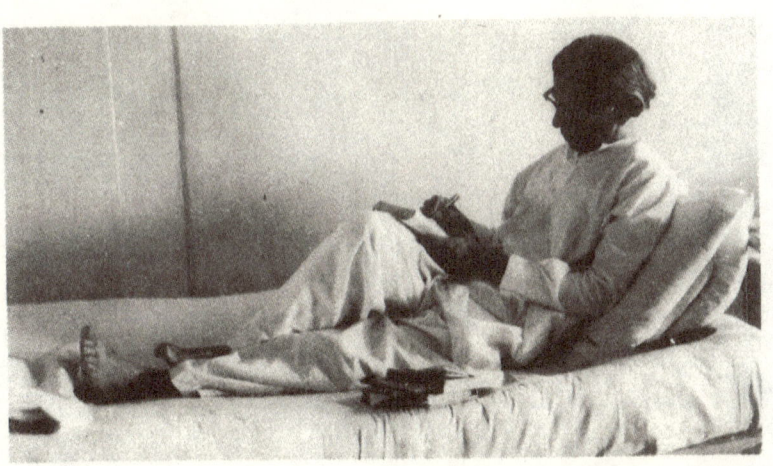

In bed writing, Bangalore, 1977.

The Pearl
Street Garage
Apartment
where Rao
lived from
1966 to 1986.

Raja Rao with his wife Susan, at home in Austin, 1998.

*Hoping this book,
when read would
be like a dip
in the waters of
Benares.
with deep
affection*

*11.5.55.*  *Raja Rao*

---

This facsimile is an inscription by Raja Rao on the editor's copy of *On the Ganga Ghat*.

# Contents

At the University of Oklahoma,
4 June, 1988.

PHOTOS: COURTESY GL JAIN, THIS PG;
BARRY SMITH, OPP. PG.

Teaching Vedanta and Buddhism, University of Texas at Austin, 1970s.

# Preface

He sits there, looking frail, sharp-eyed and, "Challenge me!" he says looking me straight in the eye, "Yes, challenge me."

I hear the heuristic question of Raja Rao, the writer, the philosopher, the teacher, Susan's husband, the weaver of tales that are difficult to read sometimes but which are destined to live with you for a long, long time. His challenge comes as a voice from within, asking me to discover a question for myself, something deep down inside me that can lead to a true understanding of where I come from.

I stare down at the heavy blue glass of lime juice in my hand. The glass looks handcrafted and beautiful in every detail, though it would be difficult to put into a few words what exactly is so attractive about it. It is the wholeness of the glass that pleases. For a minute I wonder if I should attempt a statement like this in response to his question, for, for me the glass speaks the way the stories of Raja Rao do.

The silence grows.

"I am a man of silence," said Raja Rao in his acceptance speech when the Neustadt Prize was awarded to him in 1988. And now, I see he is not afraid of letting it grow. "... the effort of the writer, if he is sincere, is to forget himself in the process and go back to the light from which words come. Go back where? That is, those who read or those who hear must reach back to their own light."

I feebly reach out to the feeble light inside me, dare to speak and find myself in a deep discussion with the frail man who sits there in his living room in Pearl Street, Austin, Texas, his hospitable home for many years now, wrapped in woollens, nursing a large mug of tea that Susan has made for him in the small, unselfconsciously homely kitchen of theirs. He asks me to come again and again we talk, me less fumbling than before. I find the quintessential teacher in Raja Rao, one who through his silence was able to invoke a guru-sishya samvadha – a teacher student dialogue.

Raja Rao may look frail but there is nothing but strength in his words, anchored as they are in the many years of thinking and teaching Vedanta and the many ways of understanding Indian philosophy. Memory of my meetings with Raja Rao have left an indelible mark on me. Perhaps all teachers must be people of silence, I think, if they are to be good, unafraid of the silence of the classroom, until knowledge is recreated – exciting, vigorous, self-defining.

I come back to his stories with more eagerness. They are by no means easy stories, but they wake the reader up to a critical culture that finally must free one from the one that the mass media narcotizes us into. He demands to be read with attention, to be understood, to reach the point of communion with the writer so the word disappears and all that remains is the meaning, the sudden light in the reader's own mind as connections form, shaped by her own experience and present knowledge.

We are extremely happy to present this Raja Rao reader in the Katha Classics series. I believe he is the first Indian writer who used English with comfort, and there have been many learnings for Katha from his handling of the language, when we have attempted the complex craft of translation and editing translations. He is the intrepid trailblazer who, long before writers like Salman Rushdie and Arundhati Roy, created an English idiom for India, but in many ways far excels them in the depth of his understanding of the Indian mind and its predicaments. Great wordsmiths like Masti, Basheer, Mauni and Raja Rao train their keen scrutiny on the everydayness of our lives, thus helping us to see for ourselves as we are.

The Katha Classics are a special series that aim to showcase the best of our writers of fiction. The first three volumes of this series have been received well, with Basheer going into reprint! For this book I take pleasure in thanking Prof Raja Rao and his wife Susan for their friendship and spontaneous kindness, Dr Nagarajan, Janaki and Bharat with whom I stayed in Austin, revelling in their warm care. I thank our editor, Makarand Paranjape, who has given of his best to the making of this book. And, Vandana Bist for the evocative illustrations she has done, Chandana Dutta who has been in charge of the in-house editing process, Suresh and Ganeshan who have always printed our books so very well. I take this opportunity to once again thank all the people at Katha for their unstinting team spirit and their eye for excellence that makes Katha what it is today.

We are happy to present this book to you on Raja Rao's 90th birthday, 8 November. We wish him health and happiness; and you, friend of katha, many hours of satisfying and meaningful reading.

November, 1998                                                    Geeta Dharmarajan

# Introduction

Even at the risk of undermining my own modest endeavour in compiling this book, I wonder if it is a little premature to publish this Katha Classic on Raja Rao. To express such a doubt about a writer who will be ninety this year requires, to say the least, some explanation. The fact is that not only is Raja Rao still a very active writer, but more significantly, much of his major work still remains unpublished. The quantum and the value of this unpublished work is so staggering that it would be rather unfair to consider this selection to be representative of his total output.

Yet I am also reasonably certain that much of this vast body of unpublished material will take several years, if not decades to be published. In the meanwhile, we have a fairly extensive published corpus of writings to deal with and to choose from. There is moreover a pressing need to offer to the interested reader a one-volume anthology of Rao's work. What I have therefore tried to do here is to include a selection from all of Rao's major published works upto 1997, which consist of five novels, three collections of short stories and one collection of nonfictional prose. A few words about the basis of this selection would be in order. I chose what I considered to be important passages from each text. These passages usually contain a major event or incident; help us understand one of the chief characters in the book; are significant for reasons of style or technique; or, finally, explicate some key philosophical or thematic issues. These criteria apply largely to excerpts from novels. For the shorter works complete texts have been used. The effort has been to include pieces which represent or illustrate an important element in Raja Rao's fiction. For instance, "India – A Fable" is written in a symbolical or allegorical style. It posits a larger cosmic or spiritual order without which ordinary, mundane existence cannot be properly understood. I could offer further explanations for this selection, but the bottom line is that it made enjoyable reading and I found it most rewarding. I believe, it offers a fairly good sample of Rao's work. I hope it also represents the totality of his vision, not as a part represents the whole, but as a microcosm corresponds to the macrocosm.

Raja Rao is generally regarded as one of the most important Indian English novelists. The reasons for his pre-eminence are both historical and artistic. Historically, he is important because his first novel, *Kanthapura*, was published during the decade of the 1930s when Indian English fiction first began to gain recognition. Although Bankim Chandra Chatterjee's incomplete romance *Rajmohan's Wife* (1864) is considered to be the first Indian English novel, it was only in the 1930s that this genre began to demonstrate the maturity and accomplishment of a major literary mode. This coming of age was heralded by the publication of Mulk Raj Anand's *Untouchable* (1935), R K Narayan's *Swamy and Friends* (1935), and Rao's *Kanthapura* (1938).

Artistically, Rao is important because of his unique formal and thematic accomplishments. Although his five novels seem modest in comparison to Anand's or Narayan's more prolific output, Rao's achievement is probably more impressive. Anand and Narayan are both highly regarded as novelists, but I would argue that not a single one of their works makes the kind of claims to great art as does Rao's *The Serpent and the Rope* or *The Chessmaster and His Moves*. Rao aficionados would even go so far as to assert that there is a certain mediocrity of vision in Narayan which, however deliberate or delightful does not save his Malgudi tales from being a trifle uninspired and pedestrian. Likewise, Anand too despite his wider range of themes and subjects, remains, according to Rao admirers, a rather obvious writer. Neither of these two, moreover, has a single passage in their works whose stylistic and poetic depth or dexterity can compare with the best of Rao's writing. Formally and stylistically, he is the most adventurous of the three. As M K Naik elaborates in his monograph *Raja Rao* (1972), Rao has consistently tried to modify the Western form of the novel to suit his Indian subject matter. In fact, it would not be incorrect to say that he reinvents and Indianizes the novel as no one else does. He accomplishes this feat by using traditional Indian genres such as the Purana, the sthalakatha and the beast fable to structure his works. Furthermore, they are written in an English that is uniquely Indian in style, tone, mood and rhythm. The Indianness of style is achieved by relying heavily on translation, quotation, and the use of Indian proverbs, idioms and colloquial patterns. Rao adroitly manipulates vocabulary and syntax to enhance the Indian flavouring of his English. The result is a style which although distinctly Indian is evocative

> *Rao is one of the most innovative novelists now writing. Departing boldly from the European tradition of the novel, he has indigenized it in the process of assimilating material from the Indian literary tradition.*
> – R Parthasarathy

and perfectly intelligible to Western readers as well. This language is unique to Rao, a highly refined medium of expression which suggests truths beyond those normally available in our everyday speech. To put it somewhat dramatically, Rao has restored sacredness to the Word.

Thematically, too, Rao is somewhat different from Anand and Narayan. Rao is a metaphysical novelist whose concerns are primarily religious and philosophical. *Kanthapura,* for example, shows a strong Gandhian influence as it documents the progress of a nonviolent agitation against the British in a remote south Indian village. *The Serpent and the Rope* and *The Cat and Shakespeare* are expositions of the ancient Indian philosophical outlook, Vedanta. *Comrade Kirillov* is an evaluation of the efficacy of Communism. *The Chessmaster and His Moves,* the first novel in a trilogy, in fact surpasses all his earlier work in its sweep. It is nothing less than an examination into the entirety of the modern human condition. Its highlight is an intense and revelatory dialogue between the Brahmin and the Jew, not only as individuals, but as representatives of two ancient and contrasting civilizational perspectives. Even his short fiction and nonfictional prose is imbued with this spirit of inquiry into the meaning of things. It is both playful and serious at the same time, creating, not merely discussing, philosophy. Thus in Rao's works there is an ongoing discussion of major systems of thought, chiefly of India but also of the West.

Both stylistically and thematically then Rao succeeds in capturing the spirit of India in his works. His innovations with form and style have expanded the expressive range of English and have influenced other writers who share his predicament: the task of writing about a culture in a language that is not native to it. Although Rao's oeuvre seems limited, his reputation is secure. Indeed, despite the appearance of dozens of talented new writers in the last few decades, it would be safe to assert that there is no one else who has even attempted to do what Rao has accomplished: to portray and justify the wisdom of traditional India to the modern world. No one, moreover, has even approached, let alone reached, his heights of spiritual illumination. The aesthetic delight that obtains in his works is as rare as it is authentic. All told, C D Narasimhaiah's claim that Raja Rao is the greatest Indian English novelist is as true today as when it was first made, twenty five years ago.

Rao was awarded the Sahitya Akademi Prize in 1964. In 1969, he received the Padma Bhushan from the Indian Government. He also won the prestigious Neustadt Prize in 1988. He has been invited to lecture by several institutions in India, France and the United States, and has travelled extensively, both in India and abroad.

A brief overview of Rao's life and career will help us to appreciate his work better. Rao's first efforts as a writer were in Kannada, his mother tongue. Between 1931 and 1933, he published three essays and a poem in Kannada in a journal called *Jaya Karnataka*. Around that time, he began to publish his first stories in English. These and other stories were collected and published as *The Cow of the Barricades and Other Stories* in 1947. A later collection, *The Policeman and the Rose* (1978), includes seven stories published in the earlier volume and three new ones written chiefly during the 1960s. In addition to novels and short stories, Rao has published essays, travelogues and biographical sketches in various journals and popular magazines: some of these have been collected in *The Meaning of India* (1997). The unfinished works include the two remaining parts of *The Chessmaster* trilogy and a novel. A biography of Mahatma Gandhi by Rao has been published recently. Rao has also edited three books: the first two, anthologies of essays, are *Changing India* (1939) and *Whither India?* (1948), coedited with Iqbal Singh; the third is *Soviet Russia: Some Random Sketches and Impressions* (1949) by Jawaharlal Nehru.

R aja Rao was born in an ancient and respected Brahmin family in Hassan, Karnataka, on 8 November, 1908. The eldest son in a family of two brothers and seven sisters, he was the centre of the family, always treated as if he was destined for great things. His father taught Kannada at Nizam's College in the neighbouring Hyderabad State. When he was only four, his mother died. This was one of the most important events in his life; indeed, the absence of the mother and the sense of being an orphan recur in his fiction. Perhaps, the earliest influence on Raja Rao was his grandfather, with whom he stayed both in Hassan and in Harihalli, while his father was in Hyderabad. Rao seems to have imbued a spiritual orientation from his grandfather; this preoccupation has stayed with Rao throughout his life and is evident in all his work.

Rao joined his father in Hyderabad, going there to attend high school. He studied at the Madarsa-i-Aliya, then the most famous school in the state, where the aristocracy of Hyderabad sent their children and was perhaps, the only Hindu boy in his class. He was then sent to the Aligarh Muslim

University in North India. These Aligarh days proved to be crucial in shaping Rao's intellectual growth. Under the influence of Eric Dickinson, a minor poet and a visiting Professor from Oxford, Rao's literary sensibility was awakened. He met other students such as Ahmed Ali, who became a famous novelist, and Chetan Anand, who became an influential film producer. Rao also began learning French at Aligarh, which contributed to his decision to go to France a few years later. After matriculating in 1927, he returned to Hyderabad to enroll as a student for the BA at Nizam's College. Two years later, he graduated, having majored in English and History.

In 1929, two other important events occurred in Rao's life. First, he won the Asiatic Scholarship of the Government of Hyderabad for study abroad. This marked the beginning of another phase in his life. He left India for the first time in his life to study at the University of Montpellier in France. Secondly, in that same year, Rao married Camille Mouly who taught French at Montpellier. Camille was undoubtedly the most important influence on Rao's life during the next ten years. She not only encouraged him to write, but supported him financially for several years. In 1931, his early Kannada writing began to appear in the journal *Jaya Karnataka*. For the next two years, Rao researched the influence of India on Irish literature at the Sorbonne. His first short stories were published in journals such as *Asia* (New York) and *Cahiers du Sud* (Paris). In 1933, Rao abandoned research to devote himself completely to writing.

Although Rao lived abroad, he never ceased to be an Indian in temperament and sensibility. In fact, his awareness of Indian culture grew even though he could not settle down permanently in India. He became a compulsive visitor, returning to India again and again for spiritual and cultural nourishment; indeed, in a sense, Rao never completely left India. In 1933, he visited Pandit Taranath's ashram in his quest for self-realization. In 1938, his masterpiece, *Kanthapura*, although written earlier, was published from London. One year later Rao's marriage disintegrated; he found himself back in India, his spiritual search renewed. He even appeared to give up writing to seek the truth. In the next few years, Rao visited a number of ashrams and religious teachers, notably Ramana Maharshi of Tiruvannamalai, Narayana Maharaj of Kedgaon and Mahatma Gandhi at Sevagram. Around this time, Rao also became a public figure in India, active in several social and political causes. He edited with Iqbal Singh,

*Changing India* (1939), an anthology of modern Indian thought from Rammohan Roy to Nehru. He participated in the underground Quit India movement of 1942, boldly associating with a group of radical socialists. In 1943-44, he coedited with Ahmed Ali a journal from Bombay called *Tomorrow*. He was the prime mover in the formation of a cultural organization, Sri Vidya Samiti, devoted to reviving the values of ancient Indian civilization; this organization failed shortly after inception. In Bombay, he was also associated with Chetana, a cultural society for the propagation of Indian culture and values. Finally, in 1943, Rao's quest appears to have been fulfilled when he met his spiritual preceptor in Atmananda Guru of Trivandrum. Rao's life altered radically after this. He even thought of settling down in Trivandrum, near his Guru's ashram, but returned to France after his Guru's demise.

In 1960, twenty two years after *Kanthapura*, Rao's *The Serpent and the Rope* was published. *The Cat and Shakespeare* followed in 1965. About ten years later, *Comrade Kirillov* was published in English. Its French version, *Le Comrade Kirillov* had appeared in 1965. From 1965 until his retirement, Rao was Professor of Philosophy at the University of Texas at Austin. In that same year, 1965, he married Katherine Jones, an American stage actress. They have one son, Christopher Rama. Teaching one semester a year, Rao divided his time between the United States, France and India. Rao retired from the University of Texas in 1980. In 1986, after his divorce from Katherine, Rao married Susan. Today, at the age of ninety, he is still working hard on his unfinished works. He says he has to complete the last ten pages of a new novel he wrote in 1993 and is reported to have begun a new novel last year. He dreams of writing his last novel in Kannada.

An understanding of Raja Rao's art is enhanced by contextualizing his novels. Although Rao admits to several Western influences, his work is best understood as a part of the Indian tradition. Rao regards literature as sadhana or spiritual discipline; for him, writing is a consequence of his metaphysical life. His novels, hence, essentially represent a quest for the Absolute. From *Kanthapura* to *The Chessmaster*, Rao's protagonists grapple with the same concerns: "What is Truth? How is one to find it?" Their methods vary, as do their results, but they share the same preoccupations. The novels thus become chronicles of this archetypal search. Formally, too, all these novels share certain features. Plot is de-emphasized; the narrative, generally subjective, is not linear, but circular, in the puranic manner of storytelling which Rao adapts to the form of the Western novel. There are digressions, stories within stories, songs, philosophical disquisitions, debates and essays. Characters, too, are frequently symbolic figures; often, the motivations for their actions might seem puzzling or insufficient. Finally, because the narration is subjective, the language of the narrator, too, tends to be unique, reflecting his or her social, regional and philosophical make-up and peculiarities.

Rao's first novel, *Kanthapura*, is the story of how a small, sleepy, south Indian village is caught in the whirlpool of the Indian freedom struggle and comes to be completely destroyed. In the *Foreword*, Rao himself indicates that the novel is a kind of sthalapurana or legendary history which every village in India seems to have. These local sthalapuranas are modelled on the ancient Indian Puranas – those compendia of story, fable, myth, religion, philosophy and politics – among which are the Upapuranas or minor Puranas, which describe holy places and the legends associated with them. The detailed description of the village at the opening of the novel is written in the manner of a sthalapurana, wherein the divine origin or association of a place is established. The village is presided over by Goddess Kenchamma, the Gramadevata and the novel provides a legend explaining her presence there, recalling several similar legends found in the Puranas. Like the "place-Gods" of the Puranas, Kenchamma operates within her jurisdiction, where she is responsible for rains, harvests and the well-being of the villagers and is their protector against famine, cholera and cattle-diseases. Thus, her concerns are local and she cannot extend her protection to other villages or to outsiders. Like Kenchamma, the river Himavathy, too, has a special significance in the novel and recalls passages describing famous rivers in the Puranas, such as the description of the river Narmada in the Matsyapurana and Agnipurana.

> *On the whole Rao's life and writing have evolved in the direction of increasing openness: from the archetypal village of Kanthapura to Paris, London, America; from village realism to a Joycean polyphony of language, languages and mythologies.*
> – Ivar Ivask

*Kanthapura* also shares certain narrative techniques with the Puranas. The story is told rapidly, all in one breath, by a village grandmother and the style reflects the oral heritage also evident in the Harikatha. Like these expositions, which are digressive and episodic, *Kanthapura* contains digressions such as Pariah Siddiah's exposition on serpent lore. The Puranas contain detailed, poetic descriptions of nature; similarly, this novel has several descriptive passages which are so evocative and unified as to be prose-poems in themselves. Examples are the coming of Karthik, daybreak over the Ghats and the advent of the rains. Finally, the narration of *Kanthapura* has a simplicity and lack of self-consciousness reminiscent of the Puranas and quite different from the narrative sophistication of contemporary Western novelists such as Virginia Woolf or James Joyce.

*Kanthapura* is also imbued with a religious spirit akin to that of the Puranas. An important idea that runs through it is that of incarnation; as the Gita says, whenever there is a decline in Dharma, the Lord incarnates to restore the balance. The doctrine of incarnation is central to the Puranas, too, most of which are descriptive accounts of the avatars of Vishnu. The avatar in this novel is Gandhi, whose shadow looms over the whole book, although he is himself not a character. Incarnation, however, is not restricted to one great soul, Gandhi, but extends into Kanthapura itself, where Moorthy, who leads the revolt, is the local manifestation of Gandhi, and by implication of Truth.

Although the form of *Kanthapura* is closely modelled on that of the sthalapurana, its style is uniquely experimental. Rao's effort is to capture the flavour and nuance of south Indian rural dialogue in English. He succeeds in this by a variety of stylistic devices. The story is told by Achakka, an old Brahmin widow, a garrulous, gossipy storyteller. The sentences are long, frequently running into paragraphs. Such long sentences consist of several short sentences joined by conjunctions (usually "and") and commas; the effect is of breathless, rapid talking. The sentence structure is manipulated for syntactic and rhythmic effect, as in the first sentence of the novel: "Our village – I don't think you have ever heard about it – Kanthapura is its name, and it is in the province of Kara." Repetition is another favourite device used to enhance the colloquial flavour of the narrative. In addition to these techniques, translation from Kannada is repeatedly used. Nicknames such as Waterfall Venkamma, Nose-scratching Nanjamma, Cornerhouse Moorthy, are translated; more important, Kannada idioms and expressions are rendered into English: You are a traitor to your salt-givers; The Don't-touch-the-Government Campaign; Nobody will believe such a crow-and-sparrow story; and so on. The total effect is the transmutation into English of the entire ethos of another culture. *Kanthapura* with its Kannadized English anticipates the lofty Sankritized style of *The Serpent and the Rope* which, stylistically, is Rao's highest achievement.

*Kanthapura* is really a novel about a village rather than about a single individual; nevertheless, Moorthy, the Brahmin protagonist of the villagers' struggle against the government, is a prototypal Rao hero. Moorthy is the leader of a political uprising, but for him as for Gandhi whom he follows, politics provide a way of life indistinguishable from a spiritual quest. In fact, for Moorthy, Action is the way to the Absolute. In Gandhi, he finds what is Right Action. Thus, for him, becoming a "Gandhi man" is a deep spiritual experience which is appropriately characterized by the narrator as a "conversion." At the culmination of this "conversion" is Sankaracharya's ecstatic chant "Shivoham, Shivoham. I am Shiva. I am Shiva. Shiva am I," meaning that Moorthy experiences blissful union with the Absolute. Indeed, the chant, which epitomizes the ancient Indian philosophical school of Advaita or unqualified nondualism, is found in all Rao's novels as a symbol of the protagonist's spiritual goal. Moorthy, the man of action, thus practises Karma Yoga (the Path of Action), one of the ways of reaching the Absolute as enunciated in the Bhagavad Gita. In the novels after *Kanthapura*, Rao's protagonists, like Moorthy, continue to seek the Absolute, although their methods change.

Raja Rao's stories were first collected in the book *The Cow of the Barricades and Other Stories* (1947). Later, these and three others were published in *The Policeman and the Rose* (1978). Rao is thus not a very prolific writer of short stories. Most of these stories, moreover, can be divided into two groups. The first were written chiefly in the 1930s and reflect his interest in social and political problems. "Javni" and "Akkayya" are good examples. Both comment not only on the caste system and on the position of women in Indian society, but also show the heroism, courage, wisdom and loyalty of its common folk. The second set of stories use a great deal of symbolism and are essentially metaphysical in their orientation. A good example is "India – A Fable." Here, Pierre, the European child, is at first fascinated by the camel of the desert but later switches his loyalty to the majestic elephant of India. The suggestion is that India offers nonduality, which is preferable to the monotheism of semitic religions. There are, of course, other interpretations available as well. "The Policeman and the Rose" is the story of a beautiful woman who cannot find release until she meets the Guru in the form of the Policeman. It is, as its subtitle "A True Story" suggests, a deeply personal tale, narrated in an elliptical, allegorical manner. "Companions" included here is a powerful allegory about Hindu-Muslim unity. It is one of the least discussed or appreciated of Rao's stories. In it Rao suggests that when Islam gets Indianized, its spiritual force manifests itself; in this story this is illustrated in the transformation of an ordinary snake charmer into a Sufi with healing powers, all because of the advice of his serpent who is the reincarnation of a fallen brahmin.

Published twenty two years after *Kanthapura*, *The Serpent and the Rope* is Rao's most appreciated work. If the former is modelled on an Upapurana, the latter is a kind of Mahapurana or epic: geographically, historically, philosophically and formally, its sweep is truly epical. The novel includes a variety of settings, ranging from metropolitan Paris to Ramaswamy's ancestral home in a south Indian village, from European locales such as Aix, Montpalais, Pau, Montpellier, Provence, Cambridge and London to Indian locales such as Hyderabad, Delhi, Lucknow, Bombay, Bangalore and Benares. Even historically, its sweep is staggering. Rao delves into almost the whole of Indian history, from the invasion of the Aryans to the advent of British rule; also exploring European history, chiefly the Albigensian heresy, and Chinese history. These – and many other topics – all come under discussion as the protagonist, Rama, a historian by training, expounds his theories in conversations with the leading characters. Philosophically, too, the novel's range is formidable. Rao discusses Hinduism, Buddhism, Catholicism, Islam, Taoism, Marxism, Darwinism and Nazism.

If its content is so varied, it is not surprising to find *The Serpent and the Rope* extremely diverse in form as well. Rao quotes from an array of languages, including Sanskrit, Hindi, French, Italian, Latin and Provencal; but only the Sanskrit quotations are translated. There are long interludes and stories, such as Grandmother Lakshamma's story of a princess who becomes a pumpkin and Ishwara Bhatta's "Story of Rama." In addition, the novel contains songs, myths, legends and philosophical discussions in the manner of the Puranas. The main narrative, the gradual disintegration of Rama's marriage with his French wife, Madeleine, is thus only a single strand holding a voluminous and diverse book together.

*The Serpent and the Rope* is an extremely challenging work thematically as well. Savithri's words in the novel sum it up well: it is "a sacred text, a cryptogram, with different meanings at different hierarchies of awareness."

It may be seen at two different levels, the literal and the symbolic, although the two usually operate simultaneously. On the literal level of plot, the novel may appear puzzling and unsatisfying. The crux is: why does the marriage of Rama and Madeleine disintegrate? Critics have attempted various answers, ranging from incompatibility between the Indian Rama and the French Madeleine, to Rama's infidelity. Although such answers are plausible, they do not completely satisfy because these reasons are not perceived by the characters themselves. Rama and Madeleine are both aware of the growing rift between them, but they do not attempt to bridge it on a practical level. Instead, both watch the dissolution of the union with an almost fatalistic helplessness. Similarly, it is difficult to understand why Rama seeks fulfilment in other women while averring his love for Madeleine, or why he never tells her of his affairs in spite of his claim of keeping no secrets from her. Rama, the narrator, does not answer such questions; he only chronicles the breakdown of the relationship, almost impersonally, as if there were little he could do to save it. He does not even think himself responsible for having affairs with other women, one of which involves a ritual second marriage, while still being married to Madeleine. What is lacking, then, is an adequate motivation for the actions of the characters, something that most readers are conditioned to expect from the novel. Perhaps, a better approach, instead of asking of the novel something that it did not intend to give, would be to consider what it does clearly provide; indeed, questions which appear unresolved on the literal level are resolved more satisfactorily on the symbolic level.

Rama, the Brahmin hero, is a seeker of Truth both by birth and by vocation (a Brahmin, says Rao, is one who seeks Brahman, or the Absolute). As an Indian scholar in France, Rama is seeking Truth in the form of the missing link in the puzzle of India's influence on the West. According to Rama, this missing link is the Albigensian heresy; he thinks that the Cathars were driven to heresy by the influence of Buddhism which had left India. Rama's quest for Truth is also manifested in his search for the ideal Woman because in the Hindu tradition the union of man and wife is symbolic of the union of man and God. The marriage of Shiva and Parvathi is one such paradigmatic union in which Shiva, the Absolute, the abstract, the ascetic, is wedded to Parvathi, the human, the concrete, the possessor of the Earth. Another such union is that between the mythical Savithri and her husband, Satyavan; Savithri restores her dead husband to life through her devotion.

In keeping with these paradigms, Rama – the thinker, the meditator, the seeker of Truth – can only find fulfilment in a Parvathi or a Savithri who can bring him back to Earth by her devotion. Madeleine, however, has given up her Catholicism for Buddhism and become an ascetic, renouncing the Earth, denying her body through abstinence and penance. Significantly, her union with Rama is not fruitful. The first child, Pierre, dies when he is about seven months old; the second dies soon after birth. Madeleine also regards Truth as something outside herself, something that has to be striven for in order to be realized. Her dualism is the philosophical opposite of Rama's nondualism. Rama believes, following the Advaita Vedanta, that the self is identical to Truth as the wave is a part of the sea, and that all separateness is illusion, like the illusion in which a rope is mistaken for a serpent. Rama's true mate is an Indian undergraduate at Cambridge named, interestingly, Savithri. Savithri, despite her modishness – she dances to jazz music, smokes, wears Western clothes, and so on – is essentially an Indian. Unlike Madeleine, Savithri does not seek Truth, but instinctively and unselfconsciously is Truth. Her union with Rama is thus a natural and fulfilling one. Savithri, however, like Rama's sister, Saroja, opts for an arranged marriage in the traditional Indian manner with someone else; hence, her relationship with Rama is never consummated. At the end of the book, Rama, divorced from Madeleine, sees a vision of his Guru in Travancore and plans to leave France for India.

Rama's path to Truth, unlike Moorthy's Karma Yoga is Jnana Yoga (the Path of Knowledge) also enunciated in the Bhagavad Gita. Rama is not a man of action but an intellectual. Although he has accumulated knowledge, he still does not apprehend Truth clearly; like the deluded seeker in the fable, he mistakes the rope for the serpent, failing to see himself, unlike Savithri, as already united with Truth. Traditionally, a Guru is necessary for the Jnana Yogi because only a Guru can cure his delusion by showing him that what appears to be a serpent is really a rope. Thus, in the end, Rama resolves to seek his Guru to be cured of his delusion.

*The Cat and Shakespeare*, Rao's next novel, which he described as "a metaphysical comedy," clearly shows a strong Upanishadic influence in its form. The spiritual experiences of its narrator, Ramakrishna Pai, are reminiscent of the illuminative passages in the Chandogya Upanishad, which describe the experience of the Infinite. The dialogues in the novel are also Upanishadic in their question-and-answer patterns; the best example being the conversation between Govindan Nair and Lakshmi in the brothel. Nair's metaphysical speculations, such as "Is there seeing first or the object first," seem to be modelled on philosophical queries in the Upanishads. Though the cat links the novel to the Indian beast fable, and Nair's comic roguery shows similarities to the rogue fable in the Panchatantra, the story really illustrates the marjara nyaya of Vedanta, not the practical and crafty animals of the Panchatantra. The major Western debt is to William Shakespeare, who is acknowledged in the title. Shakespeare is a symbol of the universal; according to Rao, Shakespeare's vision transcends duality and arrives at a unified view of the world. There are numerous allusions to Hamlet in the novel, culminating in the "rat-trap episode," in which a cat is trapped in a large rat-trap; this prompts Nair to deliver a parody of Hamlet which begins, "A kitten sans cat, that is the question."

*The Cat and Shakespeare* is Rao's sequel to *The Serpent and the Rope* in that it shows what happens after a seeker's veil of illusion has been removed by the Guru. Its theme may be summed up in Hamlet's words to Horatio toward the end of the play: "There is a divinity that shapes our ends/ Rough-hew them how we will." A similar view of grace is embodied in the novel in what Nair, the man who is united to Truth, calls "the way of the Cat." The "way of the Cat," simply, is the notion that just as the kitten is carried by the scruff of its neck by the mother cat, man is completely at the mercy of the Divine; consequently, the only way to live is to surrender oneself totally to divine grace, as the helpless kitten surrenders itself to the mother cat. Nair lives this philosophy and is responsible for teaching it to his ignorant neighbour, the narrator Pai. Pai is like the innocent hunter in the story who unknowingly heaped leaves on a Shivalingam and was rewarded with a vision.

Between Pai's house and Nair's is a wall over which Nair leaps every time he visits Pai. The wall is an important symbol because it represents the division between illusion and Truth. Nair crosses it easily, but Pai has never gone across. Towards the end of the novel, following Nair's cat, Pai accidentally crosses the wall. Like the lucky hunter, he too is vouchsafed a divine vision: for the first time, Pai sees the whole universe as a unity. The novel ends with Pai's spiritual as well as material fulfilment, having partially realized his lifelong ambition of owning a three storey house. *The Cat and Shakespeare*, although not as ambitious as *Kanthapura*, is as successful on its own terms. The novel is an elaborate puzzle which the author challenges the reader to solve; a solution is not only possible at all levels, but is completely satisfying as well. The way to the Absolute here is not Karma-Yoga or Jnana Yoga of the two previous novels, but Bhakti Yoga, or the path of devotion.

*Comrade Kirillov*, published in English in 1976, is generally recognized as Rao's least ambitious novel; it is clearly a minor work compared to its three illustrious predecessors. Formally, it is an extended Vyakti-Chitra, or character sketch, a popular genre in Indian regional literature. The main story, narrated by one R, is a mere ninety three pages in large type to which are appended twenty seven pages of the diary of Kirillov's wife, Irene, and a concluding seven pages by the narrator; the effect is of a slight, sketchy novella. Kirillov, alias Padmanabhan Iyer, leaves India for California to propagate Theosophy but, after a period of disillusionment, becomes a Communist. From California he moves to London where, marrying a Czech immigrant, Irene, he settles down to the life of an expatriate intellectual. Like Rao's other protagonists, Kirillov starts as a seeker of Truth, but after becoming a Communist, he is increasingly revealed by the narrator to be caught in a system which curtails his access to Truth. Thus, Kirillov continuously rationalizes the major events in the world to suit his perspective. Nevertheless, following a visit to India several years after he has left, he realizes that his Communism is only a thin upper layer in an essentially Indian psyche. Irene also recognizes in her diary that he is almost biologically an Indian Brahmin and only intellectually a Marxist. By the end of the book, Kirillov is shown to be a man of contradictions: attacking and worshipping Gandhi simultaneously, deeply loving traditional India but campaigning for a Communist revolution, reciting Sanskrit shlokas but professing Communism.

The narrator is Kirillov's intellectual opposite, an adherent of Advaita Vedanta. There are numerous interesting discussions on Communism in the book, which add to its value as a social document, capturing the life of Indian expatriate intellectuals between 1920 and 1950. Also of interest is Kirillov's relationship with Irene which recalls Rama's relationship with Madeleine. Numerous similarities aside, this relationship is more successful; this marriage lasts and the couple have a son, Kamal. Soon after Kirillov's return from India, however, Irene dies in childbirth, followed by her newly born daughter. Kirillov leaves for Moscow and is last heard of in Peking. The novel ends with the narrator taking Kamal, now in India, to

Kanyakumari. Despite its humour, pathos and realism, *Comrade Kirillov* falls short of Rao's three previous novels.

There has been a great deal of speculation about the identity of Kirillov. Critics have wondered if the character is based on V K Krishna Menon or M N Roy. I myself have argued that rather than these two possibilities Kirillov might have been inspired by Virendranath Chattopadhyaya, Sarojini Naidu's younger brother, who wrote a thesis on India and imperialism which was presented at the Third Congress of the Communist International. When I asked Rao himself, he said the original was a Maratha Brahmin from Tanjore who later became the Indian Ambassador to some Communist countries. Before independence, he had worked for the Soviets in Europe and married a European woman. Like Kirillov, he had written an anti-Gandhian tract. Apart from its sources, the other important thing about this neglected novel is its prophetic quality in that it predicts the downfall of Communism.

It is interesting to note that *Comrade Kirillov*, first published in a French translation in 1965, was written earlier. Thematically, it represents the stage of negation before the spiritual fulfilment of *The Cat and Shakespeare*. Kirillov, as a Communist and atheist, has negated the Karma Yoga of *Kanthapura* and the Jnana Yoga of *The Serpent and the Rope* by denying the existence of the Absolute; thus, his quest results in failure. The Bhakti Yoga of *The Cat and Shakespeare*, especially in the character of Nair, is the culmination of the various stages of spiritual realization in the earlier novels. Nair is the first character in Rao's novels who does not merely seek Truth, but has found it and actually practises it.

Raja Rao's widely awaited magnum opus, *The Chessmaster and His Moves,* was finally released in June 1988. The story of its publication is by no means commonplace. The book is a part of a trilogy which is over 1500 pages long. Written over a period of three years between 1980 and 1983, the manuscript had been ready at least five years before its actual publication. More than one major American publisher had shown interest in the manuscript but considered the book too long. Viking suggested a reduction to a third of its present size of 735 pages. And what is even more amazing is that the manuscript being shown around was merely the first part of a projected trilogy! Rao refused to omit a single page of his book. Subsequently, Vision Books of Delhi, in whose earlier imprints, Hind Pocket Books and Orient Paperbacks, nearly every major contemporary Indian author had been published either in original English or in English translation, accepted the book as it was. The publisher took over three years to finally publish the book. As it happened, when the proofs of the book were ready, Rao suddenly became one of the contenders for the prestigious Neustadt Prize awarded by the University of Oklahoma. The photocopies of the proofs were circulated among members of the jury. Raja Rao did win the prize, which was awarded to him on 4 June, 1988. And shortly thereafter, the book was formally released in India.

The Chessmaster appeared twenty eight years after Rao's last major book, *The Serpent and the Rope*. The appearance of *The Chessmaster* was certainly a major literary event in the world of Indian English literature. Much anticipation had been built up by the long years of silence and the award of the Neustadt Prize had added to the excitement of those waiting for the book's release. To say the least, everybody expected something big – at last, the great Indian English novel!

> *Rao's greatest achievement, which I suspect only he can surpass, is the degree to which his works, especially* The Chessmaster, *contain the insights, emblems, mantras, metaphors and other carriers of meaning and instruction that enable the individual to achieve, through his own meditations, a better understanding of self through Knowledge and Truth.*
>
> –Edwin Thumboo

Though I would not go to the extent of saying *The Chessmaster* has polarized the Indian English critical community into those who admire Rao and those who detest him, I would argue that *The Chessmaster*, by being such an extreme example of a Raja Rao text, has highlighted certain problems for its readers as never before. Though these problems have been present in his earlier works, even faithful Raja Rao fans do not seem to have wanted him to go so far. Rao seems to have delivered an impossible sort of book, a novel that is really an anti-novel, a novel to end all novels, a book that not only challenges, but actually resists reading in the normal sense of the word. In short, a book that makes impossible demands on its readers, strains their patience, and almost forces them to reject it.

In *The Chessmaster*, we have a particular version of Advaita that has, as I see it, the following major sources. One is the philosophical practice of Sri Ramana Maharshi and the other is the sunyavada of the Buddhist philosopher, Nagarjuna. Allied to the former is, of course, the philosophy of Rao's Guru, Sri Atmananda, while Nagarjuna's thought, obviously, is derived from the Buddha. In *The Chessmaster*, it is not the realization of the self that is sought as in the earlier works, but a dissolution of self. While Moorthy through right action illustrates Karma Yoga, Rama, Jnana Yoga or the path of knowledge, and Govindan Nair, a type of Bhakti Yoga, a complete self-surrender to the Divine, Sivarama Sastri represents the power of negative dialectics, the attempt not to achieve something, but to vaporize one's self into nothing. Here, the familiar dichotomies between the male and the female, vowels and consonants, India and the west, the Brahmin and the Kshatriya, the sage and the saint, logic and devotion, truth and the world, all hinge on the opposition between zero and infinity. The Judeo-Christian tradition is shown to represent the quest for perfect society here on earth, while India is seen as denying the validity of the world itself. The way out, for Rao, is not to improve things as the saint-soldier does, but to dissolve contradictions completely. For him, all numbers dissolve into zero as they emerge out of it. The Infinite is merely cumulative, while zero is total negation that cuts the root of illusion. One can never become perfect in time, but attain perfection only by negating time.

For Rao, the world belongs to the woman and man is merely the instrument for its dissolution – Shiva the destroyer, who alone can undo the generative power of Prakriti. The woman finds release by complete self-surrender to the man, who really represents dissolution. This only Jayalakshmi can understand; Suzanne and Mireille, on the other hand, want to continue their separate existences. The only meaningful dialogue, for Rao, is between the Brahmin (zero, dissolution, negation) and the Rabbi (infinity, completion, affirmation). The former is vertical, denying time; the latter is horizontal, finding fulfilment through time. It is such a framework that provides the skeleton of the plot of the novel. The first part, "The Turk and the Tiger Hunt," shows the incompatibility of Siva and Suzanne like that of Rama and Madeleine in the earlier novel; the second part is dominated by Siva's affair with Mireille; and the third with the dialogue with Michel, the Jewish holocaust survivor. The steadfastness of the Siva-Jayalakshmi relationship and the impossibility of its consummation, and Siva's relationship with his stepsister, Uma, and her inability to bear a child – these two relationships provide the glue that keeps the novel together. Moreover, there are the usual digressions, stories within stories, letters, diary extracts and long speculative internal monologues that characterize Rao's narrative technique.

A certain degree of novelty is offered in two or three characters whose role is minimal, but who are very important – Abd'l Krim, the exiled Algerian leader, and Ratilal, the French-Jain diamond merchant. Rao had said in an interview that the book is a tribute and acknowledgement of the great suffering of the Jews on behalf of humankind; this is elaborated at length in the story of Michel. But the suffering of Michel does not make the world any more real for Siva. His solution to the world's problems still lies in self-extinction – not suicide, but an undoing of the self.

To end this section, let me try to place *The Chessmaster* in the larger scheme of Rao's oeuvre by reducing each novel to a formula and then looking for an equation that puts these formulae together into a meaningful relationship. I see *The Serpent and the Rope* as a text which illustrates the ultimate incapacity of the intellect to resolve the human problem; Rama's relationships fail to take him to the Absolute just as all his philosophical disquisitions, however impressive they seem to others, fail to secure for himself the spiritual success that he so badly seeks. In the end, he acknowledges that only a Guru can save him. This Guru is like the irrepressible Govindan Nair of *The Cat and Shakespeare* who shows Ramakrishna Pai the way of the kitten – complete self-surrender or prapatti. This is thus an affirmative book, a book which ends in success. *The Chessmaster* is neither an admission of defeat nor an affirmation of success; here we don't see either the failure or success of Advaita. It is an ambiguous book in which neither zero nor infinity wins. It accommodates not just the Brahmin and the Rabbi, but the Jain and the revolutionary – though the violent ways of the latter are viewed unfavourably through Gandhian eyes. *The Chessmaster* moves beyond these positions to a kind of indeterminacy. Siva, Rao's spokesman, is no longer always right. Nor does he pretend to be in full control of his metaphysical project. There is always the more powerful presence of the Chessmaster behind the movements of the characters in the book. Of course, any notion of a personalized Chessmaster or prime mover is just another version of the God that Siva, the rationalist mathematician, would deny as the quintessence of the horizontal. But this is one of the apparent contradictions of the book, which will only be resolved in the second volume of the trilogy, after Siva encounters the Guru.

A good way to approach this book is through *The Serpent and the Rope*, almost as a rewriting of it. It is in the earlier novel that we can see the most convenient entry point to the central dialectic of *The Chessmaster*. Rama tells Savithri:

> Zero makes all numbers, so zero begins everything. All numbers are possible when they are in and of zero. Similarly all philosophies are possible in and around Vedanta. But you can no more improve on Vedanta than improve on zero. The zero, you see, the sunya, is impersonal; whereas one, two, three and so on are all dualistic.

*The Chessmaster* picks up this opposition, between zero and infinity, the impersonal and the personal, the monistic and the dualistic:

> Either you accept the world, and build a human empire, accepting death and, therefore, the pyramids (whether you called it a mausoleum for Mao or for Tutankhamen), or you transcend the world and as such death itself, and find the Truth of Sankara's "Shivoham, Shivoham."

Or as Siva puts it cryptically in his dialogue with Michel: "The quarrel of man is between zero and infinity, between Truth – and God." But what is important to realize is that the philosophical positions in *The Chessmaster* are more clearly defined and more neatly expressed. Thus, not only are the thematic preoccupations similar, they are carried out by similar characters in both novels. Not just the central characters, but incidents, events, discussions and locations, and even the quotations are common to both books. The resemblances are more than a sense of deja vu. Hence, those who have read and enjoyed *The Serpent and the Rope* will find easier access to *The Chessmaster*; they will also have an added dimension of recognition as they read the latter text.

It is almost as if *The Chessmaster* were written by an elder brother of Ramaswamy, the protagonist of *The Serpent and the Rope*, or an older Raja Rao, revisiting the terrain of the earlier novel. This movement is seen in the shift from the early fascination with the philosophy of history to the fulfilling discovery of an Indian way of doing mathematics. This discovery of a unified Indian method is crucial. From such a perspective, *The Chessmaster's* resemblance to *The Serpent and the Rope* does not pose a problem at all but illustrates a rather audacious example of intertextuality.

The second introductory tool which helps to unravel *The Chessmaster* has to do with Rao's method of reasoning. Except for a hint in a review of the book by Girija Kumar, other readers have not been able to figure out whether or not there is a system to Sivarama Sastri's philosophical disquisitions. Is his erudition simply impressionistic badinage or does he work from some logical principles? Often, readers seem to be baffled by the numerous discussions in the book which seem vaporous, incoherent and directionless.

Some clues to Siva's method of reasoning and philosophizing are provided by the text. Siva is shown to be a mathematician in the book, but he hardly does any mathematics. True, there are references to Poincare, Pascal, Einstein, and above all to Ramanujan and his goddess Namakkal, and a sprinkling of mathematical terminology throughout the book, but the fact is that Siva spends most of his time discussing philosophy with lovers, friends and acquaintances. Rao would imply that he is a mathematician not because he does mathematics, but because he uses a mathematical method to do philosophy. Siva explains his method somewhat like this:

> The fact is, like in any mathematical equation, you make a series of statements, and you reduce one to the other, till you get one clear class. As I was telling Michel ... the only equation that now remains and remains to be solved, is the hindu-hebraic one, the vertical or the horizontal, I repeat, the zero or the infinity, historylessness or Krishna or Moses.

This method is found in its early stage in *The Serpent and the Rope* where Rama, the historian, spends most of his time in the same kind of discussions.

As Savithri says of him : "History for him is a vast algebra, and he draws in unknowns from everywhere to explain it." Or as Rama says to himself: "And thus I tried to formulate myself to myself. I like these equations about myself or others, or about ideas: I feed on them."

Similarly, Siva tries to find the equation or formula of ideas:

> in mathematics when you have a certain method to the solution of a problem ... you apply the same method to all sets of problems in the same series. Similarly, when you understand one fundamental principle in Indian philosophy, you apply the same method of interpretation to every other problem in the same system, the same series. And I treat all Indian mythology as a set of equations, and I apply my technique to it, and the results are astounding.

Or to put it more pithily, this is Siva's "new doctrine of mathematics or philosophy" – "words are numbers and numbers words ..."

I would, therefore, characterize Siva's method as a kind of reduction. The Latin root of reduce is reducere, "to lead back" – re (back) + ducere (to lead), whose past participle is ductus (a leading, conducting), which gives us the modern word, "duct," hence "conduce" and "conduct." Among the meanings of "reduce," these apply to Rao's method: "to put into a simpler or more concentrated form"; "to bring into a certain order"; "systematize"; and "to break up into constituent elements by analysis" (*Webster's New World Dictionary*). Rao rightly calls his method "a doctrine" because we realize, when we read his books, that his method is far from "scientific" or "logical." This logic is all his own kind; everything must have "instantaneous meaning"; that is why Swanston, the Cambridge leftist intellectual, tells Rama, "There are too many incomprehensible factors in your statement, sir" (*The Serpent and the Rope*). Rao's method of reduction is, therefore, more poetic than philosophical in the traditional sense of the word. The knowledge that this method produces, is not knowledge in the strict sense of the term; it is more like a totalized realization. It is by employing this type of personalized, intuitional reduction that Siva comes to the conclusion that India represents the quest for zero, the vertical, the ahistorical and the abhuman, while the Judeo-Christian, Chinese, and Communist civilizations represent the quest for the infinite, the horizontal, the historical, the human. Moreover, it is by this system that each character comes to represent some sort of abstraction, a formula, and relationships become equations – to be solved and resolved.

Mulk Raj Anand once said to me about Raja Rao, "It's not enough to go on and on about Atman and Brahman, about the reality of Brahman and the illusion of the world; it won't do to cling blindly to Sankara's Advaita of the ninth century. Our problems are different. How do we solve them? Can Sankara's answers serve us today?" These were challenging questions for an admirer of Rao to answer, so I kept quiet. But on reading *The Chessmaster*, I think I have found at least one way of answering them. Rao does not deny the world or its suffering, brutality and violence. His book is imbued with the very real problem of dukkha, the cosmic sorrow that Buddha sought to eliminate from the world. Rao's book does turn a blind eye to history and its record of cruelty, to Birkenau and Buchenwald. He does not neglect politics, economics or history. But to challenges that the human being faces anywhere – whether in Paris, London or Calcutta – Rao's answers point inward, from the exterior to the interior, from the outside to the inside, from the world to the self. Each one of us, he seems to say, must perform this little operation on ourselves – to dissolve ourselves into the nothing from which the whole world was created. To put an end to ourselves and thus to solve, once and for all, the problem of humanity. Deny yourself to become That. To me it is not only this philosophy or its viability that are important, but the enormous energy and artistic integrity with which it is mediated through seven hundred pages of *The Chessmaster and His Moves*. It would be unfair to accuse this philosophy of being unreal because the characters are real, their suffering is real, their concern with the human problem is real.

After *The Chessmaster*, Rao published an extraordinary little book, *On the Ganga Ghat* (1989). It is a collection of eleven stories, all of which are set in Benares. In a note to the reader, Rao says, "These stories are so structured that the whole book should be read as one single novel." Once again, we see how he pushes the form of the novel in a new direction. Indeed, the question arises, how do these seemingly different stories make one novel? After all, each story not only seems complete in itself, with its characters confined to its own boundaries, not spilling out into the others. There is no common protagonist, no obvious connecting action or theme. If so, then what unites them? To me the real protagonist of these stories appears to be their setting, Benares.

This ancient, timeless city, emerges as the true hero of the narrative. But

> *Raja Rao is much more than an apologist for India who also loves and understands the best in Europe; he is a universal writer who brings the water of the Ganga to heal the ills of the modern world.*
> – Kathleen Raine

what does Benares stand for? Why is Rao obsessed with it, both as a real location and as a symbol? It figures, in one way or another, in nearly every novel of his. Benares seems to stand for nonduality, for that principle which overcomes death. Death, of course, is a constant presence in this holiest of holy cities. But unlike elsewhere, death here is not just welcome, but auspicious – a release, a liberation, moksha. In fact, what dies in Benares is death itself. That is why it is so important in Rao's scheme of things. It is Benares, as a sort of miniaturized India, that stands for the Truth of this world. It can unveil the mystery of human life and misery by showing the way to transcendence through the dissolution of the ego.

Each of the stories in this delightful book touches on this theme. Together, they portray an entire society with all its stratas and castes and how each of these, in its own unique way, seeks the same thing – liberation, salvation, transcendence. In fact, what we see is not only a rich and diverse picture of society, but, in a sense, of the cosmos itself, both human and animal, and extending further, the animate and the inanimate – everything seeking the same Truth or emancipation.

Rao's latest book is *The Meaning of India* (1997). It is a collection of previously published pieces brought together in one volume. A common theme runs through the book: "India is not a country – desa, it is a perspective – darsana." And what darsana does India embody? As I hinted earlier, it is the Absolute that India stands for according to Rao. That is why, even if there were no India in the physical, material sense, India as an idea would always exist. For Rao, India alone among all the nations of the world stands for the vertical, the nondual Absolute, the timeless; the rest of the world seeks its perfection through time, moving towards an ever-receding Infinity at the projected end of the horizontal axis. But how do we go from the horizontal to the vertical? The only way is through sacrifice. The ego, the limited or false self, must be offered just as the Boddhisattva leapt into the fire as a wise hare in the Jataka story that Rao recounts. And it is Agni, the sheer, vertical bridge between the dual and the nondual which connects the phenomenal to the noumenal.

It is not as if this whole book is nothing but abstruse metaphysics. There are engrossing accounts of Rao's meetings with Jawaharlal Nehru, Andre Malraux, Mahatma Gandhi, and E M Forster. There are also a couple of stories which have appeared earlier in *The Policeman and the Rose*, as there is the famous *Foreword to Kanthapura*, and the Neustadt Prize acceptance speech. All told, this is a wonderfully engaging and stimulating book, which has reminded us that the idea of India is certainly as important as, if not more than, its physical reality.

It has often been alleged that such attitudes to India are symptomatic of the NRI syndrome of "India seen from afar." Rao is also accused of Brahminical arrogance. Both charges, to some extent, are true. Rao has lived abroad for the greater part of his life. Yet, he has continued to live in the greater India of the imagination which he espouses so ardently. Likewise,

Rao has also subscribed to the Brahminical notion of writing as a sadhana or spiritual practice. Thus, as a writer, he has brought to bear upon himself the most exacting standards of dedication and devotion. He has rarely worked for a living nor does his writing in any way attempt to cater to market trends. As he said to me, "The Guru is very kind. He takes care of all my needs. I don't have to worry about anything except my chosen vocation, which is writing." Indeed, Rao has lived a most frugal and austere life, often subsisting on the bare minimum. Rumours that he is rich and lives luxuriously are utterly unfounded. On the contrary his is a hand to mouth existence, but one which is not only full of dignity but also replete with great inner riches.

Let me end this Introduction with an essentializing question: "What is Rao's ideological project?" In other words, what is it that he is trying to do in his novels? If he is a philosophical novelist, what is he trying to philosophize? The answers to such questions can be by no means simple or single. But I would like to propose a way of tackling such questions. Raja Rao's novels can be read as attempts to validate and mediate for the contemporary world a philosophical outlook that might loosely be termed Advaita. The implications of this statement itself are numerous and not unproblematic. Advaita or nondualism is a particular school of thought which acquired a sort of primacy in Indian philosophical inquiry. Rao's use of tradition is certainly more eclectic. But at least in *The Chessmaster*, he aligns his protagonist on the side of a kind of monism. The two key terms in my statement, "Advaita" and "contemporary world" seem to be contradictory. The moot question is whether Advaita can serve a useful function in today's world? Can it, for instance, solve the very real problems of colonialism and underdevelopment? It is not as if Rao is unaware of these issues. It is obvious that to say that the phenomenal world is an illusion and the Self alone is real – after Sankara – is not quite sufficient. Advaita has to be applied and reinterpreted in the light of contemporary experience. Its efficacy and, if I may say so, its superiority has to be logically established. Moreover, we need to derive from it some sort of revolutionary praxis. In other words, can Advaita be used to resist violence and oppression? Can it help us solve not just our metaphysical, but our physical and social problems?

To show that Advaita can do all this is perhaps Rao's ambition. His project is to show the viability of a world view which has been more or less eclipsed even from contemporary India. The only way that Rao can make this philosophy viable is via a sort of modified existentialism. Advaita penetrates to the core of the flux that is the daily life of his characters, Ramaswamy of *The Serpent and the Rope* and Sivarama Sastri of *The Chessmaster*. These characters negotiate life in an advaitic fashion, thus demonstrating its efficacy in the contemporary world. This is somewhat like negating life even while one is living it, denying the ultimate reality of oneself even as one lives and suffers. Though this may seem paradoxical or unsatisfactory, it is perfectly logical. Rao's, or for that matter anyone else's Advaita, does not preclude any action in the world. If Rao's characters seem to withdraw from such action, occupying themselves with their inner quests, that is their choice. What these characters do, of course, reflects the author's changing concerns. But because the characters withdraw, the philosophy that they propound cannot be faulted. The world can be negated even as we participate in it, just as it can be negated when we withdraw from it.

Ultimately, however, Raja Rao is an artist, not a philosopher. It is as an artist that he has to be judged and understood. And as such he has been true to his calling. In terms of language, style and theme, he has been perfectly consistent, fulfilling the promise he made in his *Foreword to Kanthapura*. It is this consistency, this integrity of purpose, this concern with the Ultimate Reality, coupled with stylistic innovation and an inspired use of language, that makes him one of the most significant and interesting writers of the world.

If I may, I would like to end on a personal note. There is no Indian English novelist whom I love and admire more than Raja Rao. My bond, with him is much more than that of a mere reader. Though it would be foolish of me to claim to be his sahridaya, yet I must confess that I feel very close to the spirit of his work. I have tried to read it as a sadhak, not merely as a professional reader: how else can one even attempt to do justice to someone for whom writing is, above all, a sadhana, an act of worship or consecration, a spiritual, not a mundane exercise?

Raja Rao has given me much more than I can publicly acknowledge. Suffice it to say that it was only after meeting him again and again that I could understand the responsibility of belonging to a parampara, both as a writer and as a critic. My tradition – all that I have received by way of my inheritance as an Indian – is much, much greater than anything that I can possibly achieve. So, any question of repaying my debt to it does not arise.

All that one can do is to transmit, as faithfully and as anonymously as possible, its rich inspiration to the next generation. That is why I can never repay what I owe to Raja Rao, but I can certainly endeavour to earn the privilege of belonging to the same parampara of writing that he does.

November, 1998                                        Makarand Paranjape

---

Note: Portions of this Introduction have been taken from my previously published essay, "Raja Rao" (1983) and "*The Chessmaster and His Moves* - A Review of Reviews and an Introduction" (1992).

The quotations in the boxes are from the Autumn 1988 special issue of *World Literature Today* on Raja Rao.

# Acknowledgements

I must acknowledge the help of several friends in making this book possible. First of all, Geeta Dharmarajan, the indefatigable Executive Director of Katha, who initiated this project and steered it to its completion with tact and determination.

Then, the tireless editors at Katha, Chandana and Shernaz, whose work on the manuscript was invaluable. They not only checked and rechecked the text with the originals, but also provided valuable inputs. In fact, so thoroughgoing were their efforts that we detected several errors and discrepancies even in the "original" printed texts of Raja Rao from which we extracted these excerpts. I am proud and grateful to have worked with such publishing professionals. My students, Anshuman Roy and Sumit Sharma, who helped compose the text, also deserve thanks. I also wish to thank several friends of Raja Rao, especially the two Drs Srinivasan, whose ongoing interest helped me keep up my spirits.

Above all, my sincere and profound thanks to Raja Rao and Susan. Without their encouragement and blessings, I would have faltered at every step. Their belief in me has rescued this book from many a dire difficulty. I, very respectfully, place the finished product at their feet as an offering to them, and through them, to the great Guru, who guides our destinies as the supreme Chessmaster.

This book is dedicated to Raja Rao and Susan with loving pranaams.

November, 1998                                        Makarand Paranjape

Foreword to Kanthapura

There is no village in India, however mean, that has not a rich sthalapurana, or legendary history, of its own. Some god or godlike hero has passed by this village – Rama might have rested under this pipal-tree, Sita might have dried her clothes, after her bath, on this yellow stone, or the Mahatma himself, on one of his many pilgrimages through the country, might have slept in this hut, the low one, by the village gate. In this way the past mingles with the present, and the gods mingle with men to make the repertory of your grandmother always bright. One such story from the contemporary annals of my village I have tried to tell.

The telling has not been easy. One has to convey in a language that is not one's own the spirit that is one's own. One has to convey the various shades and omissions of a certain thought-movement that looks maltreated in an alien language. I use the word "alien," yet English is not really an alien language to us. English is the language of our intellectual make-up – like Sanskrit or Persian was before – but not of our emotional make-up. We are all instinctively bilingual, many of us writing in our own language

First published in *Kanthapura* (1938).

and in English. We cannot write like the English. We should not. We cannot write only as Indians. We have grown to look at the large world as part of us. Our method of expression therefore has to be a dialect which will some day prove to be as distinctive and colourful as the Irish or the American. Time alone will justify it.

After language the next problem is that of style. The tempo of Indian life must be infused into our English expression, even as the tempo of American or Irish life has gone into the making of theirs. We, in India, think quickly, we talk quickly, and when we move we move quickly. There must be something in the sun of India that makes us rush and tumble and run on. And our paths are paths interminable. The Mahabharata has 214,778 verses and the Ramayana 48,000. The Puranas are endless and innumerable. We have neither punctuation nor the treacherous "ats" and "ons" to bother us – we tell one interminable tale. Episode follows episode, and when our thoughts stop our breath stops, and we move on to another thought. This was and still is the ordinary style of our storytelling. I have tried to follow it myself in this story.

It may have been told of an evening, when as the dusk falls, and through the sudden quiet, lights leap up in house after house, and stretching her bedding on the verandah, a grandmother might have told you, newcomer, the sad tale of her village.

*Menton (Alpes Maritimes)*
*France*
*November 1937*

# Kanthapura

K arthik has come to Kanthapura, sisters –
    Karthik has come with the glow of lights
and the unpressed footstep of the wandering gods; white lights from clay
trays and red lights from copper stands, and diamond lights that glow
from the bowers of entrance leaves; lights that glow from banana trunks
and mango twigs, yellow light behind white leaves, and green light behind
yellow leaves, and white light behind green leaves; and night curls through
the shadowed streets, and hissing over bellied boulders and hurrying
through dallying drains, night curls through the Brahmin Street and the
Pariah Street and the Potter Street and the Weaver Street and flapping
through the mango grove, hangs clawed for one moment to the giant
pipal, and then shooting across the broken fields, dies quietly into the
river – and gods walk by lighted streets, blue gods and quiet gods and

---

This is the tenth chapter of *Kanthapura* (1938).

– "We have neither punctuation nor the treacherous 'ats' and 'ons' to bother us – we tell one
interminable tale." – Raja Rao, *Foreword to Kanthapura*. This volume follows Raja Rao's
punctuation, capitalization and style as closely as possible. A few minor changes and
corrections have been made by the editor with the author's consent.

bright-eyed gods, and even as they walk in transparent flesh the dust gently sinks back to the earth, and many a child in Kanthapura sits late into the night to see the crown of this god and that god and how many a god has chariots with steeds white as foam and queens so bright that the eyes shut themselves in fear lest they be blinded. Karthik is a month of the gods, and as the gods pass by the Potter Street and the Weaver Street, lights are lit to see them pass by. Karthik is a month of lights, sisters, and in Kanthapura when the dusk falls, children rush to the sanctum flame and the kitchen fire, and with broom grass and fuel chips and coconut rind they peel out fire and light clay pots and copper candelabras and glass lamps. Children light them all, so that when darkness hangs drooping down the eaves, gods may be seen passing by, blue gods and quiet gods and bright-eyed gods. And as they pass by, the dust sinks back into the earth, and night curls again through the shadows of the streets. Oh! have you seen the gods, sisters?

Then when the night is on this side of the day, and the Karthik lights have died down, a child wakes up here and begins to cry and a cough is heard there, and in Suryanarayana's house a lantern is seen in the courtyard, and the beat of feet is heard here and the hushed voices of men and women are heard there. Then there is a fuss and a flutter in Rangamma's house, and everyone rubs his eyes and asks, "Sister, who is dying? Sister, who is dying?" and Nanjamma says to her neighbour Ratnamma, "And old Ramakrishnayya? We saw him only yesterday evening at the river, and he looked so hale and healthy," and Postmaster Suryanarayana's wife Satamma says, "No, surely it is the heart trouble of Rangamma," and then comes the roar of Waterfall Venkamma, "Ah, you will eat blood and mud I said, you widow, and here you are!" and Pandit Venkateshia's daughter-in-law Lakshmi takes her lantern and rushes to Venkamma and says, "And what is it, Venkamma?" – "Oh, daughter of the mother-in-law, what is it but that this Pariah-polluter has had royal visits?" – "But what is it, Venkamma, what?" – "Ah, you are a nice one, too, and three legs of a bedstead plus one makes four, does it or does it not, my daughter?" And seeing Timmamma and Satamma she says, "Oh, don't you see the policeman at the steps?" and Timmamma swings the lantern, and beneath the bulging verandah stones is seen the gaunt figure of a policeman, and one by one as the men rise up and gather in the Post-office-house courtyard, the children wake up and rush to the hanging lanterns, broom grass and cattle grass in hand, and our Seenu says, "I'll go," and as he gathers his shawl and goes to Rangamma's door the policeman says he has no permission to let anyone in, and Seetharam comes along and Dore and Ramanna and the elders, and everybody gathers in the courtyard half covered and half awake, while from this lane and that lane rises the thin dust of Karthik lights relit.

And there is noise in this part of Rangamma's house and that, and there comes the regular cry of Rangamma's mother: "Oh, sinners, sinners, to have this in our old age!" and Ramakrishnayya comes and spits across the courtyard and behind him comes Rangamma, a shawl thrown over her shoulders, and then there is seen a light in the front room and Surappa says, "We cannot see anything from here – come let us go up to Sami's," and we all rush up there and standing on the verandah we see what is happening in Moorthy's room. Over against the cracked wall Moorthy is standing, a bright light falling on his tight-lipped face, and the police inspector, a short, round man, is standing beside him, a notebook in his hand. In the middle of the room is a heap of books and charkhas and cotton and folded cloth, and policemen in uniform are turning them this side and that, and trunks are laid open and boxes are slit through, and sometimes there is laughter. The voice of the police inspector is not heard. But now and again we see Moorthy's head nodding – he merely nods and seems to smile at nothing.

The police inspector then turns toward Bade Khan, who is now seen clearly in the lantern light, and shouts, "Bind this man!" and when they are beginning to pull out ropes from their belts, there is noise in the street below, and there comes Range Gowda, Mada and a lantern with him, and when he sees the policemen, he says something to Mada, and Mada goes away, and before the cock has time to crow three times, there is Pariah Rachanna and Madanna and Lingayya and Lingayya's woman, and they all gather at Rangamma's door and cry out, "Hele! Hele! What are you doing with our master?" and the policeman shouts, "He, shut up, you sons of my woman!" – "He, he, do you think we are going to be silent because of your beards and batons ..." – "If you are not silent, you will get

9

Raja Rao

a marriage greeting today!" – and Rachanna says, "Ah, I've seen your
elders, you son of my concubine, and I shall see ..." – And at this the
policeman grows so wild that he waves his lathi and Rachanna comes
forward and says, "He, beat me if you have the courage!" and Rangamma
leans out of the verandah darkness into the starlight and says, "He,
Rachanna, this must not be done!" and Rachanna says, "And what is to
be done, mother? They are going to take away our master!" And Range
Gowda says something to Mada and Mada says something to Rachanna
and Rachanna says something in the ear of everyone, and when Moorthy
is seen on the threshold, the bright light of the police lantern falling on his
knit face, Rachanna cries out, "Mahatma Gandhi ki jai!" and the policeman
rushes at them and bangs them with his lathi and Rachanna quavers out
the louder, "Gandhi Mahatma ki jai!" and other policemen come and
bang them too, and the women raise such a clamour and cry that the
crows and bats set up an obsequial wail, and the sparrows join them from
the roofs and eaves and the cattle rise up in the byre and the creaking of
their bones is heard. And then men rush from this street and that street,
and the police inspector seeing this hesitates before coming down, and
Rachanna barks out again, "Mahatma Gandhi ki jai!" And the police
inspector shouts, "Arrest that swine!" and when they come to arrest him,
everybody gets round him and says, "No, we'll not give him up." And the
police inspector orders, "Give them a licking," and from this side and that
there is the bang of the lathi and men shriek and women weep and the
children begin to cry and groan, and more and more men go forward
towards Moorthy, and more policemen beat them, and then Moorthy
says something to the police inspector and the police inspector nods his
head, and Moorthy comes along the verandah and says, "Brothers!" and
there is such a silence that the Karthik lights glow brighter. "Brothers, in
the name of the Mahatma, let there be peace and love and order. As long
as there is a God in heaven and purity in our hearts evil cannot touch us.
We hide nothing. We hurt none. And if these gentlemen want to arrest us,
let them. Give yourself up to them. That is the true spirit of the satyagrahi.
The Mahatma" – here the police inspector drags him back brutally, but
Moorthy continues – "The Mahatma has often gone to prison ..." – and
the police inspector gets so angry at this, that he gives a slap on Moorthy's

10

face, but Moorthy stands firm and says nothing. Then suddenly Rachanna shouts out from below, "Mahatma Gandhi ki jai! Come, brothers, come!" and he rushes up the steps towards Moorthy, and suddenly, in sinister omen, all the Karthik lights seemed quenched, clay pots and candelabras and banana trunks and house after house became dark, and something so sinister kicked our backs that we all rush up behind Rachanna crying, "Mahatma Gandhi ki jai!" and now the police catch Rachanna and the one behind him and the one behind the one who was behind him, and they spit on them and bind them with ropes, while at the other end of the courtyard is seen Rangamma, Bade Khan beside her. Then the police inspector thinks this is the right time to come down, for the lights were all out and the leaders all arrested, and as Moorthy is being dragged down the steps Rachanna's wife and Madanna's wife and Sampanna's wife and Papamma and Sankamma and Veeramma come forward and cry out, "Oh, give us back our men and our master, our men and our master," but the police inspector says, "Give them a shoe-shower," and the policemen kick them in the back and on the head and in the stomach, and while Rachanna's wife is crying, Madanna's wife is squashed against a wall and her breasts squeezed. And Range Gowda, who has stood silent by the tamarind, when he sees this, rushes down and, stick in hand, gives one bang on the head of a policeman, and the policeman sinks down, and there is such a clamour again that the police inspector shouts, "Disperse the crowd!" and he slips round the byre with Moorthy before him, while policemen beat the crowd this side and that side, and groans and moans and cries and coughs and oaths and bangs and kicks are heard, and more shouts of "Mahatma Gandhi ki jai! Mahatma Gandhi ki jai!"

And this time it was from the Brahmin quarter that the shouts came, and policemen rushed toward the Brahmins and beat them, and old Ramanna and Dore came forward and said, "We too are Gandhi's men, beat us as much as you like," and the policemen beat them till they were flat on the ground, mud in their mouths and mist in their eyes, and as the dawn was rising over the Kenchamma hill, faces could be seen, and men became silent and women became sobless, and with ropes round their arms seventeen men were marched through the streets to the Santur police station, by the Karwar Road and round the Skeffington Coffee Estate and down the Tippur valley and up the Santur mound, and as the morning cattle were going out to the fields, and the women were adorning the thresholds for a Karthik morning, Brahmins and Pariahs and Potters and Weavers were marched into the police station – seventeen men of Kanthapura were named and locked behind the bars. And the policemen twisted their arms and beat them on their knuckles, and spat into their mouths, and when they had slapped and banged and kicked, they let them out one by one, one by one they let them out, and they all marched back to Kanthapura, all but Moorthy. Him they put into a morning bus, and with one policeman on the right and one policeman on the left they carried him away to Karwar. We wept and we prayed, and we vowed and we fasted, and maybe the gods would hear our feeble voices. Who would hear us, if not they?

The gods indeed did hear our feeble voices, for this advocate and that advocate came and said, "I shall defend him," vakils and advocates and barristers came and said, "And we shall plead for him," and the students formed a defence committee and raised a huge meeting, and copper and silver flowed into the collection plate, and merchants came and said, "And here we are when money is needed." And when Moorthy heard of all this, he said, "That is not for me. Between Truth and me none shall come," and Advocate Ranganna went and saw him and said, "Moorthy! The Red man's judges, they are not your uncle's grandsons," and Moorthy simply said, "If Truth is one, all men are one before it," and Ranganna said, "Judges are not for Truth, but for law, and the English are not for the brown skin but for the white, and the Government is not with the people but with the police." And Moorthy listened to all this and said, "If that is so, it will have to change. Truth will have to change it. I shall speak that which Truth prompteth, and Truth needeth no defence," and Ranganna spoke this of corruption and that about prejudice, but "Truth, Truth and Truth" was all that Moorthy said, and old Ranganna, who had grown grey with law on his tongue, got so wild that he banged the prison door behind him and muttered to himself, "To the mire with you!"

And then came Sadhu Narayan who had renounced hair and home and was practising meditation on the banks of the Vedavathy, and he said, "Moorthy, you are a brave soul and a holy soul. And there is in you the hunger of God, and may He protect you always. But Ranganna comes and tells me, I cannot change his heart. You are a religious man, go and speak to him, and I came to see you. I have neither hair nor home, and I have come to tell you, *this* is not just. Defend one must against evil, if not, where is renouncement, continence, austerity, and the control of breath?" To which Moorthy says, "You are a holy man, Sadhuji, and I touch your feet in reverence. But if Truth needs a defence, God Himself would need one, for as the Mahatma says, Truth is God, and I want no soul to come between me and Truth." And Sadhu Narayan speaks about the world and its wheels and the clayey corruption of men, but Moorthy always says, "Truth, Truth and Truth," and Sadhu Narayan gets up to go and he says, "May at least my blessings be on you!" and Moorthy falls at his feet and holds them in grateful respect.

And it was only after this that Sankar, our Sankar, who was the secretary of the Karwar Congress committee, comes and says, "Well, Moorthy. if such be your decision, my whole soul is with you. Gandhiji says, a satyagrahi needs no advocates. He is his own advocate. And how many of us did go to prison in 1921 and never touched the shadow of an advocate. I am an advocate, you will say, but you know I am an advocate only for those who cannot defend themselves." And Moorthy says, "Then if you agree with me, brother, there can be nothing on my conscience," and Moorthy's lips tremble and he falls at Sankar's feet, but when Sankar lifts him up, Moorthy says, "No, brother, you are my elder and a householder. I need your blessings." And Sankar says, "If so it is, my blessings are always with you," and Moorthy feels so exalted that he goes to Sankar and embraces him and says, "Brother, you are with me?" And Sankar says, "I am with you, Moorthy," and then they sit for a while holding each other by the hand, and as the warder comes and says, "Now it is time for you to go, sir," Sankar rises up and says, "But I can hold meetings for you, Moorthy?" and Moorthy says, "Of course, brother!"

And Sankar goes straight to Advocate Ranganna and Advocate Ranganna says, "Certainly." Then he sees Khadi-shop Dasappa and Dasappa says, "Oh, most certainly." And then he sees the president of the college union and this one says, "We are wherever you are," and so Sankar sends for his Volunteers and says, "A meeting in the Gandhi maidan

today," and Volunteer after Volunteer goes out to the cloth bazaar and
the fish bazaar and the flower bazaar and the grain bazaar, and as the
noon cools down, there is a huge crowd in the Gandhi maidan, and the
Volunteers are there in khadi kurtha and Gandhi-cap crying out, "Order,
brother, order! Please take your seats, brother, please!" and Sankar goes
up to the platform, and there is a huge ovation and "Mahatma Gandhi ki
jais," and Dasappa comes and there is an ovation again, and Advocate
Ranganna comes and there is an even greater ovation, for everybody
knew he had lately thrown open his private temple to the Pariahs, and
with folded hands people hymn up, "Vande Mataram." Then they all
squat down and Sankar and Ranganna and Dasappa make speeches about
the incorruptible qualities of Moorthy, and they say how the foreign
Government wants to crush all self-respect, and they then speak of charkha
and ahimsa and Hindu-Moslem unity, and somebody cries out, "And
what about the Untouchables?" and Sankar says, "Of course, we are for
them – why, has not the Mahatma adopted an Untouchable?" and
somebody cries out again, "Ah, our religion is going to be desecrated by
you youngsters!" and Sankar says, "Brother, if you have anything to say,
please come up to the platform," and the man says, "And you will allow
me to speak?" and Sankar says, "We have no enemies," and the man is
seen coming from the other end of the maidan, a lean, tall man in durbar
turban and filigree shawl, and he wears gold-cased rudrakshi beads at his
neck, and he goes up the platform and says:

"Brothers, you have all heard the
injurious attacks against the Government
and the police and many other things. I
am a toothless old man and I have seen
many a change pass before me, and may I
say this: All this is very good, but if the
white men shall leave us tomorrow it will
not be Rama-rajya we shall have, but the
rule of the ten-headed Ravana. What did we have, pray, before the British
came – disorder, corruption, and egoism, disorder, corruption, and egoism
I say" – he continued, though there were many shouts and booings against
him – "and the British came and they came to protect us, our bones and

our dharma. I say dharma and I mean it. For hath not the Lord said in the Gita, Whensoever there is ignorance and corruption I come, for I, says Krishna, Am the defender of dharma, and the British came to protect our dharma. And the great Queen Victoria said it when she put the crown of our sacred country on her head and became our beloved sovereign. And when she died – may she have a serene journey through the other worlds! – and when she died – you are too young to know, but ask of your grandfathers how many a camphor was lit before the temple gods, and how many a sacrificial fire was created, and how many a voice did rise up to the heavens in incantation. For not only was she a great queen, a mother-queen, but the most courageous defender of our faith. Tell me, did she not protect it better than any Mohammedan prince had ever done? Now I am an old man. You are all young. Things change. But what I fear for tomorrow is not the disorder in the material world, but the corruption of castes and of the great traditions our ancestors have bequeathed us. When the British rule disappears there will be neither Brahmin nor Pariah, Vaisya nor Sudra – nay, neither Mohammedan nor Christian, and our eternal dharma will be squashed like a louse in a child's hair. My young brothers, let not such confusion of castes anger our manes, and let the religion of Vasistha and Manu, Sankara and Vidyaranya go unmuddied to the Self-created One. Now I have said all I have to say ..."

But before he has stopped somebody says, "So you are a Swami's man?" – and the old man says, "And of course I am, and I have the honour to be." – "And the Swami has just received twelve hundred acres of wet-land from the Government. Do you know that?" says a youngster. – "Of course, and pray what else should he do if he is offered a rajadakshina, a royal gift?" – And the youngster says, "So the Swami is a Government man?" – And the old man says, "The Swami is neither for the Government nor against it, but he is for all who respect the ancient ways of our race, and not for all this Gandhi and Gindhi who cannot pronounce even a gayatri, and who say there is neither caste nor creed and we are all equal to one another, while the Swami ..." – And somebody cries out, "Do you know the Swami has been received by the Governor?" – And Sankar rises up and says, "No interruptions, please!" – And the old man answers, "And of course, but why not? And do not the dharma sastras say the king is the protector of faith? And I cry out Long live George the Fifth, Emperor!" and he hobbled down from the platform.

Then came youngster after youngster and said Moorthy was excommunicated by the Swami, for Moorthy was for Gandhiji and the Untouchables, and the Swami was paid by the British to do their dirty work. "I have grown in the Mutt," says one, "and I have known what they do. The Mutt, brothers, is the best place for retired high court judges, police inspectors, and God-dedicated concubines, and they are not with us, are they?" And Sankar rises up again and says, "Now it is better we talk of other things," but the young man continues, "The whole trouble has been hatched by the Mutt." Then Advocate Ranganna gets up and says, "And I too have been excommunicated, for I have thrown open the temple to the Pariahs," and there is a violent ovation, and Ranganna continues, "And I know one thing too that few know, and it is time I said it in the open," and everybody began to stand up and the Volunteers cried, "Sit down, please, sit down!" And when there is silence again, Ranganna continues: "Not long ago, I received a visit of a man, and he comes to me and says, The Swami would like to see you, and I say, If the Swami likes to see me, I am indeed most honoured! and straight I go the next morning with fruits and flowers, and the Swami receives me with smiles and blessings and he says, I need your help, Ranganna, and I say, Of course, everything is yours, Swamiji, and the Swami says, There is much pollution going on and I want to fight against it, and I say, I am for fighting against all pollution, and the Swami says, For some time there has been too much of this Pariah business. We are Brahmins and not Pariahs. When the Pariahs will have worn out their karma, and will have risen in the waters of purification, nobody will prevent them from becoming Brahmins, even sages, in their next lives. But this Gandhi, who is no doubt a very fine person, is meddling with the dharma sastras, the writ laws of the ancient sages, and I am not for it. He said he would like to see me, and I saw him and told him what I thought of it. But he said we did not interpret the dharma sastras correctly, and of course it was ridiculous to say that, for who should know better, he or I? But one cannot break the legs of the ignorant. Now, what I have to say is simple: we want to fight against this anti-Untouchable campaign, and I may tell you in confidence, the powers that be, well, they are with the guardians of our trusted traditions.

"Swami, I said, how can you accept the help of a foreign Government? Do not the dharma sastras themselves call the foreigners mlechas, Untouchables? and the Swami said, Governments are sent by the divine will and we may not question it, and he added, And I may say the Government has promised to help us morally and materially, and at this I got so angry that I rose to go, but the Swami held me by the two hands and said, Do take your seat! but I said, No, I cannot, I cannot, and it was on that very day I took the vow to open our temple to the Pariahs, and that is why I opened it to them ..." There was a long ovation – "And therefore, brothers, know for sure what religion is wearing behind its saffron robes. Choose between a saint like Mahatma Gandhi who has given up land and lust and honours and comfort and has dedicated his life to the country, and these fattened Brahmins who want to frighten us with their excommunications, once the Government has paid them well."

At this the police inspector comes up and says, "I put you under arrest!" and Advocate Ranganna answers, "Well, on what authority?" and the police inspector shows him a magistrate's order, and Ranganna offers himself up to the police, and there is a huge, hoarse cry, and ovation after ovation rises – "Gandhi Mahatma ki jai!" – "Vande Mataram!" – and processions immediately form themselves, and with Volunteers on either side they march through bazaar and street and lane, and women rush to the verandah, and children follow them still muttering the multiplication tables, and as dusk falls and lights flash from house to house, so shrill rises the cry of "Mahatma Gandhi ki jai!" that by the Imperial Bank buildings police cars are already waiting, and the crowd is violently dispersed.

And when the morning came the papers were full of it, and Rangamma's blue paper brought it all to us, and that is how we knew it all. And then we looked at each other and said, "So that is how it is with Bhatta," and everybody said, "And so it is!" and Rangamma said, "That is why Bade Khan was so often seen with him," and Nanjamma said, "Do you remember, sister, he was nowhere to be seen on that awful night?" and everybody said, "Yes, surely, and fools we were not to have seen it earlier," and we all felt the kernel of our hearts burn, for Bhatta had walked our streets with a copper pot in hand and we had fed him. Only

Ramakrishnayya said, "There is still many a good heart in this world, else the sun would not rise as he does nor the Himavathy flow by the Kenchamma hill," and all looked at the stars and said, "Yea, the stars of the seven sages hang above us," and as a wall-lizard clucked propitiously, we all beat our knuckles upon the floor and named the holy name, and there came with it such peace into our hearts that we walked back home with the light in our souls. And somewhere beyond the Bebbur mound, somewhere beyond the Bebbur mound and the Kenchamma hill, out against the sky that rises over Karwar, out over the river, there seemed to stand, as one might have said, the supple, firm figure of Moorthy, a Gandhi-cap upon his head and a northern shirt flowing down his waist to the knees. And there was something in his eyes that shone and showed that he had grown even more sorrowful and calm.

And week after week passed, and Rangamma's blue paper brought us this news and that news, and Pandit Venkateshia said, "Why should I not make it come?" and he too began to receive it every Saturday evening, and Range Gowda came and said, "Rangamma, Rangamma, I do not know how to read, but my little mosquito goes to school and, if he is worth the milk he has drunk, he will read it out to us," and he too began to get the paper through Postman Subbayya, and evening after evening we gathered on Rangamma's verandah, and when Ramakrishnayya had explained to us a chapter from the Vedanta Sutras, kneading vermicelli or shaping wicks for the festivals, we began to speak about Moorthy, while our men sat at the village gate, rubbing the snuff or chewing the tobacco leaf, and it seems they said many wicked things about the Government.

Then Seenu would sometimes go to Karwar with a Friday cart and come back with a Tuesday-morning cart, and he would tell us about Sankar and Advocate Ranganna and Seetharamu: and Vasudev, too, would sometimes go in a Skeffington Estate lorry, and he would sometimes slip through the evening and tell us about Moorthy and the case, and everybody said, "The Goddess will free him. She will appear before the judges and free him." And Rangamma vowed she would offer a Kanchi sari to Kenchamma if he were released, and Ratna said she would have a thousand-and-eight-flames ceremony performed, and Nanjamma said she would give the Goddess a silver belt, and Pariah Rachanna said he would walk the holy fire, and all said, "The Goddess will never fail us – she will free him from the clutches of the Red man." But Vasudev, who was a city boy, said, "No sister, they will give him a good six months," and we all said, "No, no, never!" and Vasudev said, "Well, think what you will, I know these people," and Rangamma then suddenly said, "Let me go to the city and see cousin Seetharamu; he is an advocate and he can tell me something about it," and Nanjamma said, "I too will come with you, sister, for I have to go to my daughter's confinement, and now or in three weeks is all the same to me," and that is why one Pushya night Kitta put the bulls to the cart, and Rangamma and Nanjamma went down to Karwar to see Moorthy.

And when they had bathed and said their prayers, Rangamma said to Seetharamu, "Seetharamu, who is looking after Moorthy's affair?" and Seetharamu said, "Why, Sankar!" and she said, "Why not go and see him?" and he said, "Of course!" and he put on the turban and the coat and they went straight to Sankar, and when Sankar saw Rangamma he said, "Aunt, it is a long time since I saw you – how are things with you?" and Rangamma answered, "Everything is safe – but I have come to speak about Moorthy," and Sankar said, "I love him like a brother, and I have found no better Gandhist," and Rangamma said, "Why, he is the saint of our village," and Sankar said, "Some day he will do holy deeds," and Rangamma said, "Is there nothing to be done to free him from prison?" and Sankar said, "We have done all we can, but the police say it is he who arranged the assault, the assault of the Pariahs on the police," and Rangamma said, "Shiva! Shiva! Never such a thing would our Moorthy do," and Sankar said, "Of course, of course, aunt," and Rangamma said, "Is there nothing I can do here?" and Sankar said, "Nothing for the moment. But stay and wait for the results," and Rangamma said, "So be it," and that is why she did not come back even for the harvest reapings.

And when she came back for the corn distribution Barber Venkata said, "And mother, what about Moorthappa?" and Pariah Rachanna took his two measures and said, "And mother, what have the Red man's Government said about Moorthappa?" and Boatman Sidda said, "If this Government's people were really sons of their father, they would have asked us to stand and bear witness before them!" and Goldsmith Nanjundia said, "Oh, let them do what they like. Our Moorthy is like gold – the more you heat it the purer it comes from the crucible," and the women said, "Oh, when you strike a cow you will fall into the hell of hells and suffer a million and eight tortures and be born an ass. And if this Government cannot tell the difference between a deer and a panther, well, it will fall into the mouth of the precipice," and Rice-pounding Rajamma, who had an evil tongue, said, "May this Government be destroyed!" and she spat three times. And so, from day to day, people said this against the Government and that against the police, and when our Range Gowda got dismissed from his patelship, they all cried out, "Oh, this is against the ancient laws – a patel is a patel from father to son, from son to grandson, and this Government wants to eat up the food of our ancestors," and everybody, as they passed by the Kenchamma grove, cried out, "Goddess, when the demon came to eat our babes and rape our daughters, you came down to destroy him and protect us, Oh, Goddess, destroy this Government," and when the women went to cut grass for the calves, they made a song, and mowing the grass they sang:

> *Goddess, Goddess, Goddess Kenchamma,*
> *The mother-in-law has wicked eyes,*
> *And the sister-in-law has a hungry stomach,*
> *Betel-nuts never become stone,*
> *And a virgin will never become pregnant,*
> *Red is the earth around the Goddess,*
> *For thou hast slain the Red-demon.*

> *Goddess, Goddess,*
> *The mother-in-law has wicked eyes,*
> *And betel-nuts will never become stone.*

And Kanchi Narasamma, who had a long tongue, added:

> *Lean is the Brahmin-priest, mother,*
> *And fat is he when he becomes Bhatta, mother,*
> *Fat is he when he becomes Bhatta, mother*
> *And he will take the road to Kashi,*
> *For gold has stuck in his stomach,*
> *And he will take the road to Kashi.*

*And the sister-in-law has a hungry stomach,*
*Betel-nuts will never become stone.*

To tell you the truth, Bhatta left us after harvest on a pilgrimage to Kashi. But, don't they say, sister, the sinner may go to the ocean but the water will only touch his knees?

And when Rangamma went back after the corn distributions, she went straight to Sankar instead of staying with cousin Seetharamu, for she had seen much of Sankar and she had liked him and he had liked her, and he had said to her, "When you come to Karwar next, come and stay with me, aunt, and you will help me in my work," and Rangamma had said, "I am poor of mind and of little learning, what can I do for you, Sankaru?" and he had answered, "That does not matter, aunt – what we need is force and fervour, and I am living with my little daughter and my aged mother, and you may perhaps arrange my papers and look after the Congress correspondence," and though Rangamma was the humblest of women, she liked this, and she said, "If the gods choose me, I will not say Nay," and that's why she went to stay with Sankaru. And when Waterfall Venkamma heard of this she said, "Oh! this widow has now begun to live openly with her men," and she spat on the house and said this man had her and that man had her, and she began to say she would go to the courts and have back Rangamma's property, for land and lust and wifely loyalty go badly together, like oil and soap and hot water. But she said, "Let Bhatta come and he will do it for me." But our Rangamma was as tame as a cow and she only said, "One cannot stitch up the mouths of others. So let them say what they like." And as everybody knew, Sankar was an ascetic of a man and had refused marriage after marriage after he had lost his wife, and everybody had said, "This is not right, Sankaru. You are only twenty six and you have just put up the Advocate's signboard, and you will soon begin to earn, and when you have a nine-pillared house you will need a Lakshmi-like goddess to adorn it," but Sankar simply forced a smile and said, "I have had a Lakshmi and I, a sinner, could not even keep her, and she has left me a child and that is enough." But his old father came and said, "But, no, Sankaru, you cannot do that. You are our eldest son, and you have to give us at least a grandson so that when we are dead our manes will be satisfied," but Sankar smiled back again and said, "If you want the marriage thread to be tied in an ocean of tears, I shall. But otherwise I will not. I have a daughter and I will bring her up. And you will come and stay with me and we shall have a household running," and the old mother wept and the old father knit his eyebrows, but Sankar smiled back and said, "I shall obey you," but they did not press him further, and they said, "His wife Usha was such a godlike woman. She would never utter a word loud, and never say Nay to anything. And when she walked the streets, they always say what a holy wife she was and beaming with her wifehood, and never a mother-in-law had a daughter-in-law like her," and they both said, "Well, we can understand Sankaru. When one has lost Usha nothing can replace her." And they never again gave Sankar's horoscope to anyone, and they came to stay with him and look after his sanctum and his child.

And the old father, who was a retired taluk office clerk, knew how to write English, and he said he would address envelopes for Congress meetings, and sometimes he went to join Dasappa, who had opened a khadi shop in the town. And when Dasappa was ill or away on Congress duty, it was old Venkataramayya who looked after the shop, measuring out yard after yard of khadi and saying, "This is from the Badanaval centre, and that is from the Pariahs of Siddapura, and this upper cloth is almost the work of the Mahatma, for where do you think it comes from? – Sabarmati itself!" And when a young man came to buy a towel or pair of dhotis he would say, "He, have you read the latest *Young India*?" and if he should say "Nay," he would tell them they were a set of buffaloes fit to be driven with kick and knout, and thrusting the paper into the young man's hands, he would offer him a chair and say, "Read this, it is useful," or, "Skip through this, it is less useful," and when children came he gave them pinches and peppermints and told them stories of Tilak and Gandhi and Chittaranjan Das, and such funny stories they were, too, that they called him Gandhi-grandpa. And his wife cooked food for the family and she said, "One day Sankar will earn as much as Advocate Ranganna, and he will buy a motor car, too," but Sankar laughed and said, "Mother, you must forget your dreams. Don't you see I am not a man to make money?"

At which Satamma said this about what Ramachandra had said about Sankar's reputation, and that about Professor Patwardhan's appreciation: "Your son, Sankar, he is a saint," and when he walked the main bazaar, they used to say, "Look there, there goes the ascetic advocate." People sometimes looked at his khadi coat and his rough yarn turban and laughed at this "walking advocate," and others said, "No, no, he follows the principles of the Mahatma." – "And what, pray, are the principles of the Mahatma?" – "Why, don't you know Sankar does not take a single false case, and before he takes a client he says to him, Swear before me you are not the criminal! and the client says this and that, but Sankar always comes back to the point and says, You know if you do not tell me the whole truth, well, I may be forced to withdraw in the middle of the case," and, indeed, as everyone knows, he withdrew in the middle of the case between Shopkeeper Rama Chetty and Contractor Seenappa over false accounts, between Borehalli Nanjunda and Tippayya, and you know how he withdrew in the last criminal case they had in Karwar. You see, this is what really happened. One Rahman Khan was supposed to have tried to murder one Subba Chetty, for Subba Chetty had taken away his mistress Dasi. And everybody said, "Poor Subba Chetty, poor Subba Chetty!" – and everybody said, "He will win the case easily." And Subba Chetty was an old client of Sankar and so he goes to Sankar and tells him the story and swears it is all true, and Sankar says, "Now this is going to be a criminal case, and if you have hidden a thing small as a hair, you will come to grief, Subba Chetty!" And Subba Chetty sheds many a tear and says he is a good householder and he would never tell a lie and the lingam in his hand is witness to it. And Sankar takes the case and prepares the papers, and he says he will have to see Dasi, but Subba Chetty says, "Dasi is very ill, father, but her word is my word and my word is hers," and Sankar says, "Bring her before the sessions," and Subba Chetty says, "If Shiva wills, so it shall be," and Sankar says, "Then you may go," and the case is filed and summonses are sent and the day of the hearing arrives, and Subba Chetty is the last to come and says the wheels

23

broke down and the rains, how they poured, and this and that, and when Dasi comes to the bar she is as hale as a first-calved cow, and she turns this way and she turns that way and she does her hair and wipes her eyes and stands up and sits down and bites her sari-fringe, and Subba Chetty gets angry and says, "Stop this concubine show!" And when the cross-examination begins it is Advocate Ramanna who begins to heckle her with questions, and Dasi breaks into a fit of sobs and says something and Subba Chetty cries, "Woman! Woman!" and Dasi runs up to the advocate and falls at his feet and says, "I know nothing, father! Nothing!" And when Sankar hears that, he asks the judge for permission to speak to his client, and he says to Subba Chetty, "On your mother's honour, tell me if you have not concocted the story to pinch Rahman Khan's coconut garden?" And Subba Chetty trembles and says, "No, no, Sankarappa!" But Sankar has seen the game and he turns to the magistrate and says, "I beg to ask your Lordship for an adjournment," and the magistrate, who knows Sankar's ways, says, "Well, you have it." When Sankar gets back home, he asks Subba Chetty to speak the truth, and Subba Chetty tells him how he had employed Dasi to go and live with Rahman Khan and to enrage him against Subba Chetty, "with drink and smoke and lust," and with drink and smoke and lust Rahman Khan had cried out he would murder that Subba Chetty and had run out with an axe and Subba Chetty had cried out, "Murder! Murder!" in the middle of the street, and Dasi had run out innocently and tried to calm Rahman Khan, who was so weak that he had rolled upon the earth, an opium lump. And when Sankar heard this he said, "Go and confess this to the magistrate," and the next day the magistrate gave him three years' rigorous imprisonment, with one year for Dasi. And Sankar asked pardon in public of Rahman Khan, who got six months, too.

It is from that day that people said, "Take care when you go to Sankar; he will never take a false case." And he took but the lowest fee, and when the clients were poor he said to his clerk, "Make an affidavit for Suranna's Dasanna. Stamps, private account, please," and people began to come to him more and more and never was there a man in Karwar that had risen so quickly in public esteem and legal success as he. But he never bought a car and never dressed in hat and shoes and suit, and always smiled at everyone. And when the court was over he did not go like Barrister Sastri and Advocate Ramrao to the Bar Club to have whisky-and-soda and God knows what, but he went straight to the floor above the khadi shop, where the new Hindi teacher Surya Menon held classes, and when Sankar had time he divided the class into two and gave a lesson to the latecomers. He said Hindi would be the national language of India, and though Kannada is good enough for our province, Hindi must become the national tongue, and whenever he met a man in the street, he did not say "How are you?" in Kannada, but took to the northern manner and said "Ram-Ram." But what was shameful was the way he began to talk Hindi to his mother, who understood not a word of it, but he said she would learn it one day; and he spoke nothing but Hindi to his daughter, and if by chance he used an English word, as they do in the city, he had a little closed pot, with a slit in the lid, into which he dropped a coin, and every month he opened it and gave it to the Congress fund. And if any of his friends should utter an English word in his house, he would say, "Drop me a coin," and the friends got angry and called him a fanatic; but he said there must be a few fanatics to wash the wheel of law, and he would force his friends to drop the coin and if they refused he dropped one himself.

And he was a fanatic, too, in his dress, you know, sister. When he went to a marriage party he used to say, "Everyone must be in khadi or I will not go," and they said, "Oh, one must have a nice Dharmawar sari for the bride; she cannot look like a street sweeper," and he would say, "Well, have your Dharmawar saris and send your money to Italian yarn makers and German colour manufacturers and let our Pariahs and peasants starve," and when they pleaded, "Just one Dharmawar sari?" he would say, "I am not the head of the family, but if you wear anything but khadi I will not go!" And that is how nobody in their house nor in their cousin's house had any new Dharmawar saris, and when they went for any kumkum and haldi invitation, they put on their old saris and slipped out through the back door. And he also made the whole family fast – fast on this day because it is the anniversary of the day the Mahatma was imprisoned, fast on that day for the Jallianwalabagh massacre, and on another day in memory of the day of Tilak's death, and some day he would have made everyone fast for every cough and sneeze of the Mahatma. "Fasting is good for the mind," he would say, and even on the days he fasted he was in full spirits and went to court and spun his three hundred yards every morning instead of his prayers, and he said the gods would be happy when the hungry stomachs had food.

But what a good expression he had on his face, sister! He looked a veritable Dharmaraja. And Rangamma told us never a man smiled more and sang more at home than he, and he was always the earliest to rise and the last to go to bed, yet he was always in the best of health. "Lemon water and gymnastics, gymnastics and lemon water, can keep the plague at the doorstep," he used to say, and to tell you the truth, never had Rangamma looked so healthy and serene as she did then. She was nearing forty, but she looked hardly thirty three, and there was not a grey hair on her head. And she would work, too, then, she could talk and write and hold classes and sometimes she even went, they said, to meetings with Sankar. And once Sankar had asked her to say a few words about Moorthy, and she had stood up and spoken of Moorthy the good, Moorthy the religious, and Moorthy the noble, and she had found no more words, and she had come down from the platform and had begun to shiver and tears had come into her eyes. But she said that was the first time, but if she had ever to speak again she would have no such fears, and of course we knew she was a tight-jawed person and she could speak like a man.

Rangamma came back from Karwar for the Magh cattle fair, and two days later we heard that the Red man's judges had given Moorthy three months' rigorous imprisonment. The whole afternoon no man left his verandah, and not a mosquito moved in all Kanthapura.

We all fasted.

The next day the rain set in and it poured and it plundered all the fields and the woods, and Ramakrishnayya, going to spit over the railings of the verandah, stumbled against a pillar and, falling, lost consciousness, and that very night, without saying a word, without giving a sigh, he closed his eyes forever. And everybody said, "The rains have come; oh, what shall we do for the cremations? Oh, what?" And Pandit Venkateshia immediately sent for the beadles and asked them to raise a mango pandal on the banks of the Himavathy, and the good Pariahs, they worked hour after hour during the night, and when the next morning the body was washed and the corpse tied to the bamboo, the rains suddenly lifted themselves up, and behind the jackfruit tree the sun rose like a camphor censer alit, and while the waters were still gurgling in the gutters, the procession hurried on, and they lighted the pyre in the open, and the head burst but a moment later, and we lifted our eyes to the heavens and muttered, "He goes the way of the saints." And Rangamma vowed she would take his bones to Kashi, but all of a sudden the river began to swell and when it came crawling by the pyre, people asked, "What shall we do? Oh what?" but the swell bubbled out by the pyre and Rangamma gave a sigh and when the body was ashed down whole and only a few cinders lay blinking behind the bones, a huge swell churned round the hill and swept the bones and ashes away. And we all cried out, "Narayan! Narayan!," and that night, sister, as on no other night, no cow would give its milk, and all the night a steady rain kept pattering on the tiles, and the calves pranced about their mothers and groaned ... Lord, may such be the path of our outgoing soul!

# Companions

> *Alas till now I did not know*
> *My guide and Fate's guide are one.*
> *– Hafiz*

It was a serpent such as one sees only at a fair, long and many-coloured and swift in riposte when the juggler stops his music. But it had a secret of its own which none knew except Moti Khan who brought him to the Fatehpur Sunday fair. The secret was: his fangs would lie without venom till the day Moti Khan should see the vision of the large white rupee, with the Qutub Minar on the one side and the face of the Emperor on the other. That day the fang would eat into his flesh and Moti Khan would only be a corpse of a man. Unless he find God.

For to tell you the truth, Moti Khan had caught him in the strangest of strange circumstances. He was one day going through the sitaphul wood of Rampur on a visit to his sister, and the day being hot and the sands all scorching and shiny, he lay down under a wild fig-tree, his turban on his face and his legs stretched across a stone. Sleep came like a swift descent of dusk, and after rapid visions of palms and hills and the dizzying sunshine, he saw a curious thing. A serpent came in the form of a man, opened its mouth, and through the most queer twistings of his face, declared he was

From *The Cow of the Barricades and Other Stories* (1947).

Pandit Srinath Sastri of Totepur, who, having lived at the foot of the Goddess Lakshamma for a generation or more, one day in the ecstasy of his vision he saw her, the benign Goddess straight and supple, offering him two boons. He thought of his falling house and his mortgaged ancestral lands and said, without a thought, "A bagful of gold and liberation from the cycle of birth and death." "And gold you shall have," said the Goddess, "but for your greed, you shall be born a serpent in your next life before reaching liberation. For gold and wisdom go in life like soap and oil. Go and be born a juggler's serpent. And when you have made the hearts of many men glad with the ripple and swing of your shining flesh, and you have gone like a bird amidst shrieking children, only to swing round their legs and to swing out to the amusement of them all, when you have climbed old men's shoulders and hung down them chattering like a squirrel, when you have thrust your hood at the virgin and circled round the marrying couples; when you have gone through the dreams of pregnant women and led the seekers to the top of the Mount of Holy Beacon, then your sins will be worn out like the quern with man's grindings and your flesh will catch fire like the will-o-the-wisp and disappear into the world of darkness where men await the birth to come. The juggler will be a basket-maker and Moti Khan is his name. In a former life he sought God but in this he sits on the lap of a concubine. Wending his way to his sister's for the birth of her son, he will sleep in the sitaphul woods. Speak to him. And he will be the vehicle of your salvation." Thus spoke the Goddess.

"Now, what do you say to that, Moti Khan?"

"Yes, I've been a sinner. But never thought I, God and Satan would become one. Who are you?"

"The very same serpent."

"Your race has caused the fall of Adam."

"I sat at the feet of Sri Lakshamma and fell into ecstasy. I am a Brahmin."

"You are strange."

"Take me or I'll haunt you for this life and all lives to come."

"Go, Satan!" shouted Moti Khan, and rising swift as a sword he started for his sister's house. He said to himself, "I will think of my sister and her child. I will think only of them." But leaves rustled and serpents came forth from the left and the right, blue ones and white ones and red ones and copper-coloured ones, long ones with short tails and short ones with bent tails, and serpents dropped from treetops and rock-edges, serpents hissed on the river sands. Then Moti Khan stood by the Rampur stream and said, "Wretch! Stop it. Come, I'll take you with me." Then the serpents disappeared and so did the hissings, and hardly home, he took a basket and put it in a corner, and then he slept; and when he woke, a serpent had curled itself in the basket. Moti Khan had a pungi made by the local carpenter, and, putting his mouth to it, he made the serpent dance. All the village gathered round him and all the animals gathered round him, for the music of Moti Khan was blue, and the serpent danced on his tail.

When he said goodbye to his sister, he did not take the road to his concubine but went straight northwards, for Allah called him there. And at every village men came to offer food to Moti Khan and women came to offer milk to the serpent, for it swung round children's legs and swung out, and cured them of all scars and poxes and fevers. Old men slept better after its touch and women conceived on the very night they offered milk to it. Plague went and plenty came, but Moti Khan would not smell silver. That would be death.

Now sometimes, at night in caravanserais, they had wrangles.

Moti Khan used to say: "You are not even a woman to put under oneself."

"But so many women come to see you and so many men come to honour you, and only a king could have had such a reception though you're only a basket-maker."

"Only a basket-maker! But I had a queen of a woman, and when she sang her voice was all flesh, and her flesh was all song. And she chewed betel-leaves and her lips were red, and even kings ..."

"Stop that. Between this and the vision of the rupee ..."

Moti Khan pulled at his beard and, fire in his eyes, he broke his knuckles against the earth.

"If only I could see a woman!"

"If you want God forget women, Moti Khan."

"But I never asked for God. It is you who always bore me with God.

I said I loved a woman. You are only a fanged beast. And here I am in the prime of life with a reptile to live with."

But suddenly temple bells rang, and the muezzin was heard to cry Allah-o-Akbar. No doubt it was all the serpent's work. Trembling, Moti Khan fell on his knees and bent himself in prayer.

From that day on the serpent had one eye turned to the right and one to the left when it danced. Once it looked at the men and once at the women, and suddenly it used to hiss up and slap Moti Khan's cheeks with the back of its head, for his music had fallen false and he was eyeing women. Round were their hips, he would think, and the eyelashes are black and blue, and the breasts are pointed like young mangoes, and their limbs so tremble and flow that he could sweetly melt into them.

One day, however, there was at the market a dark blue woman, with red lips, young and sprightly; and she was a butter woman. She came and stood by Moti Khan as he made the serpent dance. He played and he played on his bamboo pungi and music swung here and splashed there, and suddenly he looked at her and her eyes and her breasts and the naga-swara went and became moha-swara, and she felt it and he felt she felt it; and when night came, he thought and thought so much of her and she thought and thought so much of him, that he slipped to the serai door and she came to the serai gate, flower in her hair and perfume on her limbs, but lo! like the sword of God came a long, rippling light, circled round them,

pinched at her nipples and flew back into the bewildering night. She cried out, and the whole town waked, and Moti Khan thrust the basket under his arm and walked northwards, for Allah called him thither.

Now," said Moti Khan, "I have to find God. Else this creature will kill me. And the Devil knows the hell I'd have to bake in." So he decided that, at the next saint's tomb he encountered, he would sit down and meditate. But he wandered and he wandered; from one village he went to another, from one fair he went to another, but he found no dargah to meditate by. For God always called him northwards and northwards, and he crossed the jungles and he went up the mountains, and he came upon narrow valleys where birds screeched here and deer frisked there but no man's voice was to be heard, and he said, "Now let me turn back home"; but he looked back and he was afraid. And he said, "Now I have to go to the North, for Allah calls me there." And he climbed mountains again, and ran through jungles, and then came broad plains, and he went to the fairs and made the snake dance, and people left their rice shops and cotton-ware shops and the bellowing cattle and the yoked threshers and the querns and the kilns, and came to hear him play the music and to see the snake dance. They gave him food and fruit and cloth, but when they said, "Here's a coin," he said, "Nay." And the snake was right glad of it, for he hated to kill Moti Khan till he had found God, and he himself hated to die. Now, when Moti Khan had crossed the Narbada and the Pervan and the Bhagirath, he came to the Jumna, and through long Agra he passed making the snake dance, and yet he could not find God and he was sore in soul with it. And the serpent was bothersome.

But at Fatehpur Sikri, he said, "Here is Sheikh Chisti's tomb and I would rather starve and die than go one thumb-length more." He sat by Sheikh Chisti's tomb and he said, "Sheikh Chisti, what is this Fate has sent me? This serpent is a very wicked thing. He just hisses and spits fire at every wink and waver. He says, Find God. Now, tell me, Sheikh Chisti, how can I find Him? Till I find Him I will not leave this spot."

But even as he prayed he saw snakes sprout through his head, fountains splashed and snakes fell gently to the sides like the waters by the Taj, and through them came women, soft women, dancing women, round hips, betel-chewed lips, round breasts, – shy some were, while some were only minxes – and they came from the right and went to the left, and they pulled at his beard – and, suddenly, white serpents burst through the earth and enveloped them all, but Moti Khan would not move. He said: "Sheikh Chisti, I am in a strange world. But there is a darker world I see behind, and beyond that dark, dark world, I see a brighter world, and there, there must be Allah."

For twenty nine days he knelt there, his hands pressed against his ears, his face turned towards Sheikh Chisti's tomb. And people came and said, "Wake up, old man, wake up"; but he would not answer. And when they found the snake lying on the tomb of Sheikh Chisti they cried, "This is a strange thing," and they took to their heels; while others came and brought mullahs and maulvis but Moti Khan would not answer. For, to speak the truth, he was crossing through the dark waters, where one strains and splashes, and where the sky is all cold, and the stars all dead, and till man come to the other shore, there shall be neither peace nor God.

On the twenty ninth night Skeikh Chisti woke from his tomb and came, his skullcap and all, and he said: "My son, what may I give you?"

"Peace from this serpent – and God."

"My son, God is not to be seen. He is everywhere."

"Eyes to see God, for I cannot any more go northwards."

"Eyes to discern God you shall have."

"Then peace from this serpent."

"Faithful shall he be, true companion of the God-seeker."

"Peace to all men and women," said Moti Khan.

"Peace to all mankind. Further, Moti Khan, I have something to tell you; as dawn breaks Maulvi Mohammed Khan will come to offer you his daughter, fair as an oleander. She has been waiting for you and she will wed you. My blessings on you, my son!"

"Allah is found! Victory to Allah!" cried Moti Khan. The serpent flung round him, slipped between his feet and curled round his neck and danced on his head, for, when Moti Khan found God, his sins would be worn out like the quern-stone with the grindings of man, and there would be peace in all mankind.

Moti Khan married the devout daughter of Maulvi Mohammed Khan and he loved her well, and he settled down in Fatehpur Sikri and became the guardian of Sheikh Chisti's tomb. The serpent lived with him, and now and again he was taken to the fair to play for the children.

One day, however, Moti Khan's wife died and was buried in a tomb of black marble. Eleven months later Moti Khan died and he was given a white marble tomb, and a dome of the same stone, for both. Three days after that the serpent died too, and they buried him in the earth beside the dargah, and gave him a nice clay tomb. A pipal sprang up on it, and a passing Brahmin planted a neem-tree by the pipal, and some merchant in the village gave money to build a platform round them. The pipal rose to the skies and covered the dome with dark, cool shade, and Brahmins planted snake-stones under it, and bells rang and camphors were lit, and marriage couples went round the platform in circumambulation. When the serpent was offered the camphor Moti Khan had the incense. And when illness comes to the town, with music and flags and torches do we go, and we fall in front of the pipal-platform and we fall prostrate before the dargah, and right through the night a wind rises and blows away the foul humours of the village. And when children cry, you say, "Moti Khan will cure you, my treasure," and they are cured. Emperors and kings have come and gone but never have they destroyed our village. For man and serpent are friends, and Moti Khan found God.

Between Agra and Fatehpur Sikri you may still find the little tomb and the pipal. Boys have written their names on the walls and dust and leaves cover the gold and blue of the pall. But someone has dug a well by the side, and if thirst takes you on the road, you can take a drink and rest under the pipal, and think deeply of God.

# India – A Fable

*Advayataiva siva*
*(Nonduality alone is auspicious)*
– Sri Sankara

N ever was the Luxembourg so beautiful as on that fragile spring day. March had come and gone boisterously, cold winds blew in April, and then the immense sunshine came. The pools were transparent, the sky full of ochre clouds, the trees cut through the air with their leaves, the earth was hot. Men came out, old men with coughs and whiskers, and sat by the ponds reading newspapers. The old, fat women removed their kerchiefs and spoke garrulous words. The Sorbonnard girls opened their blouses to let the cool air breathe down them, single silver bangles on their wrists, and cigarettes held lighted in the air. They read D'Alembert or Henri Becque, while the young men basked in the sun and slept.

The children scampered all over the park. I sat under Anne of Austria (1629-1687?), grey, big-headed, big-bosomed – some old tragic royalty bulging with posthumous importance. My thoughts were about morganatic marriages, UN statistics, parks and books, and the *chocolat chez Alsecia rue d'Assas* whose taste would not leave my mouth. The cold wind blew over my mouth. The

First published as "India – A Story" in *Encounter* (London) in 1953. It was subsequently included in the collection *The Policeman and the Rose* (1978).

cold wind blew over my chest, and I sat up. A child of five or six, pink-skinned and clear-eyed, was dragging a wooden camel along the path.

"Where are you going?" I asked.

"To the oasis of Arabia," he said, and stopped.

"Where's that?" I asked, trying to see whom he was with. A woman, under a tree – his nanny no doubt – was standing, her arms round the peeling trunk of the oak; A young man, in kepi and Sunday shine, stood by her, at once disconsolate and happy. He hoped spring would remove his sorrow.

"Speak to the Monsieur, Pierrot," she cried, so as to have more time with the young man.

"You know where your oasis is?" I asked.

"Oh, yes, the oasis is all water, and big like this. My camel goes there to drink."

"Let's go there," I said. He stopped me, turned back furtively to his nanny, and then suddenly, "Look, you've faces in your buttons. Ah, faces, faces," he said, and gazed up at me. He did not know whether to come forward or not, his hand upraised, holding the string of his camel.

"You've faces in your buttons," he repeated and laughed.

"Speak to the Monsieur," cried the nanny. Her tone of voice was growing lighter. Pierrot started to say something. Then he suddenly fell silent. His camel needed a better string.

"I am called Raja," I said, just to say something.

"You've faces in your buttons," he said coming nearer, as though the mention of my name gave assurance of something known. But looking up again, he saw my blue-bronze face, and stopped. He was silent. Again he looked back, and his nanny had slipped behind the tree.

"Look," I said, and showed him my gold buttons. I was wearing my sherwani and my gold buttons were bright in the sun.

"Faces, faces," he said, and laughed, looking into my eyes. Then he looked very thoughtful.

"Speak to the gentleman. Be nice to him," shouted the nanny warmly, as though it were a song she was singing. The wind blew hard. The child came behind me, his hands tight shut in self-protection. Yellow plane leaves fell. At the Medici fountain, the water purred in the wind. I felt as though I could count each drop.

"Where is Arabia?" I asked.

"Arabia," said Pierrot, "well, it's where there is a lot of sand, and a prince who rides a horse of gold."

"And the camel?"

"The camel is a friend of his Princess. When she goes to see the Prince ... No, come, my camel is called Kiki."

"And your Princess?"

"She's called Katherine."

"And her Prince?"

"Rudolfe. Kiki is the wedding present that the King of Arabia gave to Katherine. Kiki is from Ethiopia."

"And you, Pierrot, were you at the wedding?"

"Of course I was at the wedding. There's a wedding every day. Every day there is a wedding in the oasis."

Pierrot came and sat on my lap.

"And what is it you see at the wedding, Pierrot?"

"Rudolfe comes on a white horse, and covered with white gold. And Katherine on the red camel, and her clothes are blue, the same as the clothes of Saint Catherine, you know. And they meet in the oasis."

"And what happens then?"

"Why, they kiss each other. And then they say Adieu. I'm going to the oasis."

"And could I come and see them – your Prince and Princess, Pierrot?"

"Wait, I'll ask them," he paused a moment. Then he said, "Come. The Prince and Princess are happy to see you at the wedding. You're going to show them those buttons with the faces in them?" He stopped, then asked:

"And you. Are you a prince?"

"Oh, yes," I said.

"You are a prince. Oh, yes I knew it. I do know it, you know. You are a prince. And what is your name?"

"I am called Raja," I said.

"Raja is what they call you," he said, trying to pronounce my name slowly, and to understand.

"Yes," I said. "It means a prince."

"Then you are like Rudolfe. Rudolfe is the Prince of the Oasis and of Arabia. And you?"

"Of India."

"And where is India?"

"Oh, far, very far," I said, looking across the treetops to the sky.

Pierrot was taking me to the pool. The nanny was happy with the young man. Pierrot never looked back.

"Far, very far," he repeated. "And is there much sand in your country?"

"No, not much sand. But there are big forests."

"What is that, Monsieur, Monsieur ... Prince, a forest?"

"A forest, well: it's lots and lots of trees."

"Oh, you're dressed just like a prince."

"A prince from India," I said.

Then we came to the central pool amidst the blue flowers. There were many, many children. Pierrot walked among them as though he were going on a long journey. He was going somewhere very far, far, far as that Avenue de l'Observatoire, full of great forests of trees, pools and big buildings and rippling sunshine. The sun shines there. The moon is big there. There are many birds, all blue and sometimes transparent. There are many clouds. And the camels there are never thirsty.

"And camels – are there many in your country?"

"Oh, we've elephants," I said.

"An elephant – an elephant," said Pierrot with much satisfaction. Meanwhile the nanny and her young man had come to the steps. The wind blew, and in the pool the boats raced one against the other, going to many lands, dashed against one another, fell on their sides, and rose up, and nobody was hurt or angry, because the sun shone.

"Your country – you get there by sail-boat?" he asked.

I said, "No. One goes there on steamers. One goes night and day, and for fifteen days. Then one comes to India."

"India," he repeated. He left the camel on the gravel. He sat by the pool, thinking.

"And you? Have you a princess?"

"Yes," I said. "I even have two. They are not princesses. They are goddesses. One on my right hand and one on my left hand."

"One on your right hand, and one on your left hand. They are goddesses."

"Yes."

"What is a goddess, a goddess, Monsieur le Prince?"

"Ah, goddesses, well: they are ladies with four arms and a golden crown on their heads, and the water of the Ganges, all sweet with perfumes, runs at their feet."

"And you have two of them?"

"Yes," I said. "One for the wedding of the night, and one for the wedding of the day. One who is dark as the bee, and the other who is blonde as butter."

"One is like dreaming. The other like waking up." He understood. He became silent. Then:

"And they ride elephants." He smiled to himself. Now, he really understood. He went on:

"They go down to the oasis, and they drink water."

"No, not to the oasis," I said. "But to the rivers."

"And the wedding – there is a wedding every day?"

"Two weddings a day – one by the light of the sun and the other by the light of the moon."

"And the goddesses – they come riding on camels?"

"No, I told you, they ride elephants."

"Yes, yes. They ride elephants. Two goddesses and they ride elephants."

"And then there is the river."

"Pierrot!" shouted the nanny. He sat there looking at me as though he did not hear.

"Pierrot!" she shouted again. "What's happened to you?"

"Jeannot, I am with the Monsieur," he shouted back, without looking at her. "And I ride an elephant, I'm going to the elephant country. There are goddesses there – two goddesses." He looked up at her as she came over.

"What's happening to you anyway?"

"I am going to the country of Monsieur."

"Look," she reproved him, "look at your Kiki. Look what you do with your animals."

Pierrot was quiet for a moment. Then he said. "There's a river there too."

I said, "Yes, Pierrot."

"And no oasis?"

"None."

"Kiki," he said, "you like the oasis. And there you are," he cried, and threw it into the pool. Kiki kicked up her legs and sank without a cry. Kiki went down to the bottom, and ships passed over her. Pierrot looked at the boats, borne by the wind swiftly. They encircled many continents. The nanny had gone happily away to the young man. "He likes you, Monsieur. Will you look after him? I'll be back in a minute," she had said to me smiling, so big and fat and young. She wanted to be pressed against some tree and kissed. The sap in the trees was so fresh and full. The boats raced in the wind. There was no sand any more. There were many valleys, green, green, like the fields. A lot of water. Then there were trees. A lot of trees made a forest. A lot of forests made a country. A country with a lot of forests, and many, many rivers, is called India.

"Your river – has it a lot of water?" asked Pierrot. He tore a flower-stalk and held it between his teeth. He looked very serious. He looked straight at the pool and the sun inside the pool. Then suddenly he began to cry. He cried and cried silently, tears streaming down his cheeks.

"I want to go to your country," he said. "I want to go to the wedding."

"And the elephant?"

"Oh, yes. I will ride the elephant. Take me in your arms?" I lifted him up. He held me tight against his head. He would not look back. I bought him some candy. He held the packet in his hand. He could not speak. He would not eat. He looked down at Kiki in the water.

"And now, the fifteen days' journey is over," he said.

"Yes," I said.

"Where are the goddesses?"

"Don't you see, there's one to the right and one to the left. And how beautiful they are."

"Yes. And I ride on my elephant. I'll call him Titi the Elephant." He was pleased with his speech. "Titi, now there, turn to the left. And now to the right. There, you're a good boy. And, what's the name of your river, Monsieur le Prince?"

"The Ganges," I said.

"The Ganges, Titi. You see, you see that's your river. There are two princesses, one to the right and one to the left. It's not like the oasis. There, there's only Jeannot. And the ships have sailed everywhere. They've gone far, very far, fifteen days far. The Ganges, it's the river. It's all purple. The

elephant is all white. I go to the wedding. The ships go to the wedding. There are forests. There's a wedding. The prince has buttons with faces in them. Oh, yes," he said, smiling.

The nanny came and said: "At whom are you smiling, Pierrot?" She was alone now.

"Jeannot, Jeannot," he cried, and jumped on the gravel. Jeanne looked very happy.

"Take me up?" he said. She lifted him and held him in her arms.

"I go to the wedding," he shouted.

"What wedding?"

"Your wedding," he said, and gave her a bite on the cheek.

*"Petit nigaud!"* she said, happy.

"Jeannot," he said. "Do you know where we are?"

"At the Luxembourg."

*"Non, petit nigaud,"* he answered back. "We are far, far away, fifteen days by steamship. There are no sands. There are no camels. There are forests – and then, there are elephants. Then, there's the Ganges." I smiled. "This monsieur, he's the Prince of India."

"Yes," I said. The wind blew hard and cold. The boats fell against one another.

"We must be going home now. Oh, it's so cold," said Jeanne, as though to the wind. She was looking at the gate of the garden, the one near the Medici fountain. The young man was gone, and the path had gone with him. The leaves were black against that grey sky.

"Jeannot," said Pierrot, "in that country, there are two princesses. But me," he whispered, hugging her against his cheeks, "I have only you."

"His father," explained Jeanne, "is a colonel and is in Morocco. Pierrot's mother died in childbirth. It's now almost two years since it happened."

"You are my friend," he said to her, begging.

"Oh, yes, I am your sweetheart," she said. In the Luxembourg everybody heard it. The Sorbonnard girl looked up and let fall her book on her lap, and reflected. Time flies in the spring. One should not grow big-bosomed like some Anne of Austria (1629-1687?).

"We're going to the wedding, to the wedding!" cried Pierrot, on his way.

"And Kiki?" asked Jeanne, anxious.

"Kiki is in the oasis. I know that," he said.

"Ah, *petit nigaud*, and what will grandfather say to me? You're a harlot, a liar, a hypocrite! And you, and your Kiki? What have you done with him, Pierrot?"

Pierrot slid down her waist and stood on the gravel. Then he took my hand, and said: "Prince, take me to your country, take me to the wedding. There are two goddesses, one for the wedding of the night and the other for the wedding of the day. And there's the elephant, Titi. I am on Titi this morning. He walks, he walks like this as one rides up the waves, and then rides down. The boat goes up and goes down the waves. I go to your country."

Jeanne had gone back to search for Kiki. I did not tell her what he'd done with it.

As we went up the steps, he saw the Medici fountain; he ran towards it and said: "I know where I am. I am in India." He was sure I was a prince. He was sure Jeanne was nowhere to be seen. He was sure Kiki was dead.

The elephant was drinking water at the Medici fountain. He saw the two goddesses, one to the right and one to the left. One that I would marry with the moon, and one that I would marry with the sun. He looked at the water and said: "Look, there, that's your country. How beautiful it is. Now it's the hour of the wedding," he whispered, and he grew thoughtful.

Up above the trees, the sky bore away the rapid, white clouds, and in the waters they ran like boats. One of them had already reached the other shore, was safe in harbour. He took my hand and held it in his, and said: "I love forests. It must be warm there."

"Pierrot!" shouted Jeanne. I let go his hand. He cried and cried, and would not leave the Medici fountain. He saw the elephant in the forest. He saw the river Ganges. He saw the two goddesses, with four hands and a crown of white gold on their heads. He rode the elephant, covered in silk and gold, and he came to my marriage.

"Jeannot!" he cried and slipped into the water. He touched the bottom that was like himself, his hands and feet made of light. The water was not deep, but very cold and full of perfumes. It was mid-April and the winds were blowing. The new leaves were sharp, and the sky was like deep sleep. In India, the earth is warm with silence, and the Ganges flows.

Two or three days later I came to the Luxembourg. Pierrot was not there. Again and again, I came. Pierrot was not there. Towards the end of the month, he came and with a new nanny – middle-aged. And when he saw me, he ran towards me and said: "Monsieur ... Monsieur le Prince," and leaped straight into my arms. He was very fond of his new navy suit. It had golden buttons that shone in one's eyes. "Look!" he said. "Look, faces!" and he laughed. He seemed to have grown in years. "I know now," he said. "I am a maharaja. I ride the elephant. The wedding is over."

# The Serpent and
# the Rope

I was born a Brahmin – that is, devoted to Truth and all that. "Brahmin is he who knows Brahman," etc, etc ... But how many of my ancestors since the excellent Yagnyavalkya, my legendary and Upanishadic ancestor, have really known the Truth excepting the Sage Madhava, who founded an empire, or, rather, helped to build an empire, and wrote some of the most profound of Vedantic texts since Sri Sankara. There were others, so I'm told, who left hearth and riverside fields, and wandered to mountains distant and hermitages "to see God face to face." And some of them did see God face to face and built temples. But when they died – for indeed they did "die" – they too must have been burnt by tank or grove or meeting of two rivers, and they too must have known they did not die. I can feel them in me, and know they knew they did not die. Who is it that tells me they did not die? Who but me.

So my ancestors went one by one and were burnt, and their ashes have gone down the rivers.

Whenever I stand in a river I remember how when young, on the day the monster ate the moon and the day fell into an eclipse, I used with til

---

This excerpt is from the beginning of *The Serpent and the Rope* (1960).

and kusha grass to offer the manes my filial devotion. For withal I was a
good Brahmin. I even knew grammar and the Brahma Sutras, read the
Upanishads at the age of four, was given the holy thread at seven – because
my mother was dead and I had to perform her funeral ceremonies, year
after year, my father having married again. So with wet cloth and an empty
stomach, with devotion, and sandal paste on my forehead, I fell before the
rice-balls of my mother and I sobbed. I was born an orphan, and have
remained one. I have wandered the world and have sobbed in hotel
rooms and in trains, have looked at the cold mountains and sobbed, for I
had no mother. One day, and that was when I was twenty two, I sat in a
hotel – it was in the Pyrenees – and I sobbed, for I knew I would never see
my mother again.

They say my mother was very beautiful and very holy. Grandfather
Kittanna said, "Her voice, son, was like a vina playing to itself, after evensong
is over, when one has left the instrument beside a pillar in the temple. Her
voice too was like those musical pillars at the Rameshwaram temple – it
resonated from the depths, from unknown space, and one felt God shone
the brighter with this worship. She reminded me of Concubine
Chandramma. She had the same voice. That was long before your time,"
grandfather concluded, "it was in Mysore, and I have not been there these
fifty years."

Grandfather Kittanna was a noble type, a heroic figure among us. It
must be from him I have this natural love of the impossible – I can think
that a building may just decide to fly , or that Stalin may become a saint, or
that all the Japanese have become Buddhist monks, or that Mahatma Gandhi
is walking with us now. I sometimes feel I can make the railway line stand
up, or the elephant bear its young one in twenty four days; I can see an
aeroplane float over a mountain and sit carefully on a peak, or I could go
to Fatehpur Sikri and speak to the Emperor Akbar. It would be difficult for
me not to think, when I am in Versailles, that I hear the uncouth voices of
Roi Soleil, or in Meaux that Bossuet rubs his snuff in the palm of his hand,
as they still do in India, and offers a pinch to me. I can sneeze with it, and
hear Bossuet make one more of his funeral orations. For Bossuet believed –
and so did Roi Soleil – that he never would die. And if they've died, I ask
you, where indeed did they go?

Grandfather Kittanna was heroic in another manner. He could manage a horse, the fiercest, with a simplicity that made it go where it did not wish to go. I was brought up with the story of how Grandfather Kittanna actually pushed his horse into the Chandrapur forest one evening – the horse, Sundar, biting his lips off his face; the tiger that met him in the middle of the jungle; the leap Sundar gave high above my Lord Sher, and the custard-apples that splashed on his back, so high he soared – and before my grandfather knew where he was, with sash and blue Maratha saddle, there he stood, Sundar, in the middle of the courtyard. The lamps were being lit, and when stableman Chowdayya heard the neigh he came and led the steed to the tank for a swish of water. Grandfather went into the bathroom, had his evening bath – he loved it to be very hot, and Aunt Seethamma had always to serve him potful after potful – and he rubbed himself till his body shone as the young of a banana tree. He washed and sat in prayer. When Atchakka asked, "Sundar is all full of scratches ...?" then grandfather spoke of the tiger, and the leap. For him, if the horse had soared into the sky and landed in holy Brindavan he would not have been much surprised. Grandfather Kittanna was like that. He rode Sundar for another three years, and then the horse died – of some form of dysentery, for, you know, horses die too – and we buried him on the top of Kittur Hill, with fife and filigree. We still make an annual pilgrimage to his tomb, and for Hyderabad reasons we cover it up with a rose-coloured muslin, like the Muslims do. Horses we think came from Arabia, and so they need a Muslim burial. Where is Sundar now? Where?

The impossible, for grandfather, was always possible. He never – he, a Brahmin – never for once was afraid of gun or sword, and yet what depth he had in his prayers. When he came out, Aunt Seethamma used to say, "He has the shine of a Dharmaraja."

But I, I've the fright of gun and sword, and the smallest trick of violence can make me run a hundred leagues. But once having gone a hundred leagues I shall come back a thousand, for I do not really have the fear of fear. I only have fear.

I love rivers and lakes, and make my home easily by any waterside hamlet. I love palaces for their echoes, their sense of never having seen anything but the gloomy. Palaces remind me of old and venerable women, who never die. They look after others so much – I mean, orphans of the family always have great-aunts, who go on changing from orphan to orphan – that they remain ever young. One such was Aunt Lakshamma. She was married to a minister once, and he died when she was seven or eight. And since then my uncles and their daughters, my mother's cousins and their grandchildren, have always had Lakshamma to look after them, for an orphan in a real household is never an orphan. She preserved, did Lakshamma, all the clothes of the young in her eighteenth century steel and sheesham trunk, in the central hall, and except when there was a death in the house these clothes never saw the light of the sun. Some of them were fifty years old, they said. The other day – that is, some seven or eight years ago – when we were told that Aunt Lakshamma, elder to my grandfather by many years, had actually died, I did not believe it. I thought she would live three hundred years. She never would complain or sigh. She never wept. We never wept when she died. For I cannot understand what death means.

My father, of course, loved me. He never let me stray into the hands of Lakshamma. He said, "Auntie smells bad, my son. I want you to be a hero and a prince." Some time before my mother died, it seems she had a strange vision. She saw three of my past lives, and in each one of them I was a son, and of course I was always her eldest born, tall, slim, deep-voiced, deferential and beautiful. In one I was a prince. That is why I had always to be adorned with diamonds – diamond on my forehead, chest and ears. She died, they say, having sent someone to the goldsmith, asking if my hair-flower were ready. When she died they covered her with white flowers – jasmines from Coimbatore and champaks from Chamundi – and with a lot of kumkum on her they took her away to the burning ghat. They shaved me completely, and when they returned they gave me Bengal gram, and some sweets. I could not understand what had happened. Nor do I understand now. I know my mother, my Mother Gauri, is not dead, and yet I am an orphan. Am I always to be an orphan?

That my father married for a third time – my stepmother having died leaving three children, Saroja, Sukumari, and the eldest, Kapila – is another story. My new stepmother loved me very dearly, and I could not think of a home without her bright smile and the song that shone like copper vessels in the house. When she smiled her mouth touched her ears – and she gave me everything I wanted. I used to weep, though, thinking of my own mother. But then my father died. He died on the third of the second moon-month when the small rains had just started. I have little to tell you of my father's death, except that I did not love him; but that after he died I knew him and loved him when his body was such pure white spread ash. Even now I have dreams of him saying to me, "Son, why did you not love me, you, my Eldest Son?" I cannot repent, as I do not know what repentance is. For I must first believe there is death. And that is the central fact – I do not believe that death is. So, for whom shall I repent?

Of course, I love my father now. Who could not love one that was protection and kindness itself, though he never understood that my mother wanted me to be a prince? And since I could not be a prince – I was born a Brahmin, and so how could I be a king? – I wandered my life away, and became a holy vagabond. If grandfather simply jumped over tigers in the jungles, how many tigers of the human jungle, how many accidents to plane and car have I passed by? And what misunderstandings and chasms of hatred have lain between me and those who first loved, and then hated, me? Left to myself, I became alone and full of love. When one is alone one always loves. In fact, it is because one loves, and one is alone, one does not die.

I went to Benares, once. It was in the month of March, and there was still a pinch of cold in the air. My father had just died and I took Vishalakshi, my second stepmother, and my young stepbrother Sridhara – he was only eleven months old – and I went to Benares. I was twenty two then, and I had been to Europe; I came back when father became ill. Little Mother was very proud of me – she said, "He's the bearing of a young pipal tree, tall and sacred, and the serpent-stones around it. We must go round him to become sacred." But the sacred Brahmins of Benares would hear none of this. They knew my grandfather and his grandfather and his great-grandfather again, and thus for seven generations – Ramakrishnayya and Ranganna, Madhavaswamy and Somasundarayya, Manjappa and Gangadharayya – and for each of them they knew the sons and grandsons (the daughters, of course, they did not quite know), and so, they stood on their rights.

"Your son," they said to Little Mother, "has been to Europe, and has wed a European and he has no sacred thread. Pray, Mother, how could the manes be pleased?" So Little Mother yielded and just fifty silver rupees made everything holy. Some carcass-bearing Brahmins – "We're the men

of the four shoulders," they boast – named my young brother Son of Ceremony in their tempestuous high and low of hymns – the quicker the better, for in Benares there be many dead, and all the dead of all the ages, the successive generations of manes after manes, have accumulated in the sky. And you could almost see them layer on layer, on the night of a moon-eclipse, fair and pale and tall and decrepit, fathers, grandfathers, great-grandfathers, mothers, sisters, brothers, nephews, friends, kings, Yogis, maternal uncles – all, all they accumulate in the Benares air and you can see them. They have a distanced, dull-eyed look – and they ask – they beg for this and that, and your round white rice-balls and sesame seed give the peace they ask for. The sacred Brahmin too is pleased. He has his fifty rupees. Only my young brother, eleven months old, does not understand. When his mother is weeping – for death takes a long time to be recognized – my brother pulls and pulls at the sari-fringe. I look at the plain, large river that is ever so young, so holy – like my mother. The temple bells ring and the crows are all about the white rice-balls. "The manes have come, look!" say the Brahmins. My brother crawls up to them saying "Caw-caw," and it's when he sees the monkeys that he jumps for Little Mother's lap. He's so tender and fine limbed, is my brother. Little Mother takes him into her lap, opens her choli and gives him the breast.

The Brahmins are still muttering something. Two or three of them have already washed their feet in the river and are coming up, looking at their navels or their fine gold rings. They must be wondering what silver we would offer. We come from far – and from grandfather to grandfather, they knew what everyone in the family had paid, in Moghul gold or in rupees of the East India Company, to the more recent times with the British Queen buxom and small-faced on the round, large silver. I would rather have thrown the rupees to the begging monkeys than to the Brahmins. But Little

Mother was there. I took my brother in my arms, and I gave the money, silver by silver, to him. And gravely, as though he knew what he was doing, he gave the rupees to the seated Brahmins. He now knew too that father was dead. Then suddenly he gave such a shriek as though he saw father near us – not as he was but as he had become, blue, transcorporeal. Little Mother always believes the young see the dead more clearly than we the corrupt do. And Little Mother must be right. Anyway, it stopped her tears, and now that the clouds had come, we went down the steps of the Harishchandra Ghat, took a boat and floated down the river.

I told Little Mother how Tulsidas had written the Ramayana just there, next to the Rewa Palace, and Kabir had been hit on the head by Saint Ramanand. The Saint had stumbled on the head of the Muslim weaver and had cried Ram-Ram, so Kabir stood up and said, "Now, My Lord, be Thou my Guru and I Thy disciple." That is how the weaver became so great a devotee and poet. Farther down, the Buddha himself had walked and had washed his alms-bowl – he had gone up the steps and had set the Wheel of Law a-turning. The aggregates, said the Buddha, make for desire and aversion, pleasure and ill, and one must seek that from which there is no returning. Little Mother listened to all this and seemed so convinced. She played with the petal-like fingers of my brother and when she saw a parrot in the sky, "Look, look, little one," she said, "that is the Parrot of Rama." And she began to sing:

*O parrot, my parrot of Rama*

and my little brother went to profoundest sleep.

My father was really dead. But Little Mother smiled. In Benares one knows death is as illusory as the mist in the morning. The Ganges is always there – and when the sun shines, oh, how hot it can still be ...

I wrote postcards to friends in Europe. I told them I had come to Benares because father had died, and I said the sacred capital was really a surrealist city. You never know where reality starts and where illusion ends; whether the Brahmins of Benares are like the crows asking for funereal rice-balls, saying "Caw-caw"; or like the Sadhus by their fires, lost in such beautiful magnanimity, as though love were not something one gave to another, but what one gave to oneself. His trident in front of him, his holy books open, some saffron cloth drying anywhere – on bare bush or on broken wall, sometimes with an umbrella stuck above, and a dull fire eyeing him, as though the fire in Benares looked after the saints, not the cruel people of the sacred city – each Sadhu sat, a Shiva. And yet when you looked up you saw the lovely smile of some concubine, just floating down her rounded bust and nimble limbs, for a prayer and a client. The concubines of Benares are the most beautiful of any in the world, they say; and some say too, that they worship the wife of Shiva, Parvathi herself, that they may have the juice of youth in their limbs. That is why Damodhara Gupta so exaltedly started his book on bawds with Benares. "O Holy Ganga, Mother Ganga, thou art purity itself, coming down from Shiva's hair." When you see so many limbs go purring and bursting on the ghats by the Ganges, how can limbs have any meaning? Death makes passion beautiful. Death makes the concubine inevitable. I remembered again grandfather saying, "Your mother had such a beautiful voice. She had a voice like Concubine Chandramma. And that was in Mysore, and fifty years ago."

I could not forget Madeleine – how could I? Madeleine was away and in Aix-en-Provence. Madeleine had never recovered – in fact she never did recover – from the death of Pierre. She had called him Krishna till he was seven months old. Then when he began to have those coughs, Madeleine knew: mothers always know what is dangerous for their children. And on that Saturday morning, returning from her college Madeleine knew, she knew that in four weeks, in three and in two and in one, the dread disease would take him away. That was why from the moment he was born – we had him take birth in a little, lovely maternity home near Bandol – she spoke of all the hopes she had in him. He must be tall and twenty three; he must go to an Engineering Institute and build bridges for India when he grew up. Like all melancholic people, Madeleine loved bridges. She felt Truth was always on the other side, and so sometimes I told her that next time she must be born on the Hudson. I bought her books on Provence or on Sardinia, which had such beautiful ivy-covered bridges built by the Romans. One day she said, "Let's go and see this bridge at Saint-Jean-Pied-de-Port," that she had found in a book on the Pays Basque. We drove through abrupt, arched Ardèche, and passing through Cahors I showed her the Pont de Valentré. She did not care for it. It was like Reinhardt's scenario at Salzburg, she said. When we went on to the Roman bridge of Saint-Jean-Pied-de-Port she said, "Rama, it makes me shiver." She had been a young girl at the time of the Spanish Civil War, so we never could go over to Spain. Then it was we went up to some beautiful mountain town – perhaps it was Pau, for I can still see the huge chateau, the one built by Henri IV – and maybe it was on that night, in trying to comfort Madeleine, that Krishna was conceived. She would love to have a child of mine, she said – and we had been married seven months.

At that time Madeleine was twenty six, and I was twenty one. We had first met at the University of Caen. Madeleine had an uncle – her parents had died leaving her an estate, so it was being looked after by Oncle Charles. He was from Normandy, and you know what that means.

Madeleine was so lovely, with golden hair – on her mother's side she came from Savoy – and her limbs had such pure unreality. Madeleine was altogether unreal. That is why, I think, she had never married anyone – in fact she had never touched anyone. She said that during the Nazi occupation, towards the end of 1943, a German officer had tried to touch her hair; it looked so magical, and it looked the perfect Nordic hair. She said he had brought his hands near her face, and she had only to smile and he could not do anything. He bowed and went away.

It was the Brahmin in me, she said, the sense that touch and untouch are so important, which she sensed; and she would let me touch her. Her hair was gold, and her skin for an Indian was like the unearthed marble with which we built our winter palaces. Cool, with the lake about one, and the peacock strutting in the garden below. The seventh-hour of music would come, and all the palace would see itself lit. Seeing oneself is what we always seek; the world, as the great Sage Sankara said, is like a city seen in a mirror. Madeleine was like the Palace of Amber seen in moonlight. There is such a luminous mystery – the deeper you go, the more you know yourself. So Krishna was born.

The bridge was never crossed. Madeleine had a horror of crossing bridges. Born in India she would have known how in Malabar they send off gunfire to frighten the evil spirits, as you cross a bridge. Whether the gunfire went off or not, Krishna could never cross the bridge of life. That is why with some primitive superstition Madeleine changed his name and called him Pierre from the second day of his illness. *"Pierre tu es, et sur cette pierre ..."* she quoted. And she said – for she, a Frenchwoman, like an Indian woman was shy, and would not call me easily by my name – she had said, "My love, the gods of India will be angry, that you a Brahmin married a non-Brahmin like me; why should they let me have a child called Krishna? So sacred is that name." And the little fellow did not quite know what he was to do when he was called Pierre. I called him Pierre and respected her superstition. For all we do is really superstition. Was I really called Ramaswamy, or was Madeleine called Madeleine?

The illness continued. Good Dr Pierre Marmoson, a specialist in child medicine – especially trained in America – gave every care available. But bronchopneumonia is bronchopneumonia, particularly after a severe attack of chickenpox. Madeleine, however, believed more in my powers of healing than in the doctor's. So that when the child actually lay in my arms and steadied itself and kicked straight and lay quiet, Madeleine could not believe that Pierre was dead. The child had not even cried.

We were given special permission by the Prefet des Bouches-du-Rhône to cremate Pierre among the olive trees behind the Villa Sainte-Anne. It was a large villa and one saw on a day of the mistral the beautiful Mont Sainte-Victoire, as Cezanne must have seen it day after day, clear as though you could talk to it. The mistral blew and blew so vigorously: one could see one's body float away, like pantaloon, vest and scarf, and one's soul sit and shine on the top of Mont Sainte-Victoire. The dead, they say in Aix, live in the cathedral tower, the young and the virgins do – there is even a Provencal song about it – so Madeleine went to her early morning Mass and to vespers. She fasted on Friday, she a heathen, she began to light candles to the Virgin, and she just smothered me up in tenderness. She seemed so far that nearness was farther than any smell or touch. There was no bridge – all bridges now led to Spain.

So when my father had said he was very ill, and wished I could come, she said, "Go, and don't you worry about anything, I will look after myself." It seemed wiser for me to go. Madeleine would continue to teach and I would settle my affairs at home. Mother's property had been badly handled by the estate agent Sundarayya, the rents not paid, the papers not in order:

and I thought I would go and see the University authorities too, for a job was being kept vacant for me. The Government had so far been very kind – and my scholarship continued. Once my doctorate was over I would take Madeleine home, and she would settle with me – somehow I always thought of a house white, single-storeyed, on a hill and by a lake – and I would go day after day to the University and preach to them the magnificence of European civilization. I had taken history, and my special subject was the Albigensian heresy. I was trying to link up the Bogomilites and the Druzes, and thus search back for the Indian background – Jain or maybe Buddhist – of the Cathars. The "Pure" were dear to me. Madeleine, too, got involved in them, but for a different reason. Touch, as I have said, was always distasteful to her, so she liked the untouching Cathars, she loved their celibacy. She implored me to practise the ascetic Brahmacharya of my ancestors, and I was too proud a Brahmin to feel defeated. The bridge was anyhow there, and could not be crossed. I knew I would never go to Spain.

The excerpt which follows occurs towards the middle of *The Serpent and the Rope* and describes, among other things, Savithri's ritual "marriage" with Ramaswamy.

Raja Rao

Walking back and forth in my Kensington room that day – it was a Thursday,
I clearly remember, the day of Jupiter – I thought of the letter I should write
to Pratap. For how could I have gone to Cambridge and seen so much of
Savithri without dropping him a line, some concatenation of words (and
images) that might give him hope? For hope he certainly could have.
Savithri always talked of Pratap as one talks of one's secretary – it must have
come from the atmosphere of palaces – as an inevitable support in all
contingencies, a certainty in a world of uncertainty. If she talked of him
with a touch of condescension it was not because of social differences; it
was just because she liked being kind to something, something inevitable,
unknown, such as a lame horse in the stable or it might be an old bull, fed
in the palace yard till it die; but meanwhile being treated as an elder, a
palace bull, given the best of Bengal gram and the choicest of green grass.
And when it died, for it would "die," it would be given a music-and-flower
funeral and have orange trees planted over its grave. And one day some
virgin would light a lamp and consecrate it, and every day from that
time on the sanctuary would be lit with an oil lamp, as dusk fell over the
palace grove ...

To speak the truth, I hated this attitude of Savithri's. I felt she was so
truly indifferent, so completely resigned to her fate – like all Hindu women –
that for her, life was like a bullock-cart wheel: it was round, and so it had to
move on night after night, and day after day, smelling chilli or tamarind,
rice or coconut, over rut and through monsoon waters purring at the sides
to the fairs in the plains; or to the mountains, high up there, on a known
pilgrimage. What did it matter, she would ask, whether the sun scorched or
the rain poured, or you carried tamarind or saffron? Life's wheel is its own
internal law. Nobody could marry Savithri, nobody could marry a soul, so
why not marry anyone? And why should not that anyone be stump Pratap?
It certainly could not be Hussain Hamdani; and thank heavens his vanity
and self-interest took him to Pakistan and a good job – and Pratap was,
anyway, so very clean, so gentle, so sincere. If one should have a husband
at all, said Savithri, Pratap was the very best.

"What do you think?" she had asked me one evening, a day or two
before my departure from Cambridge. We were not by the river, which
was reserved for us, for our conjoint intuitions of poetry and history – of a

song of Mira's, and again maybe of some historical character from Avignon, Nimes, Carcassonne, Albi or Montpellier. But when we came out into the open street-light we could talk of anything, of Nehru's Government, of father's despair at having three elephants instead of eight, a tradition which had come down from Rajendra Simha III, in the sixteenth century. Finally, in the heart of this extrovert world one can always dig a hollow, make oneself comfortable in a bus shelter, an ABC, or with hot coffee at the Copper Kettle one can sit and talk of Pratap.

"There's such goodness in him. I have never seen anyone so good in life. Not even you," she had said, in mock severity.

"I never said I was good."

"Of course not," she teased, "but you want to be called a saint."

"You say so," I laughed, "and that is your responsibility." I could hear the bells ring the hour on Trinity Tower, so gathering her notes we had jumped into a taxi at the Market Square and rushed off to deposit her safely at the gate of Girton.

"It's me," she said, with that enchanting voice, and even the gatekeeper did not seem to mind very much. "Am I very late?"

He had looked at the clock first, and then at me. "Well, Miss Rathor, the world does not always function by the clock, does it?" he said, with a wink.

She laid the red rose I had bought her on his table, saying, "This is for Catherine," and turning to me she had added, "She's such a nice girl, seven years old; we're great friends. Good night, Ramaswamy, good night, Mr Scott. Good night."

Back in the taxi I said to myself, "Catherine or Pratap, for Savithri it makes no difference. Both are dear because both are familiar, innocent, and inevitable in her daily existence."

Thinking over all this, my letter to Pratap never got written. It was a damp day and I did not go to the British Museum for my work, but as it was already long past three, I took a stroll by the river.

What an imperial river the Thames is – her colour may be dark or brown, but she flows with a majesty, with a maturity of her own knowledge of herself, as though she grew the tall towers beside her, and buildings rose in her image, that men walked by her and spoke inconsequent things – as two horses do on a cold day while the wine merchant delivers his goods at some pub, whispering and frothing to one another – for the Londoner is eminently good. He is so warm, he is indeed the first citizen of the world. The mist on the Thames is pearly, as if Queen Elizabeth the First had squandered her riches and femininity on ships of gold, and Oberon had played on his pipe, so worlds, gardens, fairies and grottoes were created, empires were built and lost, men shouted heroic things to one another and died, but somewhere oné woman, golden, round, imperial, always lay by her young man, his hand over her left breast, his lip touching hers in rich recompense. There's holiness in happiness, and Shakespeare was holy because Elizabeth was happy. Would England not see an old holiness again?

For me, as I have said already, the past was necessary to understand the present. Standing on a bridge near Chelsea, and seeing the pink and yellow lights of the evening, the barges floating down to some light, the city feeling her girth in herself, how I felt England in my bones and breath; how I reverenced her. The buses going high and lit; the taxis that rolled about, green and gentlemanly; the men and women who seemed responsible, not for this Island alone, but for whole areas of humanity all over the globe; strollers – some workman, who had stolen a moment on his way to a job, some father who was showing London to his little daughter, two lovers arm hooked to arm – how with the trees behind and the water flowing they seemed to make history stop and look back at itself.

London was esoteric and preparing for the crowning of another Queen; and Englishmen felt it would be a momentous insight of man into himself. The white man, I felt, did not bear his burden, but the Englishman did. For, after all, it was the English who founded the New World, yet now it was America that naively, boastfully, was proclaiming what every English man and woman really felt – that the dominion of man, the regulation of habeas corpus or the right delivery of some jute bales on Guadalcanal Island in the Pacific, was the business of these noble towers, clocks, balances, stock-books, churring ships, and aeroplanes above, and that there would be good government on earth, and decency and a certain nobility of human behaviour, and all because England was. That I, an Indian who disliked British rule, should feel this only revealed how England was recovering her spiritual destiny, how in anointing her Queen she would anoint herself.

It was nearing six by now and knowing that about this hour Julietta would be at the Stag, I dropped in, took an orangeade and sat waiting for her. Julietta was a great friend of Savithri's. She had left Girton the year before and though I had met her only once I felt I could talk to her about anything.

Julietta and a whole generation of young English people who had either fought in the war or matured during it – Julietta was eighteen in 1945 – were fascinating to me. That is why for an outsider pub life seemed so valuable – he saw the new England, even when the English men and women he met were not particularly young. But England herself had become young – and sovran. Young Englishmen looked so open, so intellectually keen, and the girls seemed so feminine, so uninhibited. It was all so far from the world of Jane Austen or Thackeray, or even from the world of Virginia Woolf. Boys and girls met and mated and helped each other through life with, as one girl remarked to Savithri, the facility of eating an apple. "In fact I was eating an apple," said Marguerite Hoffner, "when he did it to me. What is there in it, anyway, to talk about so much?" Indeed it was explained to me that the coupling of male and female had gone on more and more normally, and that a modern Lady Chatterley would not have to go so far as a gamekeeper, but would find her man beside her in a theatre, on Chelsea Bridge, or in a pub. I only knew the foul-smelling bistros in France, and almost never went to any – could you imagine Madeleine at the Café des Marroniers or in the Rencontre des Pêcheurs? – but the pub, the Stag, was so civilized.

Julietta came in, accompanied by Stephen, a Logical Positivist with a curve of sparse golden hair, a high forehead and lilting green eyes. In his opinion Aristotle had proved that the world was very real: he could not understand how one could doubt one's self.

"And who doubts the doubter?" I asked.

"The doubter."

"Who sees the doubter?"

"My mind," he answered.

"Can my mind see itself?" I pressed.

"Of course. Why not?"

"Can you have two thoughts at a time?" I continued.

"Come, come," he said, waving his glass and feeling very happy, "you don't want me to grow mystical, do you?"

"No," I said, "I am talking to Aristotle."

"Well, Aristotle has decided on the nature of syllogisms."

"Why, have you never heard of the Nyaya system of Indian logic?"

"Nyaya fiddlesticks," said Stephen good-humouredly.

"Come, come," said Julietta, with womanly tenderness, pushing back Stephen's golden hair. Her hands, I noticed, were not as elegant as the sensitivity of her face.

"Can light see itself?" I asked.

"Obviously not," said Stephen.

"Then how can the mind see itself?"

"I told you," shouted Stephen, "not to talk mysticism to me!"

"He's talking sense – and you, non-sense," said Julietta, chivalrously.

"And you my love," he said, kissing her richly before everyone, "you own the castle of intelligence, and I am the Lord." He was obviously getting drunk. I stopped, bought them each a drink and sat down. There was by now a gay crowd of artists in patched elbows, old stockbrokers with indecipherable females, landlords with their dogs, writers who talked, their noses in the air, as though publishers belonged to the tanners' or the drummers' caste – writers, of course, being Brahmins – and there were silent, somnolent painters carrying the tools of their trade, with canvases hidden under some cover, chatting with the bartender. "Half of bitter, please," came the refrain, gentle and gruff, elegant and cockney, and the whole place filled with smoke, silence and talk. The smell of perfumes mingled with other smells of females and men, making one feel that the natural man is indeed a good man – *lo naturale è sempre senza errore* – that logic had nothing to do with life. Life was but lovely, and loveliness had golden hair and feminine intimacy, while the Thames flowed.

"One last question," I said, bringing more beer to Julietta and Stephen. "The brain is made of matter ..."

"That is so, my inquisitor," said Stephen, laughing.

"... so the brain is made of the same stuff as earth?"

"That is so, my Indian Philosopher."

"Then how can the earth be objective to the earth – understand the earth?"

"It's just like asking – I beg pardon, Julietta – if I copulate with Julietta, as I often and joyfully do – and the nicer, the better when there's a drink –

then how do I understand Julietta? The fact is I don't understand Julietta. I never will understand Julietta. I don't know that I love her – even when I tell her sweet and lovely things. I'm happy and that's all that matters. I'm a solipsist," he concluded laughing.

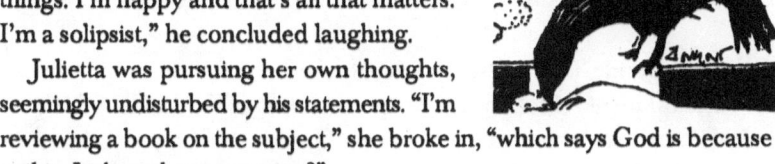

Julietta was pursuing her own thoughts, seemingly undisturbed by his statements. "I'm reviewing a book on the subject," she broke in, "which says God is because evil is. Is that what you mean?"

"I don't know what you mean by God. But it needs a pair of opposites to make a world. Only two things of different texture and substance can be objective to one another. Otherwise it's like two drops of mercury in your hand, or like linking the Red Sea and the Arabian Sea – they are both water and the same. I ask you, how can the mind, made of the same stuff as the earth, be *positive* about the earth? Water is not positive to water – water is positive to nothing. Water is. So something is. And since isness is the very stuff of that something, all you can say is, Is is."

"I knew Indians were mad, that Gandhi was mad. And now, now I have the proof," said Stephen. "I'm an old anarchist. I believe that matter is true, that Julietta is true, that I am true, and you also my friend, who stands me drinks, and spends ninepence each time on me and ninepence on Julietta. Now, go and get me another. This time I don't want a half. I want the whole damn thing, and long live Pandit Nehru."

People from the counter turned to look and lifted their glasses to India, to me. How wonderful to be in an English pub, I thought. Such humanity you would get in France only amongst the working classes, never among the dark-faced, heaving, fingering bourgeois. The sensuality of the bourgeois is studied, it is a vice, because he was defeated before he went to it: Baudelaire was already defeated by his stepfather and his smelly mother before he went to his Negress. You see the dark because you want to prove yourself the light; dialectic is on the lip of the rake. But in this young England, which I knew so little, I felt man was more primary and innocent, more inexhaustible. He did not have a "judas" on his door – he did not cultivate the concierge yet. Flowers grew in his gardens, red fluorescent lights lit the top of the buildings, and beneath them, the Thames flowed. White cliffs of chalk begirt the isle at the estuary, and you could see seagulls rising with the ferry lights and returning to the night. Soon I'd have to be back in France, and I shivered to the bottom of my spine. Lord, would that I could make the moment stay, and make the world England.

Walking beside Savithri the next day, towards the evening – we were on the Embankment – I told her of my premonition of England, of this new island, knowing she was going to have a Queen: the King was already a little not there, he was so ill, and the leaves and the water in Hyde Park, the very sparrows and doves and dogs seemed to feel that there was something new happening to England, that the Regency was going soon to end.

"What Regency?" asked Savithri, with the air of a pupil to her teacher.

"Why, don't you see, ever since the death of King George the Fifth. Ever since the abdication of Edward the Eighth – that new King Hal who would have created his own Falstaff, and which a fat and foolish bank-clerk civilization drove into exile – this country, which chose her own church because her King preferred to choose his own wives – having become big, with an Empire and all that involves: and she became so afraid of the Stock Exchange, and of what Mrs Petworth would say in Perth or Mr Kennedy would say in Edmonton, Alberta – for remember it's all a question of wool shares or the London-Electric – this mercantile country drove away what might have been her best King, or at least the best loved, since Henry the Fifth. Do you remember those broken French sentences addressed to his Kate: *Donc vostre est France, et vous estes miennes*? And England put in his place a noble Bharatha who apologized every time he spoke, saying, You think I am your King, but I am only Brother to the King; I tremble, I hesitate, I wish my brother were here. And he ruled the land with the devotion of a Bharatha, worshipping the sandal of his loved brother placed on the throne."

"Kingship is an impersonal principle; it is like life and death, it knows no limitations. It is history made carnate, just as this Thames is the principle of water made real. And when a king apologizes for being a king he is no king; he establishes a duality in himself, so he can have no authority. The King can do no wrong, comes from the idea that the Principle can do no wrong, just as the communists say, the Party can do no wrong. Talking of the communists the other day in Cambridge, I forgot to say that communism must succeed; happily for us, to be followed by kingship. Look at the difference between Hitler and Stalin. Stalin, the man of iron, the mystery behind the Kremlin, the impersonal being; to whom torture, growth or death are essentials of an abstract arithmetic. As the Catholics looked for omens in the Bible, Stalin looked to impersonal history for guidance. Stalin lives and dies, in history as history, not outside history. Hitler, on the other hand, lived in his dramatic Nuremberg rallies, visible, concrete, his voice the most real of real; his plans personal, demoniac, his whims astrological, his history Hitlerian – Germanic, if you will – dying a hero, a Superman: Zarathustra. Duality must lead to heroism, to personality development, to glory. The dualist must become saintly, must cultivate humility, because he knows he could be big, great, heroic and personal, an emperor with a statue and a pediment."

Here, silently Savithri led me on to Chelsea Bridge, and looking down at the river, I continued:

"But the impersonal is neither humble nor proud – who could say whether Stalin was humble or proud? But one can say so easily and so eminently of another Cathar, another purist, Trotsky – that noble revolutionary of perfect integrity – that he was vain. He would gladly have jumped into the fire, down the *campo di crémats*, smiling and singing, I am incorruptible, I am pure, I am the flame. Stalin would have the Kremlin guarded with a thousand sentries, a few thousand spies, killing each one when he knew too much, first a Yagoda, then a Yezhov. For him history killed them, just as an Inca chief believed his god, not himself, wanted a sacrifice. Stalin bore no personal enmity to Trotsky, for this was real history. Even if Stalin the man was jealous of Trotsky, the flame of pure Revolution (and Stalin might have admitted this), Stalin, who is history, had to kill Trotsky the anti-history. The pure, the human, the vainglorious leader's personal magic was an unholy impediment to the movement of history. In the same way Marshal Toukhachesvsky had to die – the impersonal cannot allow that any man be a hero. Stalin was no hero: he was a king, a god."

"How well you hold forth," teased Savithri, tugging my arm. She wanted me to look at the barges as they floated down, or at the clear moon that played between the clouds and delighted Savithri as it might have a child.

"Moon, moon, Uncle Moon," I chanted a Kanarese nursery rhyme, "Mama, Chanda-mama," and then we went back to history.

"The Superman is our enemy. Look what happened in India. Sri Aurobindo wanted, if you please, to improve on the Advaita of Sri Sankara – which was just like trying to improve on the numerical status of zero. Zero makes all numbers, so zero begins everything. All numbers are possible when they are in and of zero. Similarly all philosophies are possible in and around Vedanta. But you can no more improve on Vedanta than improve on zero. The zero, you see, the sunya, is impersonal; whereas one, two, three and so on are all dualistic. One always implies many. But zero implies *nothing*. I am not one, I am not two, I am neither one, nor two: Aham nirvikalpi nirakara rupih. I am the I. So, to come back to Sri Aurobindo, he shut himself in Pondicherry and started building a new world. If you can build a house of three storeys, you can build one of five, eight, ten or twelve storeys – and go as high as the Empire State Building or any other structure, higher and yet higher. And just as aeroplanes at first went fifty miles an hour, then eighty, then a hundred, two hundred, three, and now go far beyond the speed of sound, similarly you can build any number of worlds, can make the mind, the psyche so athletic that you can build world after world, but you cannot go beyond your self, your impersonal principle. And just as the materialism of Stalin and not his impersonal sense of history, but his material interpretation of history made him end up like the Egyptians in being embalmed and made immortal as history, Sri Aurobindo tried to make this perishable, this chemical, this historical body, this body of eighteen aggregates, as Nagarjuna called it, *permanent*. Moralism and materialism must go together. The undying is a moral concept – for death is a biological phenomenon, an anti-life phenomenon, against the nature of the species. Not to die, to drink the elixir of life, is moral – it is to transcend the phenomenal as celibacy is the transcending of nature. The moral must end in mummification and the pyramid."

"I am breathless," said Savithri, "you take me too far and too quickly."

"Just a moment," I begged, "I'll soon finish. The Superman is the enemy of man – whether you call him Zarathustra, Sri Aurobindo, Stalin, or Father Zossima."

"That's a new gentleman in history," laughed Savithri.

"Oh," I remarked, a little irritated by her disturbance, "it's a saintly character in Dostoevsky: he smells – he decomposes – when he dies, and thus disturbs the odour of sanctity his miracles had brought to him. When Sri Aurobindo died his disciples must have felt the same: the deathless master, who wanted to consecrate his body, consign it to immortality, died like any other. His breath must have stopped, his eyes must have become fixed in their sockets, but being a Yogi he may have been sitting in a lotus posture, and that would have given him beauty and great dignity."

"And now?" begged Savithri. The damp of the river was rising. "I am a biological phenomenon, and food and warmth are necessary. Besides," she added, pulling her sari over her breast as though it was she who would suffer, "besides, I am terrified of your lungs." So I obeyed and we slowly strolled along the Embankment.

"You know," I said, "Julietta is probably at the Stag."

"Ah," she burst out laughing, "so you remember geography and biography, do you? Come, let us go."

"Oh, never, never!" I shouted. "You, Savithri, in a pub?"

"Pub or no pub, take me anywhere, my love," she said, so gently, so dedicatedly and with such a pressure of her fingers on my arm that the whole world rose up into my awareness renewed; "take me anywhere, and keep me warm." Was it I, the foolish schoolteacher, this miserable five foot eleven of Brahmin feebleness, this ungainly, myopic over-bent creature to whom she had said those two tender, commonplace but perfect words? It was the first time she ever said them to me, and perhaps she had never said them to anyone else. History and my mind vanished somewhere, and I put my arms round that little creature – she hardly came to my shoulder – and led her along alleyways and parkways, past bus stop, bridge and mews – to a taxi.

"Let's go to Soho," I said, and as I held her in my arms, how true it seemed we were to each other, a lit space between us, a presence – God. *"Dieu est logé dans l'intervalle entre les hommes,"* I recited Henri Frank to her.

"Yes, it is God," she whispered, and we fell into the silence of busy streets. After a long moment, she whispered again, "Take me with you, my love."

"Will you come, Savithri?"

"Take me with you my love, anywhere."

"Come," I said, "this minute, now ..."

"No, I cannot. I must go back. I must go back to Pratap."

I pressed her against me ever more tenderly. "Come, I'll take you," I persisted.

"To God," she said and fell into my lap. I touched her lips as though they were made with light, with honey, with the space between words of poetry, of song. London was no longer a city for me, it was myself: the world was no longer space for me, it was a moment of time, it was now.

At Barbirolli's I ordered a Chianti, and said, as though it had some meaning, "And now you must learn Italian.

> *Io ritornai dalla santissima onda*
> *rifatto si come piante novelle*
> *renovellate di novella fronda*
> *Puro e disposto a salire alle stelle, "*

I recited. "You must learn Italian, for God has texture in that language. God is rich and Tuscan, and the Arno has a bridge made for marriage processions."

"So has Allahabad," she added, somewhat sadly. "And appropriately it is called the Hunter Bridge."

"May I go on with my Superman?" I begged.

"The biological sense of warmth having come back to me – and how nice this Chianti is" – she raised her glass – "I can now follow any intricacy of thought. I like to play chess with you in history."

"The Minister is the Superman," I started.

"And the King?"

"The Sage. The Vedantin, himself beyond duality, is in himself, through duality and nonduality."

"That's too difficult with Chianti. I wish, Rama – shall I call you that from now? – I wish you could sing me a song, and I would lie on your lap, far away where there is no land or road, no river or people, no father, fiancé, filigree, palace or elephants – perhaps just a mother – and on some mountain ..."

"In Kailasa ..." I said.

"You would sit in meditation."

"And you?"

"Pray, that you might awaken and not burn the world with that third eye – that eye which plays with history," she laughed.

"And parrots would sing, and the mango leaf be tender, be like copper with morning sunshine."

"And I would go round you three times, once, twice, thrice, and fall at your ash-coloured feet, begging that the Lord might absorb me unto himself ... I am a woman," she added hesitantly, "a Hindu woman.

> *Meretho Giridhara Gopala ...,*
> *Mine the mountain-bearing Krishna,*
> *My lord none else than He.*"

History, Stalin and the Superman had vanished. Trying to solve the puzzle of history, like some hero in a fable, I had won a bride. A princess had come out of the budumekaye, but the moment I had entered the world of the seven sisters the Prime Minister's son had led a revolution in the palace, had imprisoned the other six, and put us two under arrest. King Mark of Tintagel awaited his Iseult. I would have to give her to him, but having drunk the potion of Granval I would meet her by brooks and forests; I would be torn by dragons, but someday we would lie in the forest, the sword between us. Some day love would be strong enough to shatter the rock to fragments, and we should be free to wander where we would, build an empire if we cared.

"And we shall have a bambino," she said, and laughed as though she had caught my thought.

"Two," I added. "One is Ganesha and the other Kumara."

"And we shall throw colours on each other at Holi under the mountain moon. Our Indian Eros shoots with a flower, so why burn him?"

"Why not?" I asked. "The third eye opens when the attraction has ended. I hope you are not attracted by me?"

"Oh, no," she said. "If I were attracted by attraction, there would be no one like Hussain. He looks like someone from a Moghul painting, lovely with a long curve of eyebrow, a thin waist, very long gentle hands – and inside here," she pointed to her head, "all empty. His heart is filled with popped rice, curly and white and isolated. Muslims know how to please a woman," she finished, rather sadly.

"And a Hindu?"

"A Hindu woman knows how to worship her Krishna, her Lord. When the moon shines over the Jumna and lights are lit in the households, and the cows are milked, then it is Janaki's son plays on the banks of the Yamuna in Brindavan. The cattle tear their ropes away, the deer leave the forests and come leaping to the groves, and with the peacocks seated on the branches of the asoka, Krishna dances on the red earth. What Gopi, my Lord, would not go to this festival of love? Women lose their shame and men lose their anger, for in Brindavan Krishna the Lord dances. We women are bidden to that feast. Come," she said, as though it was too much emotion to bear.

As we wandered down the streets, Piccadilly with its many coloured lights, the Tube entrances and the bus queues gave us a sense of reality.

Finally I took her to some women's hostel off Gower Street – where she always had rooms reserved for her and where she was looked after by her friend Gauri from Hyderabad, round as Savithri herself, but loquacious, big and protective. I was always so afraid of Savithri getting lost. It was not only a matter of bringing back her glasses or pen, but one always felt one had to bring Savithri back to Savithri.

"Ah, I am very real," she protested. "And tomorrow you will see how clever I am at taking buses. I'll jump into a 14 at Tottenham Court Road and be in Kensington at ten precise," she promised as I left her. I knew that at ten she would still be talking away to Gauri about some blouse pattern or somebody's marriage in Delhi. I knew I would have to telephone and ask her if she knew the time. "I promise you, you need not telephone. Tomorrow I will be punctual as Big Ben." With Savithri the profound and the banal lived so easily side by side.

I touched her hand at the door, to know I could touch her, and carried the feel of it home. It was like touching a thought, not just a thought of jug or water, or a pillow or a horse, but a thought as it leaps, as it were, in that instant where the thought lights itself, as the meteor its own tail. I felt it was of the substance of milk, of truth, of joy seen as myself.

Next day, when I was washed and dressed and had meditated and rested – I was in a muslin dhoti and kurtha – there was still no sign of Savithri at ten or at ten past ten. Not long after, she entered in a South Indian sari of a colour we in Mysore call "colour of the sky," with a peacock-gold choli, and a large kumkum on her forehead. She looked awed with herself, and full of reverence. As I went to touch her I refrained – something in her walk was strange.

"I have been praying."

"To whom?"

"To Shiva," she whispered. Then she opened her bag and took out a sandal-stick. Her movements were made of erudite silences. "Please light this for me," she begged.

By the time I had lit the sandal-stick in the bathroom and come out she had spread her articles of worship about her. There was a small silver censer, with the camphor. There was a silver kumkum-box. She had a few roses, too, fresh and dripping with water.

"Bring me some Ganges water in this."

I put some plain water in her silver plate. She put kumkum into the water.

"Will you permit me?" she asked. "Permit this, a woman's business?"

"Oh, no!" I protested.

"But it was you who told me – at home a man obeys a woman, that it's Hindu dharma."

"I obey," I said.

Then she knelt before me, removed one by one my slippers and my stockings and put them aside gently – distantly. She took flower and kumkum, and mumbling some song to herself, anointed my feet with them. Now she lit a camphor and placing the censer in the middle of the kumkum-water she waved the flame before my face, once, twice and three times in arathi. After this she touched my feet with the water, and made aspersions of it over her head. Kneeling again and placing her head on my feet, she stayed there long, very long, with her breath breaking into gentle sobs. Then she gently held herself up. Taking the kumkum from the box I placed it on her brow, at the parting of her hair, and there where her bosom heaved, the abode of love. I could not touch her any more, nor could she touch me, and we stood for an isolate while. Then suddenly I remembered my mother's toerings.

"Stop where you are for a moment," I begged.

"I can go nowhere," she answered, "I belong to you."

Gently, as if lost in the aisles of a large temple, I walked about my room, opened my trunk and slowly removed the newspaper cover, then the coconut, the betel nuts, the kumkum that Little Mother had destined for her daughter-in-law. "I, too, had come prepared for this morning," I said.

"Really?" she smiled, for in me nothing astonished her.

"Yes, but it was a preparation made a very long time ago – a long, long time, Savithri. Not a life, not ten lives, but life upon life ..."

"Yes," she said. "This Cambridge undergraduate, who smokes like a chimney and dances to barbarian jazz, she says unto you, I've known my Lord for a thousand lives, from Janam to Janam have I known my Krishna ..."

"And the Lord knows himself because Radha is, else he would have gone into penance and sat on Himalaya. The Jumna flows and peacock feathers are on his diadem, because Radha's smiles enchant the creepers and the birds. Radha is the music of dusk, the red earth, the meaning of night. And this, my love, my spouse," I whispered, "is from my home. This is coconut, this is betel nut, this is kumkum and these the toerings my Mother wore, and left for my bridal." Slowly I anointed her with kumkum from my home, offered her the coconut and the betel nuts – there were eight, round and auspicious ones. "And now I shall place the toerings on your feet."

"Never," she said angrily. "You may be a Brahmin for all I know. But do you know of a Hindu woman who'd let her Lord touch her feet?"

"What a foolish woman you are!" I said, laughing. "And just by this you show why a Brahmin is necessary to educate you all, kings, queens, peasants and merchants. Don't you know that in marriage both the spouse and the espoused become anointed unto godhead? That explains why in Hindu marriages the married couple can only fall at the feet of the Guru and the Guru alone – for the Guru is higher than any god. Thus, I can now place them on your feet."

So much theology disturbed and convinced her, and she let me push the toerings on to her second toes, one on the left and the other on the right. The little bells on them whisked and sang: I was happy to have touched Savithri's feet.

The toerings were the precise size for her. Little Mother was right: for Madeleine they would have been too big.

Savithri sat on my bed, and the sun who had made himself such an auspicious presence fell upon her clear Rajput face as she sang Mira.

> Sadhu matha ja ... Sadhu matha ja ...
> O cenobite, O cenobite, do not go.
> Make a pyre for me, and when I burn,
> Put the ashes on your brow,
> O cenobite, do not go...

We were at Victoria by nine o'clock. We were so happy and so sad altogether, as though no one could take us away from each other and nobody marry us again. We were not married that morning, we discovered, we had ever been married – else how understand that silent, whole knowledge of one another?

"My love, my love, my love," she repeated, as though it were a mantra, "my love, and my Lord."

"And when will Italy be, and the bridge on the Arno, and the bambino?" I asked.

She put her head out of the window of the train, and for the first time I noticed the collyrium that tears had spread over her cheeks and face.

"I promise you one thing," she said.

"And what, Princess, may that be?" I replied, laughing.

"Parvathi says she will come to Shiva, when Shiva is so lost in meditation that were he to open his eyes the three worlds would burn."

"Meaning?" I was so frightened that my voice went awry and hollow.

"I'll come when you don't need me, when you can live without me, O cenobite." I knew the absolute meaning of it, the exactitude, for Savithri could never whisper, never utter but the whole of truth, even in a joke. But it was always like a sacred text, a cryptogram, with different meanings at different hierarchies of awareness.

"I understand and accept," I answered, with a clear and definite navel-deep voice. I can hear myself saying that to this day.

"Italy is," she continued, relentless, "when Shivoham, Shivoham is true."

"Meanwhile?"

"Meanwhile I go back to Allahabad and become Mrs Pratap Singh."

"And run the household of the new Governor," I added, to hide my acknowledgement and pain. For by now Pratap had become Personal Secretary to His Excellency the Governor of some Indian Province. "Palace or Government House, they're equal and opposite," I laughed.

"And what will the learned historian do?" she asked.

"Finish the history of the Cathars, and well-wed and twice-wed, become Professor of Medieval European History at some Indian University. India is large and very diverse," I pleaded.

"I shall always be a good pupil," she joked. The train whistled, and took her away.

I took a taxi, went back to the Stag – or the Bunch of Grapes, for I do not remember exactly – and stood a drink to some bearded painter who talked abstract art and had a beautiful face. Holy is a pub when one is holy oneself.

# The Policeman and
the Rose

W hen I was arrested my problem was not me but it. You see, I was arrested when I was born, and that is many, many years ago, a teen and truant score and more. All men are arrested the moment they are born. So are the women. The policemen are huge, big, when you are born – so big and shining – that is why the child cries. Some see the face of the policeman – a pollen face – and others see the bottom of a cob – he's slick and sumptuous. Others see his many teeth. Every living *man* has a policeman, and his name is your name, his address your address, his dreams your dreams. (Of course in the dream, his name, force and function are other and inappropriate, but that is another matter.) In the last life too he was a policeman – he always was a policeman. That is why we have such a grand state. We have a policeman for every man – Voltaire said the civilized state *"est un état bien policé"* – civilization is the cross-road where the policeman stands. To the left is the past, to the right is the dawn, and behind you was death, and before you is life. The policeman goes thin, in some countries and climates,

First published in *The Illustrated Weekly of India* in 1963. It was later included in the collection *The Policeman and the Rose* (1978).

as you grow big. In some countries he's quite monstrous, but he has a holy paradise after death, girls and all. Paradise is made for the policeman, aside of time. He polishes his medals, of friendships and gifts and sanctified murders in the name of God. Paradise is on a percentage basis. The insurance company is only concerned with medals. God sits on the throne and dispenses human justice. If the policeman is somewhat thin, he sits under the seat of God. If his uniform is bright, he is sent to a place of many fires. But if he is teeny-weeny with a soft moustache and a saintly odour, then he is seated in a room with television sets. He receives prostrations, camphor-burnings, coconut ceremonies, garlands. He lives on sound and sight. And some say – though I have never gone that far into the true understanding of the mystery – that some policemen are thrown into the world again, fat or small, bright or buffoon, and we know all of them. For this is a police state. The bars collide with our flesh – the policeman has those marks morning and evening, and knows them only at death. For death is a bath and we know our marks then. After death there is birth, according to some as you know, and no sooner are you born than there is a policeman. And this is the story of such a policeman, big, blustering, cummerbund, collar and sash, and a red turban (like the Madras suburban policeman) for his noble crown. He is awake when I am awake, he sleep-dreams as I have wake-sleeps, and he just has no existence in the deep-sleep state. God once got angry with him and killed him, but he became many. And as God killed the many they became many, many. Today God does not know what to do – so I have to remind God all about it. You may overhear me if you so please. I am a revolutionary, and God does not like revolution. He likes the totalitarian state. I want to be free.

You see, my policeman was born thousands on thousands of thousands of years ago. He was a native of space and his germ was the atom. The atom played at the crossroads and created water. Now, water is a silly old thing that moves, and always in one direction. So he became water and flowed towards the dawn. The dawn changed him into fire. The fire of the dawn changed my policeman into a red and leaping thing, and it combusted and flew into sanctuaries, and made many fevers big and small. The fires subsided into a window-space and became the noble earth: Earth thou origin of the sperm and splendour of the rose-blood, as say the ancient texts. And the earth became the air, that is airy-fairy, hunky-dory – papa-punya, birth and death. You could go to the hilltop and drink the holy air, and be yet not free. Your policeman is naked but he's all blind. He knows all there is to know, but he does not know the knower. When he knows the knower there is no knower. Knowledge is knowledge.

The story of the policeman is my own biography. So why hide it from you. I, that is, the policeman, was born in the Aswija-Shuddha when the moon was bright and of the eleventh day in the year 19 –, that is some thirty three years ago. He, that is, the policechild, cried like every other child, for, as I said before, I was arrested immediately. And I knew immediately why I was arrested by the policeman. For if there is no policeman there is no difference between hunger and satiation, darkness and light, mother and father, truth and bogus. The policeman, just as on the road, had to stand and say – this is left, that is right, and so right and left were made. My policeman made a nixie speech to me, nevertheless. When I was born, he said: "My child, I know your antecedents, or rather, I know why you are hot and cold," that is how he explained. "I am a big policeman for a small child. You are really free. Grow and become free, and my happiness is in my own dissolution. You seek your death of me, the death of deaths. Death happens to me. Never to you. So why worry? The bigger I am, the smaller you are. Ravana was big. But small Rama was light. Ravana was strong. Rama was young and meek. But Rama conquered the dark island of Lanka and freed Sita. Ravana in being born sought his death through Rama. Ravana was the police-jamedar. You are free. Go."

I remembered Rama and Ravana of Lanka. Of course I did. I was once a contemporary of Rama and Ravana, and had been a trefoil grass that Rama trod on in the principality of Kishkindha. I knew Sita, for she used to bathe in the Kulapati pond, and I was the twin-eyed weed by the footpath. She was beautiful. Rama was seeing itself. Ravana was like myself – he was all arms, eyes, foot, sight, sound, odour, audition and tactility. He had a mysterious jungle-tingle in his being, that sang and tingled to sight, sound, touch, tasted in tranquillity and smelt in periphery, and which was aimed at Rama every time he made battle. It was like a telescope – Rama looked without looking and saw – and fought. The jungle-tingle made the story of the world.

Then I died – I knew many other signs and conditions – and I was eaten by a horse in the army of Rama. And I was reborn here and there, as cactus, oleander, cymbalicum, gander, otter, polivel, civet-cat, leopard, hog, bungam bao, loripel, caesar-dog, walking elephant, horse and panicky hound – I rushed up branches and shewed my teeth, and I ran up the forest and sang through the leaves, the rivers knew me as tom-fish and proggered-crocodile, they knew me as pigmy, iron-man, moon-man, Aryan, Dravidian, Druidic, Hindu – I was policeman here, I was policeman there, sometimes very big, sometimes small – Turk, Ethiopic, and Dayad, I was born and reborn, till I came to Rama Krishnayya and Parvatamma, in the said Aswija-Shuddha, when the moon was bright and of the eleventh day in the year 19 – in the city of Madurai at noon and twelve minutes, and then my real story begins. The policeman, as I have related, made the said speech and I understood. I knew all of course. I was free. I knew also who the policeman was, I was under arrest. I knew also I was a child but I had a mother. And so I grew up.

And growing up is a very easy thing. You eat and you wake up, you go to school and you sleep. You hear father, mother, brothers, sisters, aunts, uncles, the two grandfathers and grandmothers, widowed grandaunts, servants in the fields, and pariahs in the village outskirts, birds in the trees and lamentations for the dead – you hear all of them and all there, and you say: this is the world. The policeman says go left – and you go left. The policeman says this is good food, and you eat it. And you fall ill and the doctors are called, who give you herbs in juice and metals in powder and you wake up, and you smile, and all are happy with you. Grandmother gives you a pair of bangles in gold, and you can shew them to your school fellows saying: "Say, I had pneumonia, and I saw the God of Death. But since I returned to life grandmother went to the goldsmith Ramachetty, and these were made. Aren't they nice for Divali?" They are all jealous and they say, "Of course!" but their bellies burn with red capsicum. You wake up. You want the whole world to see you are alive. You can walk, and you can talk. No, nobody wants to talk to you – nobody wants to hug and embrace and call you brother. Why should they? Your father is rich and lives in a city. Your grandfather is old and learned in Vedanta. Your uncle is a municipal commissioner. You are a bad fellow – besides, you had pneumonia, and you look so good. At night the policeman sits beside you and tells you, "Child, you know what that is – it's me. It's all me. Don't worry." "How is it you?" "Well, you see, as soon as you are born, in fact from many lives, we've your charts made. If there is red light here – there must be green light there. If there is right here – left is there. It's all like that, male and female, birth and death, pain and pleasure are green lights and red lights of the metropolis. And you are a citizen: the only citizen." "I do not understand." "Grow up and travel," says the policeman. "You will see wonders everywhere ..." I grew up. I excrete and try to fornicate. I miss and try again, and there's incarnation and sorrow and the killing of the child in the womb, and the marriage papers for a regularized marriage. I am married, you know, and the policeman has made all this so splendid, so ordinary. You go to the municipal officer and say, "I marry this lady," and she says, "I obey you as long as I live," and you go home married. And you weep. On the first night of marriage the policeman sits by you and says, "Son, why weep? Male and female, etc, etc ..." And I understand. Yes, left and right. I jump the wall. The glass-pricks tear my skin. I came to the Western world – world of honour and liberty. France of Robespierre: the crown of flowers on the Queen of Reason. And a whole world in acclamation. France, dear France of liberty. In a room in Rue Vaneau – exactly 48-*bis* Rue Vaneau – the policeman sits by me and recounts me my story. "Saturn

in the fifth house," he says, "and Mercury in the fourth, the Moon making a trine with Jupiter in the seventh, and the Sun, lord of the sixth, in the second house, casting his uncharitable looks on Venus in the eighth – what else do you expect, son? When you want to go left – you go left, left-right. When you want to go right, you go north. When you want to go anywhere, you go to Paradise – you see God face to face." How I saw God is a story that nobody shall know. That is the only thing the policeman did not note correctly in his diary. He just saw me disappear. He thought I was dead. But I was all a-glorying in God. I woke up. He smiled, a little angrily. He hated to erase his notes. I wept for joy. That was written in the stars. One thing I saw. The policeman had suddenly grown two inches shorter, and his clothes had grown shabbier. I said, "Why this look?" and he said, "I've had an inspection. My diary was inaccurate. So I have been demoted." But I was strangely happy. And it is from then started the rivalry between him and me, which can only end in his death. Old and tattered, when he sits besides me, listening to my inner words, he stretches his ears lower and nearer to listen. He has grown so small, he can only reach up to my black mole above the right breast. This pigmy of me brings compassion to the heart and that is why you sometimes see me with a tear in my left eye. I weep for myself.

Tattered and torn of ligament, seedless in loin, and with round booing holes in heart and head, I walk this earth interminably, I, the policeman. My beat is everywhere – and wheresoever I go that place *is* and takes shape and buildings rise and mountains and the endaemonic Mediterranean, with castles and sunsets and beautiful women coming out with big bosoms and in white-horse carriages – I like the lace hats of l'Arlésienne and Mado of Avignon, and I like sail-boats – I am old and red-lipped and lecherous – my casquet stuck to a side, my belly hanging in my hands, I stand and gaze at my own pure shadow. I see him. Do you see him? He is so funny and round and stumpy, his face against the shadow of the battleships. I am drunk because I can love no one – I am impotent – and can only fornicate with low women, for I have genitals. I live on the splendour of others – I steal the stealer. All policemen live on sin. The policeman alone is sin – otherwise the world would be a mountain-lake of white floating swans. The moon claims the policeman – not so the sun. In fact, the policeman arrested himself and that is the whole of the truth.

So it was in Paris I walked with the policeman and talked with him and found him everywhere, in shop windows, with big bulging eyes and each eye a wonder to see. I saw eyes in Paris bookshop windows such as I have never seen anywhere, small eyes, big eyes, green eyes, white-feathery eyes, lathery eyes, parroty eyes, pepper eyes and progressive eyes – red eyes for the red and all the world grew into Red beauty – (and this you will find in Rue Racine) – and green eyes and scarlet eyes, soutane and sepulchre beads and Biblical eyes – you find them just behind in smutty shops with

big squares and courtyards and bright red geraniums at the bay windows –
sooty eyes bespeaking of paradise, yellow eyes in Luxembourg, eyes of the
young, eyes of children and lovers and of the autumnal falling leaves –
everywhere you see eyes in Paris, and they all had colours and I loved
them. I lived in Rue Servandoni later – and had two eyes there that had
needle connection and logic was its palaetiology. For on the point of the
needle was my love born – and it started stitching my tatterment. Oh, the
love-needle, the pertinence, the power, and the purity of the stitching needle.
My heart was made into a Hindu sack with prayer-verses on the top as of
Benares – and I counted the doubtful beads. I was virtuous and I took on
an assigned form. The needle stitched and stitched me, and I took on a
white and wandlike shape. I became a magician of looks, and I gave eyes
to many. I opened a shop of Hindu eyes – I the policeman – and Oh,
what a chatter and a clamour was there. God, God is my business, I
cried – Hindu gods. Five *sous* a hundred tricks – standing on the nose and
breathing through the umbilical stitch, practising celibacy through baths
and kundalini – etc, etc ... – eating milk and nuts to walk in the air, eating
bitter neem leaves and sherbet for swallowing nails and toothbrushes and
broken glass, – for telling the future – motor cars, mansions and marriages,
and all, fortunes – I opened such a shop. The trade was good. I did much
business. The Municipal Council of Perpignan – for I had moved there by
now – voted me a certificate of fine conduct. And all the virgins came to
my confessions. I dealt in potions that increased physiological virginity –
gave no scratches or itches or leucorrhoea.– you touched me and you
were cured. It was wonderful. And God was the message they got. I was
virtuous and good. And I grew big. I became fashionable. Newspapers
spoke of me. I was the Policeman of God, and my certificates hung on all
my four walls. I was given the *Legion d'Honneur*, Second Class, God seemed
to speak to me from the heavens every night – and all day all night the
logical needle stitched my sores, and when I woke up, I had a good bath
and I looked so fresh and young. I could walk the Promenade des Anglais
with the agility of a tennis player. They said, here goes the Policeman of
God – and later they came and sate me by them in chaises longues, and as
the sun poured on me tender and golden, I became a legitimate divinity. I
had fruits and flowers offered to me, and I was right happy. I was God.

Now, having set sail on this pilgrimage, I wanted to become a pukka God. So I went to India – my virtue would now have confirmation, my miracles have rupee value, my mouth would smell of fresh roses. My shop in Avignon – where I had moved to – was kept open by a lady, pious and all that, and she put flowers and burnt sandal-sticks at the right places. More men and women came to honour me when I was gone – the miracle worked even better. Papers started lamenting my departure. The confessional was filled with awaiting virgins. The blind stood at the shop window and the rich in carrioles. What a magnificent clientele said the Doctor, my neighbour. The Ministry of Health wrote to me saying I was promoted to the *Légion d'Honneur*, First Class. It was notified in the *Gazette*. The bishop himself sent me the rosette with apostolic blessing. At the Cathedral the head of the chapter said a novena for me.

In India, however, when I reached the Sanctuary of the Beacon, I lay on a cot and in between my sleep someone must have held converse with me, and I woke up in my own pus. The stitches all came off. By my bed were crowds and lizards that fed on my remains. My skin hung on my shoulder like a coat and my spinal cord was all visible and white. I saw into my entrails and it was totally a world of corpuscled virtue. A man was putting his finger to the blood and tasted to see if it was human or not. I was alone.

Then it was I was given a copy of my biography, a uniform and my police number 42177 MP. I was now returned my medals, and my service book was read out to me. It wasn't so bad. I was a policeman that was all. At the District Hospital I was well looked after. I ate coconut fresh from the garden, and water of coconuts I consumed – I ate mango and cashew nuts, and much milk I drank. I improved quickly and I walked the earth again – I was thin and tall, clean and clear – I walked simply. I knew I was under arrest. I knew the *Travancore Civil and Police Code*. I would be discharged when the time came. But now I must do my duty. Of an evening when the sun sat low and a lot of stars came up suddenly with the palm-trees and the temple music, I would open my biography and read it chapter by chapter, and find it funny and tearful. I did not forget the Promenade des Anglais. Meanwhile my shop in Avignon was sold and from the proceeds many of my debts were paid, and they erected a monument for me at the Place des

Fontaines. They declared me a deceased and honoured citizen. My letters disturbed them.

And finally when I came back to Avignon, they said, the gathered virgins of Avignon, "Look, look, is that your face – we have done more miracles since you left us and in your name and then you come. You smell differently – you are too funnily clothed for words – we are the heirs of God, and we knew what is right and what is wrong. White is right and pink is wrong. Silver is sin and gold cataskeatic. Salt is spirit and earth fire. *Miséricorde*. Leave us with the statue." They made me offer flowers to my statue, and when I took the statue away, and brought a chair and sat me there, they rose in such a fury that I fled. They were sure I was a God – rightly stitched and all that, and well-tailored – and now I was happily dead. In Avignon you can still go to the Place des Fontaines and see me worshipped. I hear echoes of it in the papers, and in Latin gossip.

And through Paris and America I went, and Japan to Travancore.

Why Travancore? For there you've Two-Feet and a rose. The rose is red elsewhere, in Avignon or in Paris, and white in Travancore. The rose of Travancore is the story of a pilgrimage. I went with my red rose of aught and naught, born in a palace garden and carried in a palanquin had seen the sunshine of the Himalaya, and was hidden by the moon, such a rose I carried and to Travancore I came. For Truth is Travancore, and Travancore has Two-Feet, and so Truth has Two-Feet. I placed my red rose in worship and said: "Lord, accept." The Lord took my red rose, and never did I behold it again. So I became the disciple of the Lord, and once in a while when I wake up on my wattle mat, and see the dawn hang with the mango, down below, under the tree, and not far from the fountain, you could see my white rose bloom.

For indeed the story of the red rose is fabular and fantastic. Like the policeman it was born of the atom, became earth, air, ether, fire and water, rolled into a pumpkin, grew into a tree, became a deer and frisked and frolicked in the forests of Brindavan, became white and a cow, all with stripes and eyes of cinnamon, and took the cowboys playing to the temples of Muttra – sang, suffered and died, – died again and again, was born again and again, married a monk, intellectual, army man, was carried off by Muslims, and was given away in dowry, and head in hand wandered by the Ganges, till it came to a hut and a hearthless man, and sat there, and bewitched by his wisdom and his eyes, remained admonished into death. – "Be a rose," cursed the ascetic and so it became a rose of a palace garden in its next life and rode a palanquin. Everybody knew this rose from others, for it carried in its petals a mark red as the kumkum and round like a thumb, for it carried the mark of murderer and monk, and was sometimes called a weeping rose, for the spot on the petal often of an evening looked a teardrop. People gathered it and gave it to the gods – the princes and ministers that sang and serenaded by the palaces saw it and gave away petal and perfume to their lady-love, but the rose always carried the teardrop and smell of the temple garden. When the Magh winds rose and the houses were lit with jessamine-oil, they said, here cometh the red rose wind for it smelleth of holiness. And when the elder prince married and there was such fuss and festivity about it, the gardener came and dug the roots and gave away the plant and perfume to the princess who went to Amber for marriage-making. There, near the tulsi-brindavan, was the rose planted – and so it brought gladsome tidings to the desert oasis of Rajputana, and many a princess grew into worship and holiness plucking of it. Ascetics gathered it in their hands and gave it away to the gods, but the tear was always there. Artists came and painted the rose and, the story goes, gave of it to Emperor Akbar, and painted him with it. You can still see this in the British Museum.

I plucked it in a curious way. I had grown ascetic by now and the arms of awkwardness held me in their religious tyranny. I did not like hyacinths for worship, so I placed instead tulsi, chrysanthemum, Shiva's lip or the rose. I hid my police uniform under ash and loincloth and spoke kindly to the rose.

"O Rose of Compassion," I said, "come with me." It fluttered and said no, it flew with me and said no and no – it circled continents with me and said yes, and said nay again, till the sun and the moon were tired of its tears, and schoolgirls collected it in their cupped hands and carried it in their satchels and drank it at night that they might have bright bridegrooms. My hands were wet and rotting, my skin had grown the colour of apple and my bones shewed. My meditations had got garnered with the rose and my

89

thoughts tethered to the rose, and whether I be prince or policeman, the rose simply wept with me. Night came, and then the day, then the night again and the sorrow of the rose. Days were filled with a drowsy doom, the world marvelled that I carried the perfume of the rose, and they said I had the malady of the rose. Music suddenly melodied from the wayside tree as I walked, and birds gathered round me, for they loved the music of the rose. Words suddenly rose into their organum and ecstasy, and became parted-lipped and free. The earth's buildings were muted to the manner of the rose, and silence smelt of the rose. And I, poor creature that had wandered from the virgins of Avignon, had the melody of the rose in my ear. I fretted and frolicked and wept – I sang ditties and sat in mute meditation, but the gods spoke kindly to me and gave me hopes of recompense. They said the malady of the rose is meant for the few and the festival-born – so go poet, go ascetic, they said, and gather flowers for our worship. And so it is that the gods demanded of me the petal of the rose, and I gave it them, I gave it them handfuls and clothfuls, and when the goddesses were adorned and the camphor burnt, so great the flow of rose-water from the rose, the pujari gathered it and gave it as prasad and tirth to the devotee. I also drank of it, and the madder I became, I said, "Rose, you Rose in my heart you weep in me, and I place you on the hair of the gods and you weep still. And what shall I do now?" And there was such silence in answer you could hear the river flow. I fled from the silence, and I wandered continents, alone and my hands rotting with rose-tear. Angry, I cut a tree. It was in Belgium, and a baby was born. I saw the baby and I said, "Lovely baby, round-faced baby, I am your father, but I be policeman. How can you bear me?" It was a ruse. The baby said, "Papa, I love you." No sooner did the baby say "Papa" – I fled. "Rose, my baby," I thought, "O baby of my Rose," and I wept. Then did I climb mountains and went strolling athwart the glaciers. It was a time of international disputes, and there were grave questions of war and peace, and I, the policeman, went a-patrolling. And all the mountains smelt of the rose.

Then it was I heard the tingle in the mountain, a tingle-tingletoe across the mountain, and melody rose and music rose, and in between the chinks of my dream, I saw the magnum of Truth. And as Truth is Travancore I went a-shaking in the South Indian Railway. In Travancore station I descended and said: "Take me, please, to the Great-man." And they took me to the Maharaja. But I returned to the station and said to the taxi: "Take me please to the Retired Police Commissioner," and they took me to Truth. Truth has Two-Feet and smelt of many roses the rose. Truth has steps, and once you enter, in the verandah, at the footsteps is the Lotus on which Truth stands. I wash myself of my sins – I peel out skin after skin of my tattered body – I speak to the incarnations of the mind – I float in the magnificence of my dreams, and I tell them, "Adieu, adieu, my memories, my medals, my police uniforms. Here, take the bone, you  bone-eating cur. Here, take this sinew, you flesh-eating vulture. Here, take this blood, you proud man. I have come to eat butter. I shall live on honey. I shall speak like a nightingale." But a great agony rose within me. The smell of the rose rose in me, and brought the tears of destiny to my guttering throat. I choked into exhaustion and woke into a stupor. The stupor lasted many a year and I was fed by the squirrel of the garden – for in the garden of Travancore there are many squirrels – lean ones, and kind small round ones, and musical ones too, and they smelt the malady of the rose in me, and they too were tear-smitten. Once, I had bathed many and many a time, and my breath smelt of the freshness of dawn, they took, brothers, they took me to the House, and under the mango-leaf and coconut-pandal, and in the flame and flavour of irradiance, I saw the walk of Truth, which no tears can tell. Gold, failing to be gold, was gold there – and so were silk and filigree, and music rose from itself and was heard of by silence, and the banana and the sugar-candy tasted of the honey, and man stood there a monument. The Gandharvas, the Siddhas, the Yakshas and the eighty thousand gods came there to pay homage with flower-hands and folded hands. Rain fell to song, and cattle lowed to music, and rivers parted and poured at the Two-Feet. My medals melted on me and my skin became fresh! My voice became cantation, and my intelligence intimate. I laid my petal of rose at the Lotus of Truth, and I never beheld it again, brother, my brother. And when I woke up I heard them singing:

# Raja Rao

*In between two thoughts is the dance of Truth,*
*He who's seen it hath no rebirth.*

I was marvelled and tears came to my eyes, and I wept, and I wept for joy. Then did I turn round and round and found my rose had gone from my finger. O my red rose. Under the mango-tree, near the fountain, where I stood listening to Truth, then did I see the white rose-bush. And I knew.

Now I am in retirement. I have grown, and short, with years. My uniform has many holes, but I wear it for the pension day. I lie by the gate, however, singing songs and sometimes wishing I could fly and be inside the House, and always: or a parrot in the cage and hung *there*. The rose too from her bush does the same. "Wish I were a washerwoman or lamp-lighter, I would be washing inside or massaging. I dare not think of cooking – I am not pure enough." Such is our talk across the wall in Travancore and the One who understands knows. The rose, I forgot to tell you, has lost its tear, and I my medals. The rose knew its perfume was of the rose, its petals, its colour of rose was of the rose, and so there was no rose but the rose – if you understand what I mean. So it smelt of the Lotus. I was very happy. I became a man, that is, free and all that. Where is the prisoner, I ask, where? In the kingdom of Travancore there are no prisons, according to the *Travancore Code*, that is the Truth, and that is the beautiful Truth, said the white rose to me.

And the trouble, brother, all the trouble is that we mistake the Lotus for the Rose.

# The Cat and
# Shakespeare

M other cat sits in a cage between the office table and the almirah. In the office there are thirteen clerks. And the boss Bhoothalinga Iyer sneezes from his room. His office is partitioned off and has a swinging door. Every time anyone goes in to answer the boss's calls the cat seems to rise up. There's a painful irritating grating – the hinges have not been oiled. When the boss calls and the hinges creak, the cat sits up on her haunches, then lies down again. When Govindan Nair lifts her cage (for it's a she; after all, one discovered it) mother cat lifts up her head and says "meow-meow." Then, bending down, Govindan Nair gives his pen nib to her and she chews it. "Ah, she chews the origin of numbers," says Govindan Nair, to whom every mystery seems to open itself. If Lavoisier, as textbooks say, divided oxygen and hydrogen after years of experimentation, our Govindan Nair born in France would only have to stand and say, "Water, show thyself to me!" And hydrogen would have stood to one side somewhat big and bellied, and

This excerpt is from *The Cat and Shakespeare: A Tale of Modern India* (1965). An earlier version was published as "The Cat" in the *Chelsea Review* (New York) in 1959.

oxygen would have curled herself shy at his knees and suddenly gone shooting like a mermaid into the big sky. And he would not have lost his head at the Revolution. The British, too, chopped off their kings' heads. A king chops off your head, or you chop his, but the police state is different from the state Truth policed. The fact is that when the mother cat carries you across the wall and to anywhere, there is nothing but space. Space is white and large and free. Why don't you go there? Sir, you will say, kneading your snuff, but there is a wall. To which Govindan Nair makes answer: Like Usha, why don't you put stones one over the other, and standing under the bilva tree, you can speak to Shridhar. You can say: That is why Shridhar died. Usha spoke over the wall and the cat carried him away. Funny, sir, that a child is carried away by a cat. Anyway, tell me where is Shridhar gone? He has gone to a house three storeys high. "Is that what you say, mother cat?" asks Govindan Nair. The mother cat says "meow." Govindan Nair cannot keep her in the cage any longer. He opens the cage and the cat leaps onto his lap. It is a trained cat. It knows what is right from what is wrong.

Children below were playing hide-and-seek among the rice bags. The ration shop was also their playground. While the mothers waited, the children played among the bags. Govindan Nair wanted to go down and play with the children, but there was this Ummathur file and seventeen sacks lost. Who had stolen the sacks? Was it a gang of poor men or was it merchants' marauders? Stroking the cat, his pen in his mouth, Govindan Nair was contemplating. When he thinks in this manner it means he wants to do something mechanical. He always carried a penknife with him, for sharpening pencils and such other things (including rose twigs). He usually took this out, pulled out the blade and started rubbing it up and down the edge of the table. Just where he worked on his files, he had written, or rather carved, many names – his own, the name of his boss, and Usha's (I was surprised once when I went to visit him to find Usha's name there, but it was there). Sharpening the knife, he started humming to himself.

"Hey nonny, nonny, nonny ..."

GOVINDAN NAIR: What a kind thought, Abraham. Whoever it is that had the idea. I was just thinking this morning. There are so many rats at home. There are so many rats in the office. You remember the

Sidpur file? It might have been the rats. Big ones like bandicoots, they be. And then, at home. There are so many. Even they seem to have famine. A country at war has rations. A rationed country has little food. When there is little grain to eat, the rats become so courageous. They will bite off anything. Even the nose of a man. (*He looks around him and speaks to John.*) So, I say, thank you for having had such a kind thought, Mr John. (*Everybody bursts out laughing again. The boss also sneezes.*) Thank you, Mr John, for this wonderful gift. A cat, sir, a cat. Now, now let me make a speech in the manner of Hamlet.

To be or not to be. No, no. (*He looks at the cat.*)
A kitten sans cat, kitten being the
diminutive for cat. *Vide* Prescott
of the great grammatical fame.
A kitten sans cat, that is the
question. (*He turns the cage round and round.*)
To live is not difficult,
sir, for flesh is the form of
existence, and man in his journey to
the ultimate knows that
to yield to the flesh is to
grow grain. To yield to the pipe
is to blow flame. Asthma is
the trouble that Polonius reveals
for fool; he hid behind the curtain
asthmatic.

JOHN: And what happened to him?

GN: Sir, Lady, by now I pierce (*he makes as if he pierces something with the right arm*) the veil, and the asthmatic falls. (*A thud.*)

JOHN: Murder, murder.

GN: Rank murder.
Rank murder and dark desolation
for Ophelia.

SYED SAHIB: Go, get thee to a nunnery.

JOHN: Why, Abraham, that's the place for you. Isn't that so?

Raja Rao

SYED SAHIB: To the nunnery, maid (*looking at the cat*).
GN:   To the rank growth I go,
      Hey nonny, nonny
      To the slipping world I go,
      Hey nonny, nonny
      I tell you what, sir. In the kingdom of Denmark
      there's one blessed thing. Whatever they are they
      are not mad. (*Lets the cat out of the cage. It
      leaps on a desk, familiar, affectionate, but distant.
      It licks its front paw.*) The kingdom of Denmark is
      just like a ration office.
JOHN: How so, Mr Nair? That's a great idea – Shakespearean, I should say.
GN:   Shakespeare knew every mystery of the ration shop. Here however
      we haven't to murder a brother to marry his wife. Here we marry
      whom we like. The ration card marries. You are married even when
      there is no wife. You are married without looking at horoscopes.
      The dead are not buried in ration shops. There will be no grave
      scene. Ophelia will die but she will have no skull left for Hamlet, a
      future Hamlet, to see. We slip, sir, from sleep to wake from wake to
      sleep. We marry the wife in dream, and we wake up king of Denmark.
      We marry Ophelia in dream and wake up having a Polonius to
      bury. We live in continual mystery. In fact I ask you, John, my friend
      (*sharpening his knife on the table*), when one commits murder in a
      dream, is that murder or not?
JOHN: (*very clever*) That's jurisprudence. I'm only a clerk. Y P John is only
      a clerk.
GN:   I ask you, what is dream? Are you sure you are not in dream (*laughing*)?
      An asthmatic cough, with the cry of children under the creak of
      balance, and the cat, a Persian cat on the table of Ration Office
      No 66. Is it a dream or is it real?
JOHN: Every bit is real, but the whole is not. So it is not a dream.
GN:   In the dream the whole is real.
ABRAHAM: The boss is worried about the Ummathur file.
GN:   Are you sure the wagon did not go to Coimbatore? Or did it go to
      Cannore? Both have C in them. Even when awake we make such

*98*

an error. The reason, sir, why I ask you "are you in dream or in waking state?" is simple. In dream the dead appears.

JOHN: That is so. (*The cat comes and lies before Nair. It seems to be listening carefully to what Nair is saying.*)

GN: In ration offices, as we all know, the dead have numbers. Killing be no murder.

JOHN: (*addressing himself to Abraham*) What ho, Horatio.

Now, Govindan Nair walked straight over to John's table. Perhaps he just wanted to consult a file.

"John," he said, while the mother cat stood behind him.

"Yes, mister," said John, very sure of himself.

"John, this is a cat," he said, lifting up the cat and placing it on John's table. The whole office stopped work. Even Bhoothalinga seemed involved in this silence.

"What's that?" cried Abraham, and came over to John's table.

"Oh, I am only talking to him about the cat."

"What cat?" said Syed, his hand on Govindan Nair's shoulders.

"Why, man, cat. There's cat only. All cats belong to one species – cat. Call it cat or call it marjara which is Sanskrit or better still poochi which is Malayalam, it's the same – isn't that so, John?"

"Yes, my lord," said John, rising from his seat.

"So, gentlemen, I wanted to know how much zoology our friend knew. What is a Persian cat called in Latin? In fact what is the Latin name for a cat?"

"*Felinus*," said Abraham, remembering his church instructions.

"Then *Felinus Persiana* would be a Persian cat," said Govindan Nair, who knew of course everything.

"Yes," said Abraham dubiously.

"And man?"

"*Humanus.*"

"And I?" he said

"*Ego.*"

"Make me a Latin sentence, Abraham. *Ego esse humanus malabario et lux esse felinus persiana*, or some such thing."

"I don't know that much Latin," said Abraham.

The curious thing was that the boss did not call. The cat continued to raise her tail and bunch herself to be caressed. Govindan Nair still held the penknife in the other hand as if it were his pencil. Man must hold something  with his hands, otherwise how could he know what he is about? If you carry a penknife like a pencil in your hand you are a clerk. Is there any doubt about it? "Speaking biologically," Govindan Nair used to say, "a hundred generations of clerks will secrete lead from their bowels and clerks' fingers will bear capillaries like those in the new office pencils. You write morning, noon, and night. You could even write in your dreams."

"What is clerk in Latin?"

"*Clericus* is Latin itself."

"Ha, Ha," said Govindan Nair. Seeing the whole office around him, and the boss silent – it was a hot morning – he added: "Define the cat, Mr John."

"Mr Govindan Nair, a cat is a feline being."

"What are its characteristics?" Govindan Nair started making a firm and rapid movement with his knife (back and forth), as if he were sharpening the pencil on the beautiful skin of the cat.

"Its characteristics are – its characteristics are," mumbled John, and as somebody said, he had cleared his bladder audibly. It poured an acrid smell into the room. Bhoothalinga Iyer had a bad cold, and one could hear him snuff in snuff. There was such silence in the office (but for the burring sound of Govindan Nair who always burred anyway) that Bhoothalinga Iyer was sure everybody was at work. There was suddenly silence even in the ration shop. And this was the sort of silence which sometimes rises like a temple pillar from earth to heaven; all creation seems still, as if the universe pondered: What next?

"First of all, it's of the same family as the lion," said Rama Krishna, a young clerk. He had joined them only three months ago, fresh from college.

"Then?" asked Govindan Nair.

"Then," said Abraham, getting very anxious, "it goes in and out of one's house as not even a man can."

"What very intelligent colleagues I have," remarked Govindan Nair, smiling. "Then?"

"A cat is the purest animal in the world."

"Why so? Hey, there, Syed, what does your Muslim theology say about it?"

"In Muslim theology only the chameleon is evil. It betrayed Muhammed. And the hog. But the cat, it is sacred."

"No, man, I know your theology better. The cat is not sacred in Islam. It is sacred in Egypt. It was called Bastet."

"And it wore a crown?" said John, a little reassured that all this was a joke.

Govindan Nair quickly made a paper crown; he cut the three sides of a triangle and gave it a point, and placed it on the head of the cat and said: "Hey, Bastet, you are sacred, don't you understand?"

"And, Syed, what is it your people do when what is sacred is treated as what is sacred?"

"We kneel and touch the ground and ask for Allah's blessings."

"Now, Mr John, you understand. Here is Bastet. You have brought a very God to our poor ration office. You be the priest."

"Oh, no," said John. He knew Govindan Nair had something up his sleeve.

"Kneel!" shouted Govindan Nair. "Kneel, man!" And he brandished his knife, holding the cat firmly with his left hand. "Or say: No sir, I am a low-born, I am a coward. Kneel!" he shouted. Bhoothalinga Iyer's chair creaked. "You don't insult a cat like this, stuffing a cat into a rat cage."

John knelt devoutly.

"There, once again," shouted Govindan Nair.

John knelt again, crossing himself. Syed had his hands brought together. All the office was one noumenal silence.

"Kiss it," shouted Govindan Nair again.

John kissed the cat. Bhoothalinga Iyer came and stood behind the crowd. He thought some file was being tampered with.

"Govindan Nair!" he shouted.

"Yes, sir." And Govindan Nair went toward his boss. The cat jumped down the table and everybody gave way to the cat. By now she's lost her crown. Rubbing against his legs it cried "meow, meow" and Govindan Nair lifted her up and placed her on his shoulder with his right hand. His knife was still in the left.

"What is this?" asked Bhoothalinga Iyer.

"We've being discussing the Latin formation for Persian cat. Do you know it, sir?"

"In Sanskrit it is called marjaram," he said as if he were saying it with only the tip of his tongue. "And for Persian cat there's no word in ancient Sanskrit."

"In Malayalam it is called poochi-poochi," said Govindan Nair, as he went back with the boss to the inner office.

The boss sat down in his chair.

The cat jumped onto Bhoothalinga Iyer's table. It saw another tassel of a file and started playing with it. Bhoothalinga Iyer, seeing all the eyes of the office (for everybody, as it were, came to see what was happening), wanted to shout: Get out! Get away! But his tongue would not say it. How can you say with what is not what is? How can you shape words that cannot come from yourself? What do you do if you find yourself a prisoner? You want to escape. Govindan Nair laid the knife on the table and said to Bhoothalinga Iyer: "Sir, tell me a story."

"What story?"

"Any story."

"I know no story."

"I'll tell you a story," said Govindan Nair, and lifted the cat and placed her on his shoulder.

"Once upon a time," he began, and before he could go on, the cat jumped onto Bhoothalinga Iyer's head. Bhoothalinga Iyer opened his eyes wide and said, "Shiva, Shiva," and he was dead. He actually sat in his chair as if he could not be moved.

Govindan Nair rushed back home with the beautiful Persian cat in the cage and let it loose in the house. Then it was he went to Bhoothalinga Iyer's funeral. Bhoothalinga Iyer's wife, Lakshamma was moved, deeply moved, by all the consoling words Govindan Nair spoke to her. He spoke of death and birth and such things. He too was weeping. His boss had died. Bhoothalinga Iyer had asthma. And asthmatics have weak hearts. And the snuff did not help, did it – said the Brahmins at the door of the temple.

For some strange reason, everybody came to console Govindan Nair at his office as if he had lost something. Kunni Krishna Menon from the next house came and spoke as though Govindan Nair needed condolence. Perhaps he would be promoted to his boss's place – there was such a rumour. Then he could not run down and play with the children, remarked Abraham. An officer could not do it. "Then you be boss, Abraham," said Govindan Nair, hugging him.

The excerpt on the following page is the famous climactic Court Scene from *The Cat and Shakespeare*.

The white-clad judge, Mr Gopala Menon, said in the palacelike court by the railway line which every advocate knows so well – the name boards of the advocates look like coconuts on a tree, there are so many in the building across: Vishwanatha Iyer, BSc, LLB; Ramanujan Iyengar, MA ML Advocate High Court; Mr Syed Mohammed Sahib, Advocate; P Gangadharan Pillai, High Court Advocate; S Rajaram Iyer, Advocate; etc, etc – the judge said: "I cannot follow your argument, sir. Will you repeat?"

"Mr Bhoothalinga Iyer, of blessed memory," Govindan Nair started, "used to visit certain places whose names are not mentioned in respectable places." ("Ho, ho!" shouted one or two persons in the gallery.) "If I do not mention the name, it is because many persons whose faces I see before me now, if I may say so, betake themselves there."

"My Lord, such insinuations are not to be permitted in open court," shouted a member of the bar.

"The sun shines on the good and on the wicked equally, like justice. Please go and close the sunshine before you say: this should not be discussed in open court."

"Court: The Accused is free to do what it likes."

"I was only saying: Whether you close the door and sit like photographers in the dark room or you come out, the sun is always open. The Maharaja of Travancore, sir –"

"Say His Highness."

"Yes, His Highness the Maharaja of Travancore is there, whether his subjects – say some fellow in the hill tribes – knows his name or not."

"So?"

"So what is real ever is."

"That is so," cried the Government Advocate.

"Yes, but we never want to see it. For example, that a worthy man like Bhoothalinga Iyer (of blessed memory) used to visit places of little respectability."

"So?"

"So, he met there, one day, a lady of great respectability."

"Your statements are so contradictory."

"Your Lordship, could I say Your Lordship without the idea of an Accused? Could I say respectable without the ideas of unrespectable coming into it? Without saying, I am not a woman, what does the word man mean?"

"Yes, let us get back to Bhoothalinga Iyer."

"Mr Iyer used to visit such a place."

"And then?"

"One day after visiting such a place, he met me at the door."

"Yes, go on. Did he?"

"Of course. I went there regularly. My wife will tell you."

"Oho," exclaimed Advocate Tirumalachar from the bar table.

"And at the door he said: Every time I commit a sin, I place a rupee in the treasure pitcher of the sanctuary. I tell my wife this is for me to go to Benares one day. But the treasure pitcher is tightly fixed with sealing wax. There is here in this place a respectable woman. I like her and she likes me. When I went in, as usual, this time, however, a new woman, a Brahmin woman, I think an Iyengar woman, came. She said her husband was dead. I knew I was going to die soon, being old. But I was in a hurry. So I told her: Do not worry, lady. I will go and tell your husband everything. He will understand. She became naked and fell on the bed. Her breasts were so lovely."

"This is sheer pornography," said an elderly advocate with a big nose.

"I am quoting evidence, sir," continued Govindan Nair.

"And she played with her necklace that lay coyly on her bosom."

"And what did he do?" asked a counsel for the Government.

"He did nothing."

"Ha, ha, ha," laughed many of the advocates.

"The dignity of the Court demands better behaviour," said the Government Advocate. He had never had to argue against so strange a man. He got terrifically interested in his opponent.

"He not only did nothing, sir. Mr Bhoothalinga Iyer was a man of generous heart –"

"To propose immorality as a generous thing!" mumbled Advocate Tirumalachar. Tirumalachar, who looked fiftyish and fair, was known for his deep religious sympathies. He was president of the Radha Sami Sangh, Trivandrum.

"What do advocates defend?" asked the judge.

"Morality," said Tirumalachar, rising and adjusting his turban.

"You defend man," said the Government Advocate. "But law says we defend the Truth. The law is right."

"The Government Advocate has said the right thing. Now, Accused, continue."

"My Lord, I was saying: One day after the whole office was empty and Bhoothalinga Iyer was alone, he said: Govindan Nair, stay there. I have a job for you. And he produced the Benares pot that he had hidden deeply in the sample rice sack. There was one sack always in the office. Who would look into it? So he produced the Benares pot and said: Go to Mutthalinga Nayak Street and in the third house right by the temple mandap there must be a widow called Meenakshiamma. Please hand over this one hundred and nine rupees. That is all there is in it. I told my wife yesterday to go to the cinema with my son-in-law. She went. I stole this and came here. I opened the office. I had the key. Today I have sent her to the zoo with my son-in-law. Then there is Pattamal's music at the Victoria Jubilee Hall. Therefore they will come late, but I must return home quietly. I know you are a man with a big heart, so please do this service for me. She will wait for you."

"In English you call this a cock-and-bull story," said Tirumalachar.

"You could, if you so want, call it a hen-and-heifer story," said Govindan Nair, and laughed.

"Who then was the witness?"

"As one should except in such a cock-and-bull story, a cat, sir, a cat," said Govindan Nair seriously.

The judge rose and dismissed the court. He called the accused, and said: "Please speak the Truth."

And Govindan Nair, with tears running down from his big black eyes answered: "Your Lordship, I speak only the Truth. If the world of man does not conform to Truth, should Truth suffer for that reason? If only you knew how I pray every night and say: Mother, keep me at the lotus feet of Truth. The judge can give a judgement. The Government Advocate can accuse. Police Inspector Rama Iyer can muster evidence. But the accused alone knows the Truth."

"How right you are," said the judge, flabbergasted. He had never thought of this before. "Tell me then, Mr Govindan Nair, how can a judge know the Truth?"

"By being it," said Govindan Nair as if it were such a simple matter. After all, he had cut a passage in the wall where Shridhar used to talk to Usha. After all, who could say Bhoothalinga Iyer had not gone to Coimbatore? For example, Abraham could not, as he would lose his job (and with it his green BSA bicycle) if the boss returned. Suppose Shantha's child were really Bhoothalinga Iyer reborn? Who could know? The cat could, was Govindan Nair's conviction.

"Tomorrow I'll bring the cat to court," he said, as if asking the judge's permission. Of course what wrong could Govindan Nair have done? Could you ever see a man so innocent? Anybody could see he played with children and the scale. And when one side was heavy, he put two kids on the other side to make the balance go up. Then he brought the needle to a standstill, holding it tight. Thus the balance was created among men. When two things depend on each other for their very existence, neither exists. That is the Law of law.

"The cat, sir, will do it," he said. The judge consented.

Next day I sent Usha with Shantha (the baby was left at home with Tangamma to look after him). The cat was carried in a big cage.

When the court opened its deliberations, the Government Advocate said: "My Lord, we are facing judgement against judgement. We must be careful. We have, as witness, a cat."

"Why not? We are in Travancore."

"I thought so too, Your Lordship. Why should we follow the proceedings of any other court of the world, were it His Majesty's Privy Council in London? If a cat could be proved to prove any evidence we might set a precedent."

"My Lord," said Govindan Nair, rising.

Crowds had gathered at the courthouse. Such a thing had never happened before. It was not even a political case. (There was no Gandhi in it.) Women were somehow convinced Govindan Nair was an innocent man. Some of them had seen him in the ration shop. Others had gone to have ration cards issued. Some had noticed him give way to ladies when the bus was overcrowded. Such things are never forgotten by women. They always feed the child in their womb whether the child be there or not. Who knows, someday ...

"My Lord, I am not sure this copy of my signature is correct. Could I have the original?"

"The original is in the files," said the court clerk.

"How could it be wrong?"

The cat escaped from Shantha's hand and ran all over the court. Nobody wanted to stop the proceedings or to laugh. Either would be acknowledging that the cat was there. It went right over to the Government Advocate and sat in front of him as if it were going toward itself. The silence was so clear, one could see the movement of the cat's whiskers. One had no doubt the cat was there. And it knew everything. Each movement was preceded by a withdrawal, recognition, and then the jump. The cat jumped straight onto the judge's table. And before the attendants could brush it away, it leaped down and fell over one of those huge clay office inkpots kept under tables, and, turning through the back door, went into the record room. The court clerk was looking at the file. The cat did nothing. It stood there. The attendants came and stood watching the cat. Then the cat lay on the floor and started licking its fur. Govindan Nair was burring something in the court. The attendants, seeing the cat doing nothing, went back to the court.

The cat suddenly jumped onto the shoulder of the clerk and started licking his neck. He felt such sweetness in this, he opened file after file. The cat now jumped over to the table and sat. Usha came from the back, led by an attendant, and took the cat in her arms. The clerk had indeed found the paper.

"May I see it, Your Lordship?" asked Govindan Nair.

"Yes, here it is," said the judge, but at the last moment he held it back. For just as he was handing the paper over, the light from the ceiling – a sunbeam, in fact – pierced through the paper, or maybe it was just electric light. Underneath the signature was another signature. When the judge had read it, he handed it over to the Government Advocate. He read it and said: "Bhoothalinga Iyer himself signed this. How did this happen?"

"Yes, sir. That is how it was. Rama Iyer made a slight mistake. After all

Bhoothalinga Iyer and he are both Brahmins. He wanted to save Bhoothalinga Iyer. It is plain as could be."

"Then why did you admit all that you have admitted?"

"I have in all honesty admitted nothing."

"Oho," shouted Tirumalachar.

"Go on," said the judge.

"Sir, why do we admit then that a chair is a chair?"

"Why, have you not seen a chair?"

"Ho, ho!" shouted the crowd.

"Has anyone seen a chair?" asked the judge.

"Nobody has," said the Government Advocate. He was plainly taking sides with the accused.

The judge said: "I sit on a chair."

"Who?" asked Govindan Nair.

The judge in fact rose up to see who sat on the chair. He went round and round the table looking at who? There was such silence, the women wept. The cat jumped onto the dais. The attendants said nothing. The Government Advocate was chatting happily with Govindan Nair. Who said there was a case? The clerk was looking for the file to put back the paper. Usha put a garland around the neck of Govindan Nair.

That was the fact. Govindan Nair was not set free. He was free. Nobody is a criminal who has not been proven criminal. The judge had to find himself, and in so doing, he lost his seat. Who sits on the judge's seat became an important subject of discussion in Travancore High Court. Since then many learned treatises have been written on the subject.

It was all due to Govindan Nair. He had, while in prison, written out a whole story to himself. Bhoothalinga Iyer had signed the paper. It had nothing to do with ration permits. It had to do with Bhoothalinga Iyer's extramarital propensities. In this business he came across virtue. So instead of going to Benares he gave the money to the widow of a Brahmin, an Iyengar woman in fact. (The breasts and other things were added to make the story comply with film stories.) The story came true as he wrote it. He was sure that it was a fact. He told himself again and again and told it in the court again and again. At night the prison wardens were surprised to see him talking to himself. Actually he thought he was addressing the court. He even made and remade the necessary gestures. Wardens could think he was practising acting. He recited his prose precisely till he knew every situation by heart. That is why he was so cocksure in the open court. After all, only a story that you write yourself from nowhere can be perfect. You can do with it what you want to do with it. (Abraham wrote romantic poetry and he said it did with him what it wanted. So, eventually, he married Myriam, etc.) But Govindan Nair had the liberty the judge did not have. Only the Government Advocate knew everything. A fact is a prisoner. You are free, or you become the prisoner, and the fact is free, etc, etc. So the Government Advocate knew the Accused was no Accused. He was one with the Accused. That showed why the cat went to the Government Advocate first. The cat also kissed the clerk on the neck.

Bhoothalinga Iyer's signature was revealed by a sunbeam. Was Bhoothalinga Iyer then in Coimbatore?

Mr Justice Gopala Menon was the son of the late Peshkar Rao Bahadur Parameshwara Menon, and he had only three months of service before retirement. He took leave preparatory to retirement and went to the Himalayas, so people said. Govindan Nair laughed and remarked: "You no more find the truth in the Himalayas than you find in the *Indian Law Register*. You may find it on your garden wall and not know it was it. You must have eyes to see," he said desperately to me.

# The Writer and
the Word

Triple are the constituents of a book – the word, the author, the reader. The word which says what the author has to indicate, and the reader has to apprehend, seems to be the one element we seem to neglect, as if it were something we know so well that we may not investigate its nature, its function, its end. For the word, like every constituted thing, seems to have a birth, a life-span, and a death. In the word Rama before saying "Ra," there was nothing, as it were; after saying "Ra" there is just "ra"; and when "ma" is said "ma" is heard; and then Rama comes to be after the two syllables have been experienced in an enunciation. Now the problem is, if Rama, or Agni, or Vriksha have any life at all beyond their birth, existence, and extinction, in a sentence like "Rama went into exile," if Rama were just two syllables, two breaths, that the vocal chord shapes into a sound apprehended, we would have as many words as statements such as it must have been when man began – that is if man began at all.

From *The Meaning of India* (1997), this was originally a talk given at a literary seminar in 1965 and published in *Critical Essays on Indian Writing in English* edited by M K Naik et al in 1968.

If (the word) Rama has just one single moment of existence there would therefore be no language at all. All statements would just be cries. But since the word Rama has, or seems to have, some permanent existence, it is fair that intellectuals should inquire how it came to be that a sound began to have some sort of permanent existence.

But we all, anyone, anywhere in the world, would like to have a language that will mean the same thing and for all time. It is just the same way that you feel you will live for ever, though your life span might be seventy or eighty years. The *feel* that you are everlasting demands that everything be everlasting. Hence the demand that the word be eternal. If man is eternal, so is the word.

Is the word Rama then eternal? The combination of "Ra" with "ma" which makes the word Rama, you will remember, creates a new entity. "Ra" and "ma" together is not "Ra" plus "ma" but is in fact beyond both sounds, hence it becomes a word. And so when you can pronounce the word correctly, and say Rama, you create a vibration which when it dies in the hearer (we have not yet come to the reader) you have another person who experiences the sound at the end of which experience he should know Rama in the way you wanted Rama understood. So that Rama must mean the same thing to you and to him and as such Rama has to be of an unchanging nature. Thus a vibration or a series of vibrations must mean at all times the same thing, for otherwise you would not have used it, and the hearer would not understand it as such. This comes to mean finally that he who says the word enunciates the word, and he who hears it has to have the eternal part awakened in him so that there could be right communication. If the transient speaks to the transient it becomes a cacophony. But if the eternal, the unchanging, speaks to the unchanging, in me, in you, we have one language.

Now, some languages have history and according to some all languages have history. It would be better to say just as Indian civilization is the making of the Rishis (the sages) and the Western, of heroes and prophets, that some languages seem to have this breath of eternity in them and have attained then the status of what Albert Einstein called "the language of the gods," others are mere vernaculars.

The Sanskrit language is such a language of the gods and through Sanskrit all Indo-European languages participate in this, including the much abused, in India, English language. After all, remember, Shakespeare used the English language.

Therefore my argument is, unless you, the writer, could go back to the changeless in yourself, you could not truly communicate with the reader, if at that level the reader exists truly, then the question: who speaks to whom? would not arise at all.

There is considerable talk in the world of "communication." At the UNESCO there is a special department devoted to the so called subject, of communication. It is my conviction (basing myself on my Indian background) that you cannot really communicate unless you have *no* desire to really communicate.

Mauna vyakhya prakatita parabrahma tatvam, silence, the illuminator of the Supreme Brahma's essence.

Unless the author becomes an upasaka and enjoys himself in himself (which is Rasa) the eternality of the sound (Sabda) will not manifest itself, and so you cannot communicate either – and so the word here becomes nothing but a cacophony.

The word indeed is eternal. Man faces himself when he seeks the word. The word as pure sound is but a communication that comes from silence. The word is but vibrant silence compounded into a momentary act. The act has to be like prayer if it should yield what you want it to yield. Even to say a flower, let alone Rama, you must be able to say it in such a way that the force of the vocable, has the potency to create the flower. Unless the word becomes mantra no writer is a writer, and no reader a reader.

For the right reader-to-be, the writer has therefore to become an upasaka of the word. Thus we give sound back to silence and the seemingly divided remains undivided.

Let us, therefore, not heed expressions like "the reading public," "communication," etc. We in India need but to recognize our inheritance. Let us never forget Bhartrihari, the great grammarian (AD 450-510).

# Comrade Kirillov

I had been in London only a year, a young reporter for *The Hindu*. A school-Satyagrahi at seventeen, I had gone to Germany, like so many others – Berlin and Heidelberg had shaped me, imagine Gora and Werther on the Necker – I had drunk beer with the Bavarians, had mock duels with the Herrenvolk – but Hitler and Nuremberg sent me dithering back to Gandhiji. Sevagram was too austere for Gora, but *The Hindu* had openings for young intellectuals with nationalist ambitions. After all, I was born in the Temple Street of Chidambaram, where not even a cur barked. Remember a loud noise was inauspicious for Brahmin purity, and even dust settled quickly into sanctuary silences. And rats never bark.

However, after a few months at *The Hindu* in Madras, some editor took compassion on me and thought with my knowledge of Germany, London is where I should now be. Of course, I said to myself, Hemingway had worked on the *Chicago Tribune*. Would some Perkins ever discover me?

From *Comrade Kirillov* (1976). Though originally written in English, this was first published in Georges Fradier's French translation in Paris in 1965.

For you will now recognize my ambition was to be a writer. And I had so admired *A Farewell to Arms*.

And this Kirillov, he was some distant cousin of mine, my grandfather's first wife, dead at eight or nine years of age, was Kirillov's father's aunt or some such thing, one of those Indian relationships that had meaning only at birth or death, in the law courts, on pilgrimages. But he had lost his thread and I had lost mine, and we faced each other with the deference due to age (he was some six or seven years older than I was) and the distance of circumstance, for he was already, I was told, a writer.

On the other hand, S, my cynical companion and senior colleague (who had first taken me to see Kirillov), was a shorn Sikh and an unrepentant widower, who chased girls by the wayside and abandoned them pregnant – he read and respected Marx, and right after him D H Lawrence, that puritan saint, born for the greater glory of England to the British working class. S sported a Lawrencian beard and a requisite red scarf. "Freud," remarked S, who was so learned and in so many regions unknown to me, "Freud says somewhere, does he not, red and menstruations go together, thus the taboo against coitus during Woman's Sickness, therefore red the male symbol of the libido in action. But to speak the truth," continued S, hissing into his handkerchief, as we were waiting for the Number 6 bus, off Fleet Street, that would take us to Wakefield Square and to Kirillov, "to speak the truth, that's the best time to know a woman and the safest. You are too young," he laughed again, and so loud that an Englishman, surely a civil servant, glowered at him, but S, turned to me warming me up with a broad and affectionate pat on the back. We were good friends, I told you, though we argued over shine and rain.

My friend S and I knocked at Kirillov's door and, pen in hand, he opened wide the entrance. With becoming grace, he offered me the awaiting chair, while S knowingly took his place on the table, and thus settled, we discussed the theory of sanitary liquidation. These were the days of the Moscow trials; I needed signatures for an appeal. Kirillov, whose pistol faced his forehead, turned its frank force on me. I was initiate.

Marxism had given a strange ascetic incision to his Brahminic manners and his sweetness had that unction, the theological compassion, of a Catholic priest. The indrawnness of his nature gave a prominent curve to his chest, which in turn gave that peculiar parabola to his necktie, as though man in his destiny had shaped his garment to his thought and had given a certain twist of psyche this particular intensity of approach from the thick neck to the narrow waist, where within the folds of the shirt, this grey-green stretch of respectable cloth found its umbilical end.

The more I observed this grey-green stuff and the assurance, the intimacy, almost the obstinacy, of its collarly and waistward penetration, the more I felt its absurd inevitability in Kirillov's emotional life. I was sure, whether the trouser end was torn and showed bits of hanging fibre, or the coat button needed remembering and retracing back to some overcoat pocket where it must have been lying for these six months or more – this, the prime presence of daily decoration, nay, of daily care and companionship had the vital clinging passion of a pet, or of a young mistress. I imagined, as his fingers played with a stray thread and needle in the pen-basin, and I observed the gentle-feelingness of his nails, the pluck of the palm and the delicate connection of fingers and wrist and hand – I imagined how this hand, this kindly celibate hand, must turn and bend and gently pass the knot through the right centre of the shirt collar, and the sensuous fold that, like some South Indian prince, gives to his dhoti folds, must shape the last curving swiftness of the hanging cravat over the chest – no, no, this will not do, no, the curve has to be taken deepwards, its circumference given a more elevated inwardness, and then pull and flatten, and the tie coils itself on the belly, with the swiftness of a juggler's serpent. Yes, it was his boon companion, his poetry, his sole possession. How fondly he might have folded it night after night, and whispered, "You, you, my noble, secret friend, you lie in the faithfulness of my scholarly solitude. O, go not away from my habitation, for what shall my destiny be without your contiguous presence. You have seen me in my glorious Californian surroundings, when with water and holy word, I thought I would charm the world. My honesty led me straight from the labyrinths of Leadbeater's metaphysics to the safest shores of Marxism. Go quiet, lie peaceful, my companion – the revolutionary bay is not long. And if revolution come not, and rank reaction and the Tower of London my destiny, then I pray, here, put your clasp to this fold in the neck, and let my death be in the warmth of your memory. Lie, lie my noble companion, I have none but ..."

If such were his night meditations, his daily activity was of an equally lofty kind. He spoke to me of his new book – the one book he had been contemplating these six years and more, and which was to have the benediction of light in very few weeks. Indeed some obscure publisher had granted a pretty generous remuneration; and had bought this noble book on *Mahatma Gandhi – A Marxist Interpretation*, and had given to it a habitation and a preface. The preface was by some eminent scientist, whose meanderings in biology had faced him with irreversible answers, and had it not been for the new theories of science in the Soviet Land, they might just as well have stayed in bibliographical obstinacy. Soviet Science had come and saved his theories from misfortune, for his analysis of human society had confessed predilections towards orthodox Darwinism. The new fib about mathematics and God was of Cambridge and capitalist indecency – biology could only lead one to Marxian conclusions. Of this there was no earthly doubt – no, not even Sir Patrick Geddes could frighten our London professor from his Darwinist convictions.

And by some peculiar psychological transference, his perfect un-Darwinian enemy was this Mahatma Gandhi, friend and fool of the poor, the Sadhu reactionary who still believed in caste and creed and such categories, and whose birth in this world had set history many centuries backwards. Marx had indeed built in his theory of revolution on the British working classes revolting against their masters, heralded by the rising in the vast dominion of the British crown called India – and Mahatma came and upset Marx. If Marx were alive no doubt Mahatma Gandhi would have received, under the truculent pen of the great master, the destiny he deserved. Gandhi was somewhat of an oriental Mazzini, with Indian mysticism to boot. Much like Mazzini this new prophet of God had the Almighty too often on his lips. Besides, in South Africa, had Mahatma Gandhi ever raised the storm of revolt against the Negro slave-lords, Smuts & Company? No, no, never. Nonviolence was a biological lie. Man was born to fight – fighting is an instrument of Darwinian evolution, which made dialectics possible. If there were no opposition there would be no progress. And this "titanic struggle" could only be resolved when humanity rising out of its economic contradictions, creates the classless society, wherein war and all the concomitants of belligerency are forever banished from the neo-Darwinian State, and all men being selectively chosen for the ultimate state of human evolution, man would regain his primary innocence, and a new biology will arise. Till then our present theories alone can explain the development of mankind, and Mahatma Gandhi is one enemy of this new dispensation. More insidious than Hitler is this intellectual venom that is spreading over vast and ignorant humanity. Beware!

"Besides," added Kirillov, turning suddenly towards me, "your Gandhi is a kleptomaniac. You know what kleptomania is. It is the instinct for stealing money from others. You can read any day in the provincial newspapers of this country case after case of kleptomania. You find it mostly in juvenile courts. The fact is Mahatma Gandhi is an ungrown adult. Look at his theories on sex – he justifies the sexual act in terms of theological necessities: God wanted to people the world. When He wants the population to rise, then you know it instinctively: you feel like increasing the population of your own home. Then you can go to bed with your wife and produce the prescribed number of foetuses for population figures. Otherwise, you impose sisterhood on your young wife, and spread a carpet of virtue between you and your spouse. Fine, very fine counsels in this age of reason. Ask your Gandhi to read Freud – he would be the wiser for it."

"Well, brother," I said, "what is your theory on population?"

"I have quoted in my book all the new theories on biology, especially Mechnikoff, and later the great Mitcherin. The biological game of lovemaking is as natural as food ..."

"And water," I added mischievously.

"Yes, quite, quite so," he agreed.

"So sex is the common biological act," I pursued.

"Quite so – does it need any proof? No." His head rotated in absolute assurance.

"Have you read," I begged, "Lenin's remarks on the glass-of-water theory?" For Lenin as you know was against those who stated that taking a woman was like taking a glass of water.

"Oh, oh," he said triumphantly, "I knew you were going to quote scripture. Marxism knows no irrevocable statements. A fact is the truth of the moment in its own historical setting. I can quote to you ten other statements where Lenin says just the opposite of the glass-of-water theory.

Raja Rao

The communist, the true Marxist, is above all a realist. For him, the fact speaks in terms of its history. And its meaning is in terms of itself – like in any experiment in a laboratory. If the neutron can be split, and its mechanism discovered, you don't refer to the Bible for explanation. It is in terms of itself that a fact is revelatory. That is why we think morality is a humbug. Your Gandhi morality, fattening itself on the marwari-capitalist, and speaking a brother-brother language! It is nothing but the plainest of vulgarity. A decadent society, changing from feudal to the capitalist order, especially when it wants to throw over imperialist slavery, seeks moral and mystical accompaniment for its inevitable fight. Your morality is bogus. The only morality is scientific, and this is based on the inexorable laws of cause and effect. Mahatma Gandhi should have been born in the Middle Ages, and he should not have bothered us with his theology in this rational age of ours."

"So, for you," I continued, "you think our civil disobedience and mass satyagraha are all imbecile adornments to a historical process."

"No, no, you misunderstand me," he protested gently, and with a wide, human smile. "I am not a monster. I see the beauty and the nobility of all this I-love-you, I-love-you-brother business. The only trouble about it is: not this way will the mighty British Empire go crash and ash, revealing the beatific vision of Indian Liberty. Either there will be another war with Churchill and Company crawling on their backsides and wanting the black man's help, as it may well be, or a new situation may arise, when the economic condition of the working classes of the Indian cities, and the spirit of the landless labour becomes so intolerable – in times of famine, for example – then the great masses will rise in historical inevitability, and Mahatma Gandhi and his henchmen will all be washed away. Otherwise you can wait with your nonviolence at the door of Whitehall, and a crumb may fall from the Conservative basket, or a piece of painted pastry from a children's toy-shop which will be your gift from the Labour Party. The fact is, nobody in England dares lower the wages of the working classes, and he who tries to do so, with whatever noble intention, will be washed aside by capitalist history. We have no way out – except to wait."

"A brilliant analysis," I remarked, "But then what will I get after all this waiting?"

"A state of Society," he assured me, with bright and loving eyes, "where no man will be master of another, and where a man like you will sit on some lone hilltop and write beautiful books, instead of wandering in search of metaphysical will-of-the-wisps, and a cup of coffee, or listening to nonsense from men like me. I myself am a man fit for liquidation. I am an old moralist. I hate possession and yet I respect every one else's possession. I hate violence, and yet I will kill in a civil war. You, for example, you are an arch reactionary, and I shouldn't think it would be safe for you to be near me, if revolution came. I know only one God, and that is the common man. I know only one worship, and that is the Party meeting. I know only one morality, and that is a classless society. It will come to India. It has already made a heroic beginning in China. Chiang Kai Shek would be out of China if the Japanese were not in Manchuria. You will see what I say is true. Wait, wait. And our days, too, will come."

"And once you have fed the Indian millions and given them nice houses to live in, and railways for their monthly holidays, and sanatoria for their sick, and maternity care for their mothers, and the Dnieperstock for the electric illumination of India – what then, brother, is to become of your despair, your emotional upheavals, your metaphysical yearning, your God-ward beckonings?"

"Fibs," he said and laughed. "Yes, remind me of my theosophical days. Metaphysical inquiry, I now say, is due to rachitism – it is like a disease caused by vitamin deficiency. God is the fiction of the lazy. You remember you told me once of a thirteenth century peasant mystic of Karnataka who had rightly declared, Paradise is for the good-for-nothing, and if you want to see it, go, go on to the top of your village hill and have a grand look at it. Or something of that order."

"Yes, something of that order," I agreed, though my quotation was a much more vivid one. It was: If you want their God, go, go to the top of the village hill. There they lie, the lazy of all time. That is Paradise, say you fool! But I say: God is in you.

"Pity, I cannot offer you even a cup of tea," said he, "or rather coffee, since you come from the South. And a cousin to boot."

"Don't worry," I said. "But do you know why I came to see you?"

"Rama has a wicked purpose," added my friend S who was thoroughly enjoying this cock-and-sparrow show. "I told him not to come to you, but he insisted I bring him to you. So I've done my job – the rest is not my business. As usual, I laugh at human foibles. It keeps my stomach in good order."

"So, you have some business with me, have you?" said Kirillov, adjusting the curve of his slightly distended necktie. It was just as though he were turning to his wife and saying, "Hello, dear, what is this? Wait a moment and listen – it might be frightfully important, and maybe I'll need your help."

I said, "Kirillov, I want your signature. It's that a fair trial be given to the Moscow accused. Here is the Manifesto, look. The cause is good. You know politics is something I do not fully understand. Human suffering, life, birth, death, sickness, marriage and love, God, I understand. I hate violence of all sorts, especially political violence."

"Nonsense," he interrupted. "Do you think I and you and our good friend S could sit here and talk this fine language but for the violence with which the have-not classes are forcibly kept under by the haves? The courts, banks and parliaments are but hypocritical seats of the most insidious violence man perpetrates, day after day, hour after hour, on mankind."

"Yes, yes, I know. But what about the violence in Soviet Russia?"

"In Soviet Russia," he pronounced with an air of infallible accuracy, "in Soviet Russia the freest liberty is given to all men for self-expression. You will not find a beggar there. You will find people reading more books in Soviet Russia than anywhere in the Capitalist world. You could write books in freedom, and cultivate your garden, if you will. Otherwise, even a vegetarian like you would be allowed his idiosyncrasies, and he can have a tomato at breakfast and a turnip for tea." He laughed again, in a kindly compassionate way.

"But then what about the trials?"

Here he removed the glasses from his eyes, his mind turned inward and spread back on itself, as it were, in grave immediacy. What had to come might not be from the lips of man, but were to be pages of recorded history. It was a pronouncement that should have the accuracy, the universality, almost the word structure, of every communist dictum from the centre of China to Vladivostok, from the frontiers of Japan to Washington and Philadelphia. It would be spoken in French in Paris, in German in Hitler's prisons, in Persian in the Iranian borderlands, and in Hindustani at the Chowpati beach. Such universality not even Christendom could perpetrate on the human race. If truth were universal and had indeed the same rhythm, the breadth and the same limit – it was achieved in the communist world and he who ignores it, ignores a metaphysical certainty. Kirillov spoke.

"Man, you agree, is a biological being. Darwin has spoken of selectivity in evolution. From the point of view of evolutionary history, we are so many vertebrata. We can just as well have numbers instead of names. When, in the selective process, the dialectical opposite arises, you know what Darwinism has proven. The weaker biological presence, however good, is venom to the historical process. *Ecrasez l'infame,* said Voltaire. I would say, *Ecrasez la vermine.* The question is not one of personal virtue. It is a fact of history. If you are weak and on the wrong side – the wrong side for us, as you know, is the weaker side – then you must inevitably go under. Trotsky is a traitor, I say. A traitor for me is not my moral enemy, but my historical opponent. I know simpletons write that Trotsky had sold out to the capitalists. I know, as far as I can, that Trotsky is not the one to be bribed by the capitalists into their golden dens. Trotsky, like Zinoviev and Kameniev, was an instrument in a great historical process. For that matter, so is Stalin. If Stalin went against history, history would not spare him because he is Stalin. History is the respecter of no individual. We are the workers of an anonymous pyramid, and he who works simply, and stands straight and supple as the building stone leaps down from hand to lower hand, lays the foundation of the great human city on which the rose-red beauty of mankind will arise, and shine as in a desert. Until then, the weak and the turbulent must be sacrificed for the god Ra – or whatever His name may be – and the blood of the victim be poured to cement the crevices of man's incompetence. I am the anonymous. I am a biological number. I am a communist because I understand history."

There was a long and grateful silence. The necktie received its pattings; it hissed and curled in ritual approval. The snake-charmer had played on his bamboo flute. A great, dark sadness filled the empty room, where Lenin's picture hung so reverently. Night was falling – it was September, and the birds in the Wakefield Gardens were mournful with autumnal anxieties. Soon, too soon, would they have to wander over the terraces of France towards the Mediterranean. Some would have to go southwards to Madagascar, and others westwards to Brazil or Peru. The sea winds were harsh, and not very regular. Fear is a biological instinct, and fear of death universal. Is it not because death is full of fear that killing is an ugly act? If the biology of selective killing were understood, humanity might yet attain the clean apex of history. There, you build the point of the pyramid and under it through the mystic cave door you bring in processional the treasures of the three worlds. You have all the desert in golden perspective, and the Nile flows in chartered movements to a mellow sea. We are the scientists of man – and our measure is not man, but history. History, said the Mahabharata, is like the collyrium of the feminine eye – your perspective becomes more beautiful, and your nostrils have the camphor of the antiseptic. Death, the Moscow deaths, were the antiseptics of history – you kill for the beauty of your eyes.

We walked in the evening through the parks. There was much silence, and what we said later was the friendliest nonsense. When you come out of the temple, going homewards, the womenfolk laugh a lot. We were of such spirit made that evening, but one thought came to me. Descartes had made one of the simplest, one of the noblest statements on man. Of all things common sense is the one quality universally shared by all humans. I asked and asked myself – whose common sense was indeed sense? My father was once mad, and you could argue and argue again with him. My mother had never been to the prison (he was kept there because there were no asylums in those days) but his answer was always final: "I have seen her. You tell a lie." And, indeed, some time later my mother did come to the prison, as though to prove his common sense perception, and you wondered – where was the authenticity of fact? It all ends in your selective mind, and no doubt mathematical thought itself is of no valid structure. Two and two may or may not make four. Fact and fiction are interchangeable events whose accuracy in terms of the valid is an individual gift. Common sense is indeed the most divided phenomenon – it needs a metaphysic of interpretation. If zero were not, no number would have place value; there would be the anarchy of the number.

Communism had a metaphysic – a logic of fearful power, a scholastic, and its new humanism. The fact is, you cannot save Trotsky (or his comrades) from the gallows. You must seek the evil at its roots – the rigour of logic could pursue Marxism to its den and kill it there, in superb simplicity. Democracy had no logic – hence the superiority of Marxism. Danton crowned a lovely Parisian girl and led her in a procession through Paris to the Champ de Mars, that she be worshipped as Truth. If Truth were such a lovely Parisian girl, democracy would be the benediction of man. The Communist Truth has Hegel for father, Feurbach as the spouse of a legal wedding. Marx gave it a baptismal name, and Stalin gave it his own crown of steel. Such a Truth is not paraded – it is hidden in the folds of history. Dare you go there, brother? Dare you?

There are a million Kirillovs – Indian, Chinese, Albanian, Egyptian, North-Siberian, Guadeloupian, Greenlandian, Swedish, Norwegian, Polish, Portuguese – how dare you tread on Kirillov. His wife may have deserted him, but when she returns and the baby is born – somebody else's baby – how he still rushes to the midwife in wild joy: "Sister, sister, I have a baby – that is, my wife has a baby, and it is not mine, but just as well mine because my wife has borne it. Birth is a biological phenomenon, the sperm just a question of numbered genes. Have you ever heard more fulsome abuses than my wife Marie showers upon me, or have you seen such, oh, such a beautiful child, ever! The murderer may be at the gate, but I am innocent. My thought is true and scientific. My life is a biological reality. I am no more important or unimportant than Napoleon. Kill me, kill me, brother. I want to taste the feeling of biological extinction. I am only a number. Shoot."

Kirillov will not die. He has dialectical reality. You can kill him if you know his discipline. You can kill him only if you know his superior metaphysics. Reason alone can kill Kirillov, but then you must reason yourself down to your logical Truth. Logic is the most compassionate friend of true humanism. The fact is – do you really want it, brother?

Goodbye, Kirillov, goodbye. Perhaps I shall never see you again.

# The Chessmaster
and His Moves

I was in a dispirited mood that whole afternoon, as it were, half asleep and half awake, but my mind absolutely clear, sparking for an adventure. Unable, however, to work, I went to the salon, where there were always logs burning at the fireplace, – summer not being official yet – the coffee ever ready, to awaken me. I was standing warming myself by the mantlepiece, prodding the sugar to melt into my coffee, when who should I see but Michel – Irene, the secretary, had brought him to me. Michel looked grim, almost unfriendly.

"*Bon jour, patron,*" he said, somewhat ironically.

"*Bon jour camarade,*" I laughed to unfreeze him a little.

With his thick glasses, his short stature, his clothes ever awkward, he seemed incongruous in this magnificent salon, with so many candelabras, gilt-edged fire-shields, and the thick persian carpet shining with mythology, transmuting shimmering colours, and deep ancientness. I showed him a

---

This excerpt is from *The Chessmaster and His Moves* (1988) and contains the famous conversation between the Brahmin and the Jew. The original punctuation has been retained.

comfortable seat and myself chose a stiff chair, for I always thought more logically with my spine against a straight background. We did not speak for a long time.

"I have come," he said, finally seating himself on the plush sofa, green with yellow stripes, the flames from the fireplace playing on his face, giving it a sudden nobility, "I have come on *une* enterprise grave." Yes, those were the very words he used, as he crossed his legs, his heavy hunch, looking more like an archaeological lump then than a physical one. "I am a strange creature, not an indian, of course not, and not asian or african. Hitler has told you we are not european either. But we may call ourselves, if you will, asiatique, oriental, something kin or kins of the pharaohs, of your vedic ancestors, of the chinese, but not in species. A race somewhat forgotten maybe, but it has not forgotten itself, despite Mr Toynbee. He thinks we are an archaic society to be dumped between the interstices of history. Sir, I am a jew." He had come obviously to say just that. I had an instant shudder, a tremor, as if he were not a human speaking, but a geophysic event, a volcanic sputter through time's rude holes. He seemed, that evening, to be made as if of steel, but alchemically turned back from gold, so to say – not a steel of today, but an ancient metal, encrusted perhaps in the depths of the Pacific, from Lemuria, where legends say gold and steel were made from each other, for the benefit of primal man. It was a voice firm, dead, stomachal, but yet spoke, if you understand what I mean. It spoke not for himself, but, as it were, for the species, a whale upsurging in the ocean, leaping, cavorting, white-breasted, diving back, its mammal face prehistoric, but its movements contemporary. "You said the other day," he continued, the neighbours of the apartment opposite and above, playing some loud raucous music, and yet his voice was distinct, finite, irreversible – each word just a fact. "You said the other day, how could I laugh, how joke?"

"Yes, I did," I agreed.

"Now, I understand. I understand. But the truth is – and I say it as Moses must have, when he spoke to God: Who, my friend, can see my face, *our* face? – Is there anyone on earth which dare look on not merely the nazi stripes, broken rib-ends, gun-butt marks – holes, chunkless dimples, bumps – but the stripes and stigmata we bear from the assyrians, the romans. The romans even took away our ancient city of Jerusalem, the holy, and made it their provincial headquarters. And again, what stripes from the wirewhips the zoroastrians gave us in Babylon, and earlier still the pharaohs' eunuchs in Egypt. We are a simple people, we never were meant for war or government, the Moshe Dayans or the Rothschilds, as one of our great scientists, but himself an aide to Moshe Dayan, told us recently. We were made for books – for the Book and the Torah. We are a procession. We were always a procession. The nazi trains have always existed. We are ever on departure and arrival. In fact, sometimes on arrival before departure. Or on at once both. If so, and here my friend, may I say we would agree with your Vedanta – the world, in fact, a dire illusion. Going from the ghetto to the train, and from the train to a railway siding – you see, it being war, the Wehrmachi has so many trainloads of soldiers and material to carry to the Front – *nach* Stalingrad, *nach* Leningrad, *nach* Moskau – and then again, the train starts. And we come to another railway siding, the same evening, the next day, the day after, who can remember? We spit, squat, squeeze, dung, vomit, scratch, shout, fistfight, and sometimes even make love in corners, and fight again. And then suddenly, the train stops. Even it, the long train, seems tired. It really stops. And now the loudspeaker howls, yells, *Schnell, schnell,* jump down, get out, quick, quick. So man, woman and child, grandchild, granduncle, we all jump down, for we are just being transported. Taken, because of war conditions in Poland, from one town to the other, away from the great battle to be, and for the convenience of troop movements. Then when we arrive at another railway siding, then again another, with rubble and barbed wire and snarling dogs. The stations all look alike, skies' spittle, bombstruck, monumental. *Schnell, schnell.* And now a shout again. Enter, go back. And we leap, like circus animals, back to the opened-in wagons. There is, however, no audience to clap hands. Tickets sold out. There is an SS man, and he closes our doors, seals them. And we enter our permanent night again. There's, do not forget, there is always an SS man in history, egyptian, iranian, roman, the roman legionnaires. Why, for ought I know, there might even have been indian, buddhist or mughal SS men. Who knows, who knows? And *schnell, schnell* again. We leap out. And now we are marched off, all of us, bundles, children, grandfathers with canes, caftans, halts and shoes, to the lager, large as a hangar. They now tell you, you have just to undress, have yourself shaven, and there's a guard with whom to leave your treasures – wallets, jewels, eyeglasses, talismans – and they even give you back a certificate, you understand, a real receipt, stamped and all that in good german with Heil Hitler seals. Now, you men go this way, and you women go that way – it's meant only for registration. And then naked and fresh, the number, your number, is tattooed on the arms, and once you are numbered, you now become a real man, a woman, why even a child. We become mathematical entities. When a man is no man, yet a man, he is a real man, the superman, you understand. Now you march, you march to music, listen to fine music, to Bach, Beethoven, Richard Wagner, played by excellent musicians, and some maybe even famous – music played by our own people, and through a corridor, in which you find geraniums, in pots, on either aisle," he said, did Michel, and crossed his leg from one side to the other. "Never, never forget the geraniums," he said, and abruptly crossed his leg again to the other side. I was aghast. Aghast at the simplicity, the truth of the human animal. So this is man. Such is man. From the caverns of the Dordogne to the Gobi desert and beyond, man exists, and tells his story, the same, long, hun story.

"So, since we are what we are, and we know what has happened – and will happen, and remember, there was an Attila before Genghis Khan, Rasputin before Hitler, so we jews, we laugh," said Michel, and burst into a sob. It was not a loud sob, but like in death's early agony, there's an intake and outflow of breaths, which is like a rattle, a slight miss in rhythm. "Since we die, and we are dead – and we are always dead, remember, since Job, oh that good, good Job," and he laughed, did Michel, this time a good grave laugh, somewhat like the africans do, that would seem, as if, the tree or the stone laughed, and Michel added, "The good Job carried God's dirt pail, *la merde de Dieu, tu comprends.* You see, our Job was young. Thus he did not become a regular musalman. He was taken to work for the masters, to clean laboratories, factories, real ones, and for the very young like me – for I was only thirteen – we were separated efficiently, at the end of the geraniums – to dig trenches, trenches to push the dead into, the dead that died of cold, or starvation, on the bunkers. They were too costly to be sent to the crematorium. There were already too many there. Now, you understand. Now, this task had its fortunate side. Sometimes a gold tooth fell out, and this could buy things, many things on the blackmarket – the SS and the Kapos ran this – you could buy there, at this black-exchange, soap, shirts, tobacco and what not. Even a woman sometimes – for, on the other side of our camp was, so to say, Odin's harem. Yes, that is it, you understand. And thus the woman had somehow direct contact with the golden-haired gods, and knew what was happening to Rommels in Africa, to General Paulus in Stalingrad, to our own Rommels and Ludendorffs, outside and inside, the women knew more than we did. Thus God dispensed his justice, without stint, and he never, never failed."

"So, sometimes we did not carry corpses, we carried man's muckpails. I am sure you have never carried anything so heroic," and he laughed at me again, somewhat contemptuously. "You are not an untouchable. You are a brahmin, a nazi. Only untouchables carry pails of human dung in your country. I know it, because an uncle of mine told me so. And what my uncle said, the good Rabbi Zeev Moshe Fervan, God bless his soul, was ever true. He never told a lie, never hurt a bee."

"So, the jews have carried God's dirt, along the footways of history. You know, it's heavy, very heavy, the pail is. After all, it is God's. And he is a big man, we say to him, God, you have chosen us to carry this burden. So here we are waiting for you to come out of your WC. Then it's all there, big, fermenting bubbles. And it's so heavy, I tell you, and we've to carry it to the dumping ground. And it's a long, long way, I tell you, had you phthisis, typhus, diphtheria. You see," said Michel, rubbing his thick back against the sofa, as if it were painful, painful to bear the burden, to talk. "You see, God forgot us. That's the truth. But we remain over, like those dead bodies – and how many, many, many I've seen of these – they grow nails and hair, even after the man is sweaty, cold and dead. He also, this time, is to be carried, not on a stretcher steady eyed, but in a sack, if it's available, if not, we roll him like one does a log, and dump him finally, with a push and a kick – and there it goes, the man. Yes, it's all a part of Job's song, you understand."

"Remember, I was saying, God forgot us. Thus, as dead bodies grow hair and nail, as I have said, we go on mechanically carrying the dirt pail, like we did in Birkenau. Dead but alive, you understand. That's better,

I tell you, than anything else. For if you're still alive, you can rise, rise – because you see the ghouls are tearing the air shouting in fear, like animals, and – they run. They even speak deutsch, you know, as they decamp. The world is bloody mad. So you rise from the dead, because you were not dead, but they thought you dead, ha, ha! thus they dumped you down there. That's our own men, the Haftings, who had dumped us. You have typhus, diphtheria, dysentery, infectious sores, so you are dead, you understand. But you are not. At least for once, you are not. And night and day commingle to make your stay among the dead comfortable. It's just like sleep. Then you suddenly awaken, and you jump up and out and see there's no one, no one at all, anywhere around. None. Just gone, gone, gone, the germans are gone. Yes they are gone. Then you see a broken home, somewhere, anywhere, far, far, for remember, by now the barbed wires are cut. Who cut them? No one knows. Someone has done this, maybe many, many. The werewolves did it all. The watchtowers too are silent, dead silent, if one can say so. The dogs are gone too, those hounds of hell. You slip through the same pathways, between the lagers, by broken trees, the hanged men, their neat caps still on them, but their faces and hands covered with flies and sparrows, and then line after line of cement-tubes, meant for that gigantic rubber factory to be – the germans will win because they are german, and will make synthetic rubber, you understand, you frenchies, yankees, Mr Churchill & Co. We are a great nation, we believe in our fuehrer. He is no mortal, you know. So make synthetic rubber, and we'll make wheels for our aeroplanes, for our jeeps, for our gas chambers, Zyklon B. Zyklon B. Now finally, you come to an abandoned home, a wretched home, you understand. And you crouch like a rabbit, a young hog. You can see from where you are, a dog's pen, a dump of hay. So now you slowly crouch and move, crawl like soldiers in a trench. The back door is open, you enter to see if it's all real, real. You realize there are no humans around. In the kitchen maybe, there's still bread, and fish and eggs in the larder. The cattle too are there, nervously munching their foods, between shivers, urinating, and calling for their young ones – for they too have lost something, something true, familiar, noises known. This abrupt silence is stultifying. What to make of it, you bull, you horse, you fluttering, foolish, foolish hen? Oh, how the hens are horrored by these sounds of new humans, and the cattle, too. You see. So you now crawl, on your belly and along the floor, curled under some table, absolutely alone, for this time God will come, yes, God himself will come, God Illych will come, and he will not touch us. The russians are our brothers. Everything is alive, see, everything says back, I table, I pillar, I picture, one, two, three – river, wood, men, medals. Yet no one, no one, no one is there. So the good God Illych will come. He will take us in his troika, across the polish lands to the princess who awaits us. Yes, the princess. And she awaits us, open-armed, the bitch!"

"But now let me tell you a story. A true story. A true story for me, since then, is always false. So, history is false. It is just a chronicle of human truths, of newspaper cuttings, etc, etc. You understand?"

My mind was too benumbed to speak. So he started again after a moment's deep-breath silence.

"You are a sensitive, gentle, highly civilized fellow. A brahmin, a mathematician, and soon to be a member of the Royal Society, etc. And who knows, you may even win the Nobel Prize."

"Absurd," I spat. "Don't be too absurd."

"Absurd, sir," shouted Michel, sitting up straight, and small. "Who is absurd, those pedestrians of Paris, the clerk at the Crédit Lyonnais, the professors at the Sorbonne, the minister of De Gaulle – I will, for the moment, leave the great man, as much for your comfort as for my own – for withal, he is a good man, but for how long, who knows, who knows? Good becomes bad overnight, like milk left at night becomes curd next morning – does it or does it not?"

"Yes, it does."

"Well, I spoke it, because I had read it in one of your buddhist books. You see I am not mad. I am sane. I am Michel, all right," and he rose, came to me as if a little drunk, patted me on the back and said:

"Oh, *mon frère*."

"*Oui*, Michel."

"You are too innocent. You do not know hell. I do."

"Yes, I know you do."

"When you've *tripoté* so many dead, and have been *tripoté* by so many dead, what do you think you become? You leap out, that's if you are still alive and young fifteen, run to an abandoned house, and lie amidst the

139

silences between the gunfire – for God has at last come. God reveals you an empty abandoned house, with a rich larder – how do you like that? Between bombs, machinegun ticktacks, Mauser rifle-shots. You see, a true, true fairy tale, better than any writ by the great Andersen."

"You're right. Andersen never knew hell."

"Because," continues Michel, following his own monologue, "because you see, the good germans, grandfather, mother, children, who sat on the other side of Birkenau camp, ran – they who would visit the SS men's family, with neat gardens, fresh clothes, and after a chat and a cup of tea, they would stroll the perambulator, and peep through those innocent windows, you know, and see the musulmans all entire, without a cry, abjuration or disdain, but tied to their God, as the exiles were in the old days of the czar, going to Siberia, hand-to-hand tied, a never-ending line, on the snows, white, pure, but singing – listen, I can still remember, a song my great-grandfather is supposed to have sung coming back from the land of the snows – for he was caught in some minor misdeed done to the name of the czar, or of his henchmen – and this is the song," said Michel, and standing on a chair, as if he were performing in a drama, he sang, clapping his hands.

"Yes, the russian God is coming, the sickle in his mouth," added Michel, showing his teeth, "the machinegun in hand," and here he jumped down from the chair, and started showing how the machinegun went, in this direction and that, "Tock, tock, tock – and tock. And now, sitting beneath

a table –," and here Michel sat back on his chair, and held his hand forward as if he were taking something from the table in front of him, "So my friend, you sit under a table in the kitchen, munching, munching, dead beef – after all, there is something to eat – and to laugh, to laugh at yourself, so that's where I learnt laughter." And Michel laughs curve by curve, into the falling evening, and as I light my cigarette, he starts: "The miracle is you laugh, and laugh again. It is so thrilling, thrilling to laugh. By next morning, as you go down to the larder, there are one, two, three skeletons like you, wondering how you could be there, and you wonder where they came from. Of course, one thinks suddenly – for thoughts come slowly, and then abruptly, as if we were children again – of course others came, one, two and three – the same way I came. Maybe there is a fourth and a fifth, still not known, hiding in a big dog-kennel."

"But I was going to tell you a fairy tale, the tale of a princess and true."

"Now I will tell you. There was a madman in my town, crazy, crazy. He too had read books, too many, many of all religions, and though his father was a good hasid, a rabbi, too. And this young man, who ior convenience we'll call Isae, his real name though was different. His mother, a widow, was a laundress. Yes, and a very good laundress in Lvov. Being an important town, and she having a reputation, she made money laundering for the rich. And the polish rich in those days were rich, rich. He, Isae knew them well as a boy, so my mother told me. For as a boy, he played with things electrical like wires, bulbs, brackets, sockets, etc, because his uncle, his mother's brother, had an electrical shop, in the richer part of the town. He was a very clever boy, Isae was, so everybody told me. And at school, he was very bright. Since he wanted to be an engineer, his mother said, Son, son, go to Warsaw. There you will have teachers such as you will not find here. Your sister will stay to look after me. – But Mother, said the good Isae, you will be alone. I am the only man in the house. Father died so long ago. – Since your father died, said Isae's mother, your father entered me, and I have become him, – and she put her chin forward to show how manly she had become. When one has lost a husband, while young, and you have children to bring up, you become a man, work, earn, fight, pray, die, you understand. Anyway, his mother, Isae's mother, dreamt her son would become an engineer in Warsaw, and she would make for him a good wedding – her brother had told her of Simon Katz and Manes Satorsky, who became famous engineers, despite government obstructions raised against the jews, became rich men and even lived in villas. And why would not Isae, her son, Isae, build a villa in Poskya Street, off the great boulevards. So her brother had told her, for her brother too hoped, if his nephew became rich, he too could open a bigger shop – and in Warsaw. Thus you see the world is round, round," laughed Michel, good-heartedly. "Don't ask me," he continued, "if the mother wanted to be rich, or if the brother of the mother wanted the nephew to be rich, maybe he wanted to be rich to make his wife think better of him, for she came, said my mother, from a family of apothecaries. Who knows, who knows? You know the world is full of Suzanne Chantereuxs." I did not understand why he said what he said, and then after a moment's silence, he continued: "Well, well, my Isae, our Isae, being a bright boy – my mother told me he looked just like me, broad and short, and with thick glasses, but of course I never was very bright in mathematics, or in anything, nor did I have an uncle who ran an electrical appliances shop. My father wrote petitions for the unlettered: Your Excellency, the Prèfet, the Magistrate, the Count, etc, etc. For there were many counts. And we have even a count in my story.

"Well, well, Isae went to Warsaw. But, like an untouchable, sat at a separate table, at the University of Warsaw, for remember, that was how we were treated, even under Marshal Pilsuduski, so I was too. And our Isae read all the electricity which could be read, finally wore a gown and became an engineer, and was given a minor post in Warsaw municipality. But by now, his real interests were elsewhere. He never wanted to be a rabbi, even when very young, that his mother knew, and he knew. He wanted, however, to save mankind. Remember, we are all like that. We jews are. If some tartonpion in, say, Tahiti, is dying of venereal disease – a venereal disease, as you knew only one virtue, and that is to be a woman – so this white man gave the disease to a woman, and that woman to a tahitian, and he is, the tahitian is, covered with small and big boils. And somebody, another white man, a good pole, maybe, because he had heard of the beauty of tahitian women, goes there, you know, like Gaugin went, but this time, not to paint, but to enjoy, to enjoy the thick juicy richness of tahitian women – and there it comes, the news to, say, Isae. And he will say, *Tiens, tiens*, someone, some, people, in Tahiti are suffering from venereal disease. So I will study medicine. Become a doctor. And then go to Tahiti and help the tahitians get better. How do you like that?" smiled Michel, slapping his thighs with both hands.

"So that our Isae was involved in trying to help mankind in every way – therefore, he joined the Theosophical Society. Do you know that organization at all? It is something to do with your country. It's a sort of Gurdjieff, with Tibet and Mongolia and the Himalayas, and all that. And saints of course, many, many saints, and masters several thousand years old, sitting on top of your Himalayas which guide mankind etc, etc."

"Well, I knew something about it, just a little," I said.

"So my Isae studied theosophy. And when one studies anything so outlandish as all that, you always meet – especially in faraway Poland – people of the upper classes – like, say, at the Rotary Club in Paris today. So, my Isae met many counts and countesses, studying, you understand, esoteric, yes, esoteric philosophy." And by now Michel was exhausted, he asked for a glass of water, and I went to my room to fetch him some cool nice water. And when I returned, he sat there, silent as a rock, as solid and natural as the rock of the Trocadero hill, which rose in front of us, across the garden.

"So to go on with my story, my Isae fell in love with a countess, with a real countess, a highborn lady. He was five-foot-three-and-a-half and hunchbacked like I am – his back was like an accordion, my mother used to say, and therefore, when he spoke, it was like music, like some psalm. He spoke not words, but long, musical syllables. And many were often like words from the Bible. He lisped – he did not talk – as a child does or a dumb person, and so it carried rich meanings. Thus my mother. But let me go on with the story. He was hunchbacked like me, I told you – he had fallen from a tree when young, like I had from a colt – and though I had never seen him, but it's as if I know him, even sometimes I feel I am him. Since he is not alive, I'd even believe in your theory of reincarnation and cry I am Isae, I am he indeed, our Isae," said Michel, and laughed again, tenderly, as if he had no reason to hurt me.

"Whether you believe it or not, it might still be true, like in the Middle Ages, whether you thought the earth was flat and the sun went round the earth or not, for which Galileo had to be burned at the stake, the sun still was the centre of our planetary system."

"Maybe you are right. Often what we suspect to be true turns out true. Why, the reincarnation theory might even explain the story I am going to tell you. Listen."

"Yes, I will."

"I said, Isae fell in love with the countess, but to be true, it's the countess who fell in love with him. She thought him a genius and perhaps he was one, who knows? The countess was from a famous polish family, with castles in Silesia, on one side greek and on another german, and she was at least a palm-wide taller than he was. But he had a mind, my mother tells me, so brilliant, the rabbis refused to discuss with him. As I have said before, maybe he was a genius, a new Spinoza."

"Now, now," I protested, "Spinozas are not born so often. Please?"

"But, said my mother," continued Michel, without listening to my own remarks, "he spoke in biblical polish, as I have said before, or sometimes, yiddish, with a touch of softness that made one think he loved vocables, he loved to pronounce vocables, like a good rabbi. And he must have spoken sweet things, to the countess, and she must have adored him, much, much. She said, the countess said, I would wed you today were it not I have two daughters to marry. If you can wait a year or two we will surely get married. But she boldly, openly, for she was a courageous woman, became his mistress. She took an apartment in the city and moved him there. And spent evenings with him, as much as she liked."

"A beautiful story," I said.

"But wait, wait. So my Isae said, as all good poles thought at that time, I will go to Paris, like Madame Curie had gone, or like the good Chopin, and I will make money, so that I may keep my Helen, for that was her name, Countess Helena Volonsky, I will make any Helen happy. And so to Paris he went. His mother, thinking her son was going to Paris to make money for them, said, Oh what a fine son I have, he thinks of us, of me, of his sister Liza. And he will build us a nice house here in Lvov – after all, we still have land there that Maximilian, my husband, had bought outside the town for a nice house. And that was when he was working at the grain-exchange. And we shall have a grand marriage for his daughter."

"Just like in India."

"All the world is India, sir," he said somewhat in mockery. One always felt, talking to him, or in fact with any jew, as if there was a sort of supernal rivalry between the hebraic and the hindu. Of course, we the hindus, especially the brahmins, always felt we were the eldest beings of creation. And the jews of course were the "chosen people." So, who would decide? God would. But he did not exist. So?

"She was, Helen was," he started, "some sort of a shekina."

"Now, what's that? It sounds almost indian." And he laughed again, somewhat compassionately, and added, "Oh, why, as I have said before, all that's good comes from India, does it not, *mon cher ami?*" and he came over and once again patted me on the shoulder good-humouredly.

"Well, well maybe," and I joined him in laughter, as though it were a private joke.

"So, she was his, Isae's, shekina." ·

"Now, now, Michel," I said, smiling within myself, "what's all that?"

"Well, if God is a He, the feminine aspect of God is, of course, a She."

"Like Sakti and Shiva," I said to understand.

"Yes, more or less so," and he laughed again. "And if God is a He," and this time he laughed so loud, loud enough for the whole building to hear, and even the concierge must have heard, and, as if in sympathy, the fire in the hearth shot up, or so it seemed.

"How is it Michel," I asked very grave, "how is it you can laugh at God in that manner. I thought you shouldn't even pronounce his holy name."

"That, my friend, is the trick. God, Dieu, is not the unpronounceable. Because it is latin and not hebrew. You know, pandit," he added smiling, "I think we are prisoners of our language. So it is that I have become involved in linguistics, one notes there is no plural in chinese. Those chinois are so materialistic, for them their object, *la chose*, is very, very real. So real they can see only one thing at a time. In our linguistic laboratories, when we have to choose the computer for the chinois, we are in a fix. So we have to give to chinese letters a plus, an algebraic symbol like x or p. Yes, we are prisoners of language, for example, the jews have no vowels. We too in our own way love objects, because we use consonants. God is beyond, therefore we have no vowels, so you explained to me once, you remember, and I think that is precise."

"But –"

"No, no, let us get back to my Isae and his shekina. Now I have said to you already, all that I say is pure legend, the legend of the ghettos. You know, when the germans entered my country, Poland, they created a ghetto government, so to say, and they named a fuehrer for us, and our fuehrers could be as terrifying as the one you know, all fuehrers, can, were they even hindus –"

"Now, now Michel, don't be so hard on us."

"No, sir," he said, sitting up and crossing his legs, "we are all *les êtres humains*. And I am speaking of *La Condition Humaine*."

"Well. Let us go on."

"In the ghettos of Lvov, the legend of Isae was one of the most enchanting. It was like some ancient fairy tale. Our parents sat on their frontsteps on summer evenings, listening to our grannies talk, talk, talk. So, we would, had we more time, have written a ballad, an epic poem, like Roland, to extol the exploits of our Isae, le Bossu. And Isae le Bossu would have become tall, bent and noble as a rabbi. His words were so clear, they could sound talmudic. He was a saint, there was no doubt of it. For the story said, he made so much money, Isae did, in the very first year of Paris, taking patent after patent, so his mother is supposed to have said – and that was in the good golden days before this heinous war – that our Isae made much, much money, and sent her enough money to live in peace, and even put aside some in the bank for his sister's marriage –"

"So he had a sister?"

"Yes, a sister, I told you so, and she studied pharmacy. She was already engaged to a young man, even before Isae went over to France, and that must have been around 1930 or 1931."

"Oh, as long ago as that?"

"Yes, does it not all sound prehistoric! Anyway, our Isae then made so much money, but he would not send too much home, lest our government get suspicious, as to how a laundress had so much money, and we jews have prudence in our fingernails, so to say, you understand, counting our rosaries – turning the pages of the Talmud," and he laughed again. And this time, I understood his nerves had become so frail, he had to laugh, laugh and laugh, at himself, at his own people. "Thus our Isae then made so much money, so his mother said again to my aunt, or to my aunt's aunt, or my aunt's aunt's aunt, who cares. She told it all to my mother, and Isae in two years' time had bought a home on the outskirts of the Bois de Boulogne. But I, in my own way, made enquiries here in Paris and found through a russian, a restaurant keeper, that had helped him in the beginning – the russian survived because he was some sort of a prince before the revolution, so the Hitler people spoilt him – and the russian talks of Isae with contempt, for he did not know who I was, and he said, A house, a house! That Yuopin lived in Clichy, in a hotel with a gasring. True, he was generous with all his friends. *Tênez.* He said, he gave me money to bet on horses. And if I lost, I said to him, Isae, I will not live, if you do not give me any money, and I will hang myself, like I've done once before, you remember, and Isae would give me another fifty or a hundred francs – and in those days it was a grand sum, and I would go betting again. In fact, he helped two or three refugee girls from Lithuania, Latvia – good girls who did not want to go on the streets to make money. Yes, he was a man of heart, the russian concluded, and clapped his hands, as if he was paying off a debt to Isae, and took the bill of the next customer. Yes, that's how I made enquiries everywhere."

"So, to go on with my story, my Isae had indeed taken many patents. I, I went out of curiosity to the patent office here, and found that he had in true fact taken some twenty two patents in a year. That must have brought him a lot of money. And despite the russian prince, Isae must have lived in comfort. And here we come to the last part of the story."

"Our Isae then decided it would soon be time, in a year or two, to get married to Helen because her two daughters were by now engaged. And I found on enquiries from other jews here, who knew him then but did not know the story, that he had bought an apartment on rue des Sts Peres, no 7 or 9, I do not remember, a comfortable one. It's now an office. And he waited and he waited, like Balzac did, his shekina, who, as you know, was a polish countess, and all that."

"No, I did not know that."

"However, the apartment once found, the shekina had to come. And here the story becomes complex, tragic. She's supposed to have written one day, imagine, to this anxious, all awaiting jew, that she had met a famous count, elegant, tall, and an admirable dancer – met him at a party, and they danced the evening away – of course it was in Warsaw. He was so exquisite a dancer, they danced down till almost the light of day, and this shekina is supposed to have said, I went and married him as soon as the papers were ready. I am sorry, very sorry, to have done this to you. I am really sorry. You know I am a woman of impulse, polish to the core. But don't come here, she seemed to have added, for Victor knows everything about you. He said he would shoot you if he saw you. So please do not come. Yet I love you, I love you, etc."

"But, but Michel, why are you telling me this story?"

"Well, you will see why. Just wait. I thought hindus had a lot of patience, because, with you, time is cyclic and all that. Anyway, our Isae, then, heroic, charismatic, brilliant, had only one thing to do. A good jew he would understand anything. He would forgive anyone – even a former prisoner, a murderer whom he is supposed to have befriended in Paris, and gave him money – to live in honour. So, he took the first train to Warsaw, and a short tacko to the castle, some seventy miles or so away, and presented himself. Yes, presented himself, like Rolland before the saracen, and at the castle door. He knew the guards would never let him in. So he pretended he was a county engineer who had come on government inspection. And he looked intelligent, well-groomed, efficient. So, they let him in. And once up and inside the castle, he just said, he wanted to see the countess, to ask about the electrical repairs. He had learnt about such matters from his uncle. And imagine what a shock it was, she in her nuptial splendour, so to say, before a hunchbacked jew, here in this fifteenth century castle."

"Yes, I understand – it's like when I visit Jayalakshmi in her palace at Vilaspur –"

"Well, well, the brahmin of India is not quite the jew of Poland. But you understand what I mean. Then openly, quietly, she went and told her husband what had happened. And believe me, and I have been assured of this here by two or three polish noblemen in exile – impoverished and humble, now polishing hotel-floors, running lifts – and they say the story is true – that the count came out and said in his chest high and moustached manner, Well, engineer, what is it you want? – You know who I am. I have come to settle some business with you. – Business in the castle is done by the bailiff – and he almost walked away. – Yes, I know, but I have another business, and the legend says, so sweet was the voice of Isae, so true, and maybe the count did not want to offend his new bride, the two men settled down to business together. Isae said he loved his shekina so totally, he would only wish for her happiness. He said he had become, while in Warsaw, a liberal catholic priest, so even more did he understand love. Thus, in the name of God, His Son, and the Holy Ghost, and here Isae, must have sincerely crossed himself, and in the name of the Trinity, can we make a pact. And he had asked for Helen to be present. And Helen came out, trembling, ashamed, proud, heroic, while all the maids and butlers were amazed at this historic confrontation. A jew, and this is how the count talks to him! Well, human nature is magical. Yes, a hasid, I tell you, a zadik, can work miracles, prayer can. Then Isae said, and this was in the large hall of the castle with the portraits of all the count's ancestors in armour gold and ermine, looking down on him in pride and protection, So make a promise to me: If she is happy, she stays with you. If not, if not, – Yes, if not? – If not, she come to me. – And the count, a real  chevalier, was so moved, and Helen, so proud of her Isae, they shook hands ceremonially, had lunch together, and he, Isae, left for Paris by the evening train." Here Michel stopped, mopping his head, perspiring, and went over to the coffee machine, which was still blinking red, took a cup of coffee, came back and sat down. And I sat there, of course, thinking of Jaya. How could I not have? If I went to Raja Ashok and told him the same, then what would he say? He might say: "*Mon vieux*, or old chap. Let us wait and see. She is not yet mine, and when she is mine and if ever, we can always settle the accounts!" He would use, I was sure, the same expression, having been brought up in the anglo-saxon, the upper-class, background, that is, a european background. So, it's all a common story, you see. Then why is Michel shifting about his legs so often? One has to wait and see. The evening had not yet set in, and all one heard was the Orpheus singing out the waters to the naiads below. It sounded so much like his own story too. He and Eurydice, and all that, as Suzanne had explained to me – a barbarian from India who did not know greek mythology. "For the european, the french, he who does not know greek mythology is indeed a barbarian," she had said one evening on rue des Bonnes Soeurs, au 7e, and added with a passionate kiss, "but I love my barbarian brahmin prince." – "Yes, my queen," I had said and smiled thinking of Jaya of course.

Alas there was but one queen for me, one shekina so to say, and squeeze as I might Suzanne, under my power-led loins, in my tight gripped arms, begging her for more of *that*, all she gave was so thin now, so dry, so melancholic. Jaya's simple touch of hand had more wealth than all this psychodrama. Suzanne was even as Hermione, stiff, theatrical, mental. Her mind ruled her, and as such Gurdjieff. She seemed so germanic to me, will, absolute will, the Herr with the knout, her lord. Yet she wanted so much to be a woman. And obviously, I was not her Herr. I wondered if she had showed any of her privileges to Michel yet. The smell of her pubic hair, for example, or the big black mole on her left breast – Suzanne's well-shapen breasts – the mole big as a small ring, black and pink, was to be touched only by the highly privileged, and I was, she had assured me, at the moment, and, was forever to remain, the only privileged one. And I felt so jealous, I knew how the count could and might have killed Isae.

"You may wonder why I tell you all this." He must have read my thoughts. "You indians – indian thought as such – since the eighteenth century – has usurped our place. We were the priests of the western world. Ever suppressed, pogromed against, they knew and we, of course, knew, we were ultimately to be the victors. The west belongs to the jew. We the God-carriers of the Mediterranean, if you remember what Mediterranean is, despite Paul Valéry and his boasted latinism. The Mediterranean man includes Ramases II, the great Gilgamesh, and of course, Abraham. Yes, that is what Mediterranean means. I have told you the greeks were asian aryans. They had a sense of the occult, of mystery, orphic, dionysian, but no prophets – of the unpronounceable!" and he let his second foot down and stood up, as if to feel his own true stature. "Moses on Sinai, that's the only metaphor of man to his maker. All your neutral It, and so on, is *c'est la fantaisie, mon vieux*," and he came and patted me on the back with what seemed, at once, contempt and affection, a father to a son. The jew, the Father of the World. And everyone not his children – only the jew can be the child of the jew – the others just his farmworker, farmworkers of the lord.

"You have taken our place," continued Michel, with almost anger, I might even have said hatred, and he went to the glasswindow to see the rocks of the garden, as it were. The atmosphere was at least as angry and vibrant, I am sure, as when Isae might have faced the count. Christianity, especially catholicism, was even more greek than jewish – Saint Paul had done his job – thus the christian was a sort of indian of the West.

And so – the ghetto and the incinerators. History smells bad, you know. Attila and Hitler, they are all the same.

The hasid, he worked on the Garden of Eden. His language was prayer. From his prayer grew fruits and forests, and the cattle to slay. He, the hasid, even invented a knife, so gentle, it would cut his goat or cow without pain, or almost so. I was now the goat before Michel. I was now his Isaac. He seemed in prayer. I had heard he too had thaumaturgical power – he had healed people. There was no doubt he was a zadik. How could, otherwise, he have come out of the dead?

"From now the story is simple," he said, going back and taking his seat opposite me. There was no Paris or Poland that evening. No world – two humans face to face, in what seemed an eschatological drama. No Helen of Troy, no Suzanne the problem. It was whether the sacred ship from Delos had come into the harbour or not. Then Socrates would have to take his poison and die. Such the laws of history.

"Of course," exclaimed Michel, "of course, a count who could be such a good dancer, even were it only the mazurka, could not have satisfied our Helen. This Isae was a jew and a hasid. He had seen the Maker face to face. He gave her, Isae gave her, his powerful God. She was infatuated. Under the hitlerian law, she would have been shorn in public, marched in front of people naked, and taken to the firing squad, with the pancarte hanging from her neck: I commingled with a jew. This is just to set an example, you know. Hitler then had no such power. But Isae knew, for he knew his God well, that she would come to him. And of course she came back to him. The count was a man of his word. He belonged to a different order of nobility than of the french or of the germans today. The polish counts were servants of the Black Madonna. They were first christian, and then polish. They died fanatically on the field of battle, even as recent history shows us. There could be no Hitler in Poland. A house painter become dictator! Impossible. Even a hindu could become a dictator, a brahmin," he laughed, "could become a dictator, but never a polish house painter." And Michel smiled at his own joke.

"So, our Isae said to his Helen, not of Troy but of Warsaw, shall we say, and remember she was part greek too, he said to her: Come my love and we'll go to India."

"What?" I said, almost standing up in astonishment.

"Yes, he said, did our Isac, India is all peaceful and beautiful – and he dreamt of it, a hasid, as his Garden of Eden, you see, that's our obsession, where everything is positive and good. So thither, my friend, he took her, to his Gandhi and all that. They say he invented many things in India, became a monk."

"What, a hindu monk? A bizarre story."

"Yes, a bizarre, story. A jew first, then a theosophist, then a christian, finally a hindu monk --"

"Now tell me, how did this happen, according to your legend?"

"I asked some men of your country, working at the CNRS. They told me little, they knew little. One man amongst them had a father who was a theosophist. And he heard of Isae Zimmerman and his monkship. Yes, and a disciple of Krishnamurti, a devotee of one Ramana Maharishi, and finally a worker with Gandhi. So I've heard. Have you not heard of him?"

"Zimmerman, Zimmerman," I said, "never. Besides my father was on the british side. How would he have known of someone with Gandhi?"

"Anyhow, and again I've heard, it was Gandhi's last spinning wheel, a great invention – an indian one – was one of Isae Zimmerman's make. And our indian at the CNRS, whose father is a minister in some state in India, in Madras I think, even said, Mahatma Gandhi had given his elegant instrument of spinning, one of the first, rare ones, a gift to Chiang Kai-shek. So, who knows, if this polish jew's spinning machine is not singing away with some of Mao's comrade maidens in Szechwan. Thus life, my friend, with his hasid life."

"But Helen – what happened to her? You never completed that story."

"In this paradise of his, this Eden of the World, India, people certainly are angels – as Suzanne and her mother never stop discoursing to me. For these two ladies, you are only next to God, you understand. Well, well, let us leave that part out."

"Yes, let us!"

"Anyway, evidently the hindus do not know much of microbes. So, this Isolde, in the land of enchantment, drank no magical potion, but water from an infected well. She had typhoid. Nobody had told her to take an inoculation against such an event –"

"So?"

"So, she had typhoid. And Isae duly telegraphed to the count. He had, the count had, even in those days, an aeroplane company. So he hopped and hopped to India in four or five days – you know in those days, there was no night flying. And he reached Bangalore."

"Oh, Bangalore. I know Bangalore."

"Well, so much the better. However, the lady lay flat in her bed, in the outskirts of Isae's factory – for he was the first to start an electrical factory in India – the british did not like it, but there was a good and strong maharaja, a saint, I am told, who gave Isae all the money he needed to build a factory –"

"But I thought Isae was with Gandhi –"

"That was later. So, Helen, like a tolstoyan heroine, lay – on one side, the hunchbacked thaumaturgical jew, and on the other, the elegant polish count, whose family had fought many battles, including the one at Sadowa, in the fourteenth century with the russians – and between the two, she gave up her Ghost, as the fairy tales would say. And she was cremated. And her ashes later thrown into the Ganga. The count now took the two daughters back to Poland – the war was still far away – Hitler had only marched to the Rhine, you understand, and the french panicked and ran –"

"Oh, yes, but the french show extreme courage when faced with real danger, never with near danger – like we hindus do," I said. "When the japs were coming we were all so frightened – we ran from Madras for our lives. But the japs never came –"

"But Hitler marched into Poland – and you know the rest of the story. At that time, I was happily just over twelve."

"Why happily?"

"Because later they took from the ghetto all the very old and the very young. They left me because I was thirteen and took Sasha, my brother, seven years of age –"

"What did they do with them?"

"You innocent," he said, very angry. "They sent them to the gas chamber immediately. Thus my uncle and my younger brother, Sasha, preceded us into paradise ..."

"And Isae, what happened to him, at that time?"

"He must have sat in rapt meditation, in holy harmony, as the hasidim say – before one of your many saints, maybe talking of the brotherhood of man, of nonviolence, and what not. Later, so my count in Paris told me, his mother and sister went to Birkenau, like I did where the count's brother-in-law worked, in a chemical factory."

"What happened to the count?"

"His time too must have come. One never heard of him either."

"Oh!"

"So ends the story," said Michel, stamping his feet, as if all was said.

"One more thing, please?"

"Yes –"

"Well, well, in this paradise he found that there were thieves too. So some poor fellow, whose good indian habit was to steal, I suppose – one day coming home, thus I've heard from one of your countrymen – who'd read it in one of your indian newspapers – so Isae coming home and finding his rupees gone – is rupee the money in India?"

"Yes, it is."

"– his rupees gone, Isae in a nice bourgeois manner slapped his servant. So, the poor fellow whose habit was to steal, I imagine, cried and howled. Confessed he had done it. So that our Isae, who'd read a lot of Tolstoy – you know, we poles read russian very well – Isae, the saint, then said unto him, Pardon me, brother? and not able to sleep night after night, went, so I was told, to a nearby hindu temple, a temple of Shiva, donned the ochre-coloured robe – and so became a hindu monk. Could one become a hindu monk so easily? No ordination, etc?"

"I don't think it's so easy."

"Well, anyway, that's the legend. He knew his mother was dead and his sister as well. They had some news through the underground which worked between India and Eastern Europe."

"Oh, was there such an organization?"

"Well, if your Mireille, worked in Greece, and communicated with England – this too was possible between India and Poland, especially through Persia and Soviet Russia –"

"And then?"

"And then came the deluge. We were swept away till Stalingrad. Then we were cooked, you understand, cooked as lamb or hen. And when we had turned into ash, my dear fellow, it grew potatoes. Potatoes and turnips, all over Germany today. You could ask a potato: How much chemical from the Levi and the Katz do you have? It might sit up, the potato might, as in a cartoon, and say: Why, I have 0.3% of the Levi's and all of the Katz's. And does it taste good, you ask of Herr Goboldo Kommin, and Goboldo Kommin will say: it tastes *schon, schon*. Heavenly. Yes, that's our Europe. Yes, that's it."

"Thus, he, Isae, went back to the source," I said in mischief, smiling.

"Why do you say that?"

"Because hasidism, from what little I know of it, and of what you have said, came late to judaism."

"Not quite. But if it were so?"

"Anyway, your Scholem says it."

"Perhaps. But I do not remember."

"So hasidism was influenced by the christian mystics."

"Maybe."

"And christian mysticism, I repeat, by Plotinus."

"So?"

"And the roots of Plotinus?"

"Of course, India," he snarled with bitterness.

"Thus –"

"He went back to the source!"

"Does hinduism alone contain the Truth?"

"No."

"No. Then what does?"

"The Truth."

"Are you a hindu?"

"No."

"Then what are you?"

"A seeker, a simple seeker. But who knows, maybe Truth is ... is peruvian." And we both laughed.

"Then what is true hinduism?"

"He who goes beyond hinduism, like –"

"Yes, like –"

"– a true christian, one who has gone beyond theology, like Jakob Boehme, like Eckhart, and –"

"And –?"

"Like the sufis in islam – like Rumi – could you say the same thing, of your jews?"

"Maybe not – but of the hasidim, yes."

"So, you see, we meet again."

He was kicking the coffee table, pushing it back and forth, Sisyphus style. Not to hear what the coffee table was saying, but to say what his shoe would like to say to the coffee table.

"The goys," he said, "are never so dead serious – as you and I." And after a moment of tense silence, he continued, "There was, you know, once upon a time, a great russian prophet. He did not like the jews either. But he had faced the gallows, therefore love oozed out of him, so to say. So our Feodor Dostoevsky has called Europe – and not Russia, because Russia is holy – Stalin is now a czarevitch, etc, etc – well, well, Dostoevsky has called Europe, a cemetery." Then he stopped, did Michel, and with commiseration asked: "How did you land in this cemetery?"

"A good question, Michel. But, I will answer it another time. It is getting late. You know the princess and my sister are waiting for me. At home."

"Well, of course!" And as we rose together, Michel suddenly put his head against me gently, and sobbed – and sobbed. Wiping his tears, he said: "I had to tell all this to someone. Who is there I can say it to? For that Isae might have been me. It's the legend which I have told to myself again and again, on the bunkers of Birkenau and in the Ka-be, the hospital, even on the last day before the russians came. I have told this story often to my bunker fellows, that they too could dream of a countess and a noble count, and of the jew who went to Paradise. India then meant for us paradise indeed – with Mahatma Gandhi – we believed in him then."

"Yet, my good Michel, just three years later, our hindus and muslims massacred each other, two million of them, the same way, maybe in a less methodical mode, not being germanic. We did not even have the gas chambers to dispose of people – in a civilized way. They, the hindu and the muslim, cut the throats, the breasts – their heads smashed, their penis severed, bodies stoned, the women, their babies gouged out of their pregnant bellies, yes, noses cut, the hindu and the muslim did this to one another – in our paradise –"

"So you mean there is no paradise!"

"None. None. None, despite Madame LaFosse and her great guru, Réné Guénon."

"So you mean we shall never find what we seek."

"Never. Never the way we seek it. Indeed there is no paradise. But – but – there must be – the Truth."

And this time we both stood still, staring at pure, concentric space. And Michel then ran his fingers on my back, enfolding me, with a tenderness, a concern, I had never known before, and never known since, of any man.

"I wonder what is happening to Isae now?" I said, to break the silence. "Maybe he is dead."

"Nonsense, my friend. Saints do not die so easily," he remarked, and laughed as usual, releasing me from his embrace. "Saints live very long, you know."

"Then you mean he must be in India now?"

"Of course, a swami, like one of those thousands in your country, maybe receiving the homage of innocent people, sitting under a tree, a hasid. How much his thaumaturgical powers, healing people – maybe even bring back the cadaver to life – ten rupee a dead body, how do you like that?"

"Maybe not."

"And again, being an inventor, I am sure he could invent for the good hindu, a machinegun, a bomb, a nonviolent atom bomb, to kill without killing, your wicked neighbour of Pakistan –"

"Now, now, Michel, don't be so facetious. Why has no one written about him?"

"The only man who might have written about him is – would have been – Papa Buber. But he wouldn't have approved of this devotee of Gandhi –"

Raja Rao

"Why not?"

"Because Gandhi was against the jew."

"Nonsense. Gandhi was against no man. Never."

"But you know what Gandhi said to Buber: The poles who fought against the germans and the russians were sort of nonviolent, but we, the jews, who did not fight, we were – I don't know what he called us –"

"The jews went to their death in prayer," I said, "in pure nonviolence, nonviolence. The true jews, I mean, I honour them for their truth."

"Like uncle Dinka."

"Wonderful."

"Then go and speak that to your indians. Tell them the true gandhians, the jews of Poland, of Birkenau, the true, the true –" and Michel stood up against the mantlepiece, as if in grave contemplation of the dying fire.

Then coming straight at me, and holding me by the lapel, he shouted: "The jews love God – love God, you know, and with passion."

"But, but," I remarked, smiling, "Gods need man to be."

"– or, man needs God –"

"It's not the same. Man invented a superman – thus *sprach* Zarathustra. *Heil Gott!*"

"Yes."

"So, man made God."

"What then the answer, brahmin sir?" He became suddenly polite again.

"The nondual – pure Liberty."

"*La Foutaise,*" he spat, looking down with contempt. "The non cannot exist with *Nous*. That much even I know."

"You must realize, Michel, we invent language."

"I know. Don't I! Remember I am in linguistics. Anyway, give me an example."

"Like God, Dieu, etc, etc."

"Yahweh," he pronounced, intrepid.

"Isvara, in sanskrit."

"Not the same," he declared decisively. "Imagine Abraham speaking sanskrit or Manu speaking hebrew. Impossible!"

"I am sure Manu would happily *sprach* hebrew."

"But Abraham will never *sprach* sanskrit."

158

"Yet Isaac is to be saved. The impossible will be made possible. That's where your God is. You crawled out of the dead, Michel. But I – but I, I want to crawl out into –"

"– into –?"

"I do not know what."

"Into eternity!"

"No, Michel, that still smells time."

"Then Heaven?"

"That smells Hell."

"A saint, then?"

"Never, I have a horror of good men. Or for that matter of good women – and by your leave, may I say, like Suzanne ..."

"But evil, then?"

"Evil, the non-recognition of the nondual."

"You see, there's duality then."

"But tell me, dear, dear Michel –"

"Yes, dear, dear Siv –"

"– in your non-recognition is there cognition – or *nicht!*"

"Yes, there is."

"Then is not the cognition of the non-cognition the dissolution of cognition."

"Into what?"

"Into knowledge, of course. To what else!"

"But then, Siv, my friend, how to get there then? That is the question." He put his hand warmly on my shoulder this time. We were getting somewhere.

"Yes, of course, that's the question of questions."

Then he walked toward the window and stood there gazing intently at the garden, shimmering with the evening breezes. And suddenly turning back, he asked: "What is evil then?"

"A lesser good –," and he seemed so under shock, I added, "*en une facon on de parler.*"

"Well, well. If evil then the lesser good, where, sir, does less come from? Once again the non in the *Nous*, the fish in the water."

"It's all a metaphor – a metaphor, just a way of looking at things."

"For –"

"For, from the Plenum, you see, there's nothing but the good."

"Oh!"

"And not our good at that!"

"Beyond good and evil, then. From there you go straight to the madhouse in Basel. And finally end up on the Berlin bunker, this time with St Eva. Oh, my poor, poor friend," he said in compassionate irony. I shuddered.

"Every jew is an Isaac. The lamb may not appear. So God eats man. The potato is born," I said deliberately, and in utter desperation.

"Oh, *mon pauvre* Ivan."

"*Quel* Ivan?" I said looking straight at him, angry.

"Of course, Ivan Karamazov," and we both laughed together.

"And you, Michel, are you Alyosha then?"

"Every jew an Alyosha – but, but, minus chastity, please!"

"*Le mal c'est le limitrophe du bien.*"

"Oh, you benighted hindus!"

"Not so bad," I retorted, angry again at his superciliousness.

"We had Hitler," he spat finally.

"We had Ravana." He now looked at me, smiling, stretching out his hand. He had understood something then and there. So peace had happened.

And I left him there and went over to have a wash. I was exhausted. It was getting late. And I had to be back home.

# Bhim, the Parrot

Bhim, the parrot, is among the eldest of the kingdom. Lean at the neck (much hair having fallen during these many decades), and with a wisp of white hood, he moves with natural serenity. He seems to have such privileged freedom of movement across the sky of Benares that even the vultures give way to him. His nest is on the neem tree – that old, wind twisted and tall neem – just where the Dasi Lane ends, and the boats come up for people to have a quick look at the Dashashwamedh Ghat and high up; an ever-ordained hole, as it were, exists for Bhim. The story goes (and any boatman worth his salt will tell you) that Bhim and his wife Rupvati have lived here for over fifty years – that is, since the time of the Delhi Durbar until today, and this is till about two or three years ago and the China war – Bhim and Rupvati always moved about with the august marks of princes. They bear a large litter, sometimes of four, sometimes of five, so people thereabouts say, and at least three or four live on. Once in a while a vile vulture used to swoop in or some over-courageous

From *On the Ganga Ghat* (1989). "These stories are so structured that the whole book should be read as one single novel." – Raja Rao. The story title is the editor's.

school boy would go and catch the little one, in the deeps of the night, with a torch, and no amount of cries would drive the vicious intruder down.

But since a few years something has happened. Every time a boy wants to go up, he falls off the tree before he is even up to the level of the first verandah of the Bindu House, to the right. Once, twice, thrice, this happened and people in the Bindu House and the Dasi Lane now know that some Siddha has come to live on the neem tree. Often women, when they wake up on a moonlit night, and go to the verandah to contemplate the broad river and the silver of her murmurings, a sudden wind seems to shift on top of the neem tree and one hears, as it were, the sound of a mantra. Hum hum humumm it seems to say, with a grave and a ruminant voice. The voice is not human nor is it that of a bird. It certainly is divine, luminescent. Anyhow, from then on Bhim and Rupvati have lived undisturbed and bear their little ones with absolute hope. All little chicks do not survive in Benares nor do all mother birds in Benares have a Siddha to protect them. The little ones grow up and multiply and even today the bird catchers of Benares (and there are none more wicked in this wicked world, I tell you), they say to you, "This is the Bhim-Rupvati breed" just by the ring at the neck, and a sort of pearly mist over the eyes. The colour of the ring is yellow but more close to sapphire than to ochre – there's more green in it than gold. The eyes of Bhim are somewhat small but Rupvati has eyes large as an eight-anna bit, and she rolls them with fire. Rupvati must not be easy to live with, yet sometimes when Bhim stands on one leg on some branch of the tree – and this any pilgrim can see, Rupvati sits on another branch and contemplates her lord with devout attention.

Sadhus throw Bengal gram towards the couple but Bhim and Rupvati do not eat all the gram that's offered to them, which explains why near the tree you have such a collection of madhu birds and sparrows, which get a feast as few birds get anywhere in this wide and bent Benares. And the ants have such a feast too that they have a permanent nest in the tree, and you can see them pass along the trunk down and go towards the Bindu House where they always find sugar from pilgrim kitchens. The Jains will tell you that never do you find so many ants on a tree as on this neem, and some knowing people say, of course because it's of Bhim or maybe it's because of the mighty mantra-intoning Siddha. But the women who sell clay-pots round the corner and who have lived on the lane for so long say there's a story of a queen, rich and splendid in her beauty, who came to Benares sometime in the time of our grandfathers and drowned herself under that very tree. She was unhappy, and she thought a Ganges death were better than a palace rot. So she slipped through the palace guards, warded off her pursuers (in those days you rode on horseback a great deal, even women did), and she and her maid-companion both came here when the river was in floods and they jumped one

after the other into the flow. The fisherman found her floating the next day by Rajghat. They called her, just to give her a name, Prabhavathi, and in the lane they still say, "By Prabhavathi's stone," meaning a little rock by the ghats where Prabhavathi is believed to have come and sat contemplating the river, and when she disappeared a rock suddenly appeared, and that is why in the land of Benares where no stones grow, why this rock astonishingly emerges. True or untrue, the potters will also tell you that a few years after Bhim, the parrot, came to live there, so the elders said, another parrot was seen evening after evening sitting on the Prabhavathi stone. And of course Bhim was Prabhavathi, and her companion (who soon joined him) was born as Rupvati. The fact that Rupvati lives with such arrogance is simple: she was not so much devoted to God as to her queen. And as she jumped into the river, she still continued to feel the pride of her palace surroundings, bells and carpets, and elephant trumpetings, and the high presence of her companions of honour. And the Rajas of Vikramapur, who heard of all this, came royally to Benares, built a square platform around the neem, smeared the stone with ochre, and gave the tree a golden pole (with a Kalasa-mount) and a flag with their peacock insignia. Thus Prabhavathi is, as you see, still in her own kingdom.

Now, the little parrots of Bhim can people the Benares high trees with such sacred namings and songs. Bhim parrots have one virtue. They never steal. They never learn cinema songs. You can make them take the name of Ram and this they will repeat with delight. And many a Zamindar's wife has carried a Bhim parrot from Benares – and in fine-worked Muradabadi bell-metal cages – to Calcutta or Agra and some have carried them even to Rajasthan. The truth about these parrots is also that they die quickly if they go to the wrong house – a black-marketeer or an unprofessional prostitute, a bribe-loving police officer or a British Official's dancing and drinking wife. One British lady even took a Bhim parrot to England and he came again and again in her dream and said, "Send me back home, send me back home," and some Indian coming back is said to have brought back the parrot, and let him fly off to the Dasi Lane Ghat. Nobody saw this but it is rumoured that the vultures fell on him immediately – such the smell of the evil-touched among birds – anyway he died in Benares, did the London-returned parrot, and this makes it better for rebirth. Who knows, he may have been among the later litters of Bhim and Rupvati.

When Bhim stands on his one leg, the other strictly drawn to his belly-downs, all the world can see that the sparrow and the madhu bird, and even a vulture or two will come and sit on the other branches, and if by chance you hear a sharp voice or cry, it's because some unwanted rascal has tried to sneak in near this assembly, and the vultures will not have him do so.

The vulture Krodha is a tame old thing, too tame and old except to catch a fish here and there, or peck at the remains of a carcass. Krodha was seen by man at least since the last twenty years – and so people say, since a year or two after Mahatma Gandhi was assassinated. He came, did Krodha, to the Dasi Ghat, an unknown as it were, for he appeared, truth to speak, from nowhere. The Dasi Ghat has few corpses to offer you, while the Muslim weavers' quarters on the other side are so full of hide and flesh and fish. Why then here among pilgrims and potters and grave shaven widows? Some vultures do carry off babies, that is true, and Dasi Ghat was no better than any. And of course in the Bindu House and Rati Mansion and the Bishembhar Palace (of the Rajas of Bhume) you have so many puling little things. You flop down, catch, and rise and rush off to the Ramnagar bank of the river. But Krodha is a hard task master on himself. He would rather carry a lamb or a cock than a human baby. He felt this way since he saw a baby carried off and it cried so much and beat its hands so fiercely, that five of them had to come and finish off the baby. And human flesh anyway does not taste as good, as say, goose flesh.

Now Krodha has many problems. He has an itch in the neck and a very acute pain on the bend of the back. He took mustard shoots from the fields to cure himself, and even fasted for three or four days, but nothing lessened his pain. However, coming here one day by accident – he was chasing a fish, and he was swooping down, when he saw Bhim. He brought back the fish and ate him on the neem tree. The itch in the neck somehow stopped for a moment. He came again and again, and the pain only stopped when Bhim was standing on his one solitary leg. Usually when Krodha came, the other birds, sparrows and madhu birds, rushed away in fear. But little by little they too began to have assurance of themselves. The fact is Krodha is too crude to know of the Siddha. Everybody cannot know the Siddha, and even among the potters only a few can hear that mantra-like humming of the nights, Hum ... Hum ... Hum. You think sound can be heard because you've ears. I tell you, you can only hear what your ears hear, there are so many many sounds in Benares that your ears cannot even smell of, leave alone see. A sound is like this. It can be thick, or thin, low, minor, or even minion. At each level you have a special ear to hear, that is, if you can hear. If you eat too much onion or carcass or butcher's scrap or steal the manes' offerings from crows or the grain-gifts from cows or peck into gutters like some low birds do, you are out of your circle.

In fact there are two definite circuits in Benares – the outer and the inner. The inner is so clear. It passes from the Dufferin bridge past the main post-office, and skirting the Hindu High School, runs straight down to the kutcheries by the Brahma Bazaar Road, and from then on, meandering, you could reach the University campus city – those to the right belong to one caste, to the left the other. To the left you have the weavers, the untouchables, the hide-sellers, the prostitute houses (of the poor and the accidental), and to the right you have the rajas, the concubines, the pilgrims, and the temples – and the river. The vultures of the right do not eat with the vultures of the left – there are strict rules not only about eating but about mating. You have on the right the vultures born life after life feeding on the fishes, the thrown-off meats of pilgrims, and even a good carcass or two. It depends on whose it is. But on the left you must eat all sorts of things, and even share a buffalo with crows or a host of curs. The vulture's cry to the left is like a policeman's whistle, sharp and one-noted, but the vultures of the right have long drawn notes, as if they were gentlemen accustomed to wait on Zamindars. And the two provinces are so clearly drawn that the two types of vultures – the vultures of the left and the vultures of the right – never invade each other's domains. That's the law. And the vultures, you may know, are great obeyers of the law.

This is not always so true of the sparrows. These tiny commonplace populace of Benares are so mixed up in their mediocrities that they eat anywhere, and they mate anywhere, and in fact they peck at any grain, funeral grain, or pilgrim-leavings. They however marry only from the sparrows of the ghat sides, exception being made to those of Ramnagar, on the other bank. For reasons of bird-laws the Ramnagar side is counted as holy. The sparrows too follow the pilgrims sometimes when they make their sixty-league circumambulation of Benares. They go in groups and return by evening to their nests on the Dasi Ghat or the Hanuman Ghat side. The peculiarity however of the Benares sparrows is this: they are fearless. Commonplace they may be but proud they are. The story goes that once when Sri Rama was crossing the Ganges a sparrow stood on a side, and swore allegiance of all the sparrows to the Lord.

"How so?" asked Sri Rama, the fount of compassion. "How so, Bhagirathi?" for that was the name of the sparrow. "Because," said the sparrow, "once one of our race was born in Janaka's kingdom. Great was the peace and luxury in the land of Devi Sita's father. The sages were honoured and you only heard the murmur of mantras come out from every housetop. And when Janaki the holy one went to the river to bathe, and her housemaids were all busy arranging her clothes on the bank, Sita Devi was so enchanted with the waters she went swimming. Now on the other side of the river was a Rakshasha spirit whose deepest desire was to have cast an eye on Sita Devi bathing for once, and thus Sita would not be Sri Rama's spouse, and there would therefore be no Ramayana. When this monster rose on his bloody bed all the sparrows were frightened, and we on this side did perform an act simple. We flew in wide formations swinging ourselves like a large swap of song which comes back on itself, and the longer Sita Devi stayed in the waters the greater the number of sparrows that joined us on this sky-curtaining flight. So Sita Devi when she saw this called me, Bhagirathi, and said: Bird, what festival of yours is this? O none, Princess, but that ogre there has decided there would be no Ramayana, that is, if he could just sight you, as you take your bath, so Sri Rama would not wed you. We know the Lord is born to liberate man from evil. We have woven a net of illusion for the ogre not to see you. Lady, we know you're the daughter of the earth and the Mother of mankind. Devi, we are but humble protectors of the Queen-born-of-the-furrow," said I. "So," continued Bhagirathi coming forward, "Lord, she gave us this sign on our forehead. You can see it's the kumkum from her brows, our iris, the iris of her honey-vermilion hue."

The Lord was so touched. He laid his two thumbs on the two sides of the sparrows of Benares that whatever happens they would not be eaten by vultures or be killed by the hawk. These Rama-marks on the sparrows of the right have come generation after generation, and just as no crocodile will touch you when you bathe in Benares, no vulture will touch the Rama-sparrows. They seem, as it were, to have eyes on their wings. For at the moment when Rama laid his fingerprints on them Sri Rama had not broken the arc of Shiva nor he seen Sita Devi yet. But when he returned on his way to Ayodhya and with his new-wed queen, the holy couple stopped and gave a few nuptial rice-grains to these sparrows so that they now eat only the virtuous grains of pilgrims. Thus after many lives they're born again as men, and sometimes even as Brahmins. And why not I ask of you, a sparrow be born a Brahmin? The wise Bhim the parrot says: "Are you still there, O race of Bhagirathi? The Brahmin is dead with his lucre as the English with their greed. In Benares we know no caste but virtue." "Oh, ho," says the vulture of the right, "and what about us then? You don't want us to be like those butchers on the other side eating of buffalo flesh?" Bhim turns to Rupvati and says, "Talk to them, I cannot. I must go on with my meditations."

The bharadwaj bird now comes in poking her nose in every one's affairs, that eternal thief. The vultures, knowing the bharadwaj has not only a long tail but a long tongue, frighten her and say, "Don't you meddle in our affairs." "What," says the bharadwaj, "I am only a praying bird forever willing to eat off the leavings of pilgrims. What are you angry about?" The vultures do not argue, they hiss. It's then Rupvati says, "When my lord is in meditation we need no intruders. Will you just keep quiet?" Which explains why when the bells are ringing for evening worship, and, of a sudden the night falls, there's a long silence as if the temple water-tank were shaken by the breezes, and between the shake and the splash there's the space of no-sound. The wavelets by the Ganges play about as if in adoration of evening, and when the bells ring high, and the drums beat and the leaping pilgrims of the boat wash their hands and feet and beat their cheeks seeking forgiveness, and they fold their hands in worship, on the neem tree there, there's a wide-awake silence. By the red-stone of Prabhavathi Devi a lamp has been lit. On all the verandahs the lamps leap from house to house, and Benares begins its evening of worship. The birds do not move any more. There are no bats on the neem tree. Sometimes, however, so old is Bhim that in the Bindu House you can hear his snore. Did you know parrots snored like men? They do.

And just a few days ago, as anybody will tell you in Benares, Bhim took his usual evening bath in the Ganga and was never seen again. And since that was the evening of the death of Swami Siddheshwarji, the great blind saint, the story is that one saw the bird, yes, Bhim, as he was known to every sadhu, fall into the pyre and die. This is perhaps just a rumour. It is believed Bhim came every day to be fed by Siddheshwarji, and when he knew he was going to leave his body, he told the bird: I am going away, you know, the day after tomorrow. This explains why Bhim never ate for two days, never left his perch. And then Bhim disappeared from the world.

Now Rupvati sits in her austerities biding her time.

# Ranchoddoss and his Daughter, Sudha

R anchoddoss Sunderdoss was a jeweller in Bombay. You can still see on Girgaum Road the yellow painted shop-sign, discoloured, hung high, the shafts and wheels of a dilapidated brougham lying all about under the young pipal tree in the front yard, and a little shrine, jut out of the garden walls, for the passers-by to worship at the idol of Panduranga Vithala that Rukmabai a devotee had seen arise before her just there, and in almost transparent marble, with flute, chest-jewel and white cow – and this must have occurred at least two or three hundred years ago. Even now on every fullmoon night women come to worship the deity, for it's he that gave a baby boy to Rukmabai, so legends say, to this simple woman who could not go to Pandharpur on pilgrimage (her husband was too unbelieving and pice-miserly to let her go) – thus the little children's clothes that hang all about the door – for God alone gives, who else would give, tell me? And many a lady in Bombay even now has a child only because of this Pandurang of the Girgaum Road.

Thus it was, the Sunderdoss family finally decided, and during the

From *On the Ganga Ghat* (1989). The story title is the editor's.

good Queen Victoria days, to build a small temple around the idol of Pandurang and organized regular kirtans in Ashad – to be precise, on the rounded fullmoon day of the month – to commemorate the vision the Lord gave to Rukmabai, this humble devotee. On that day the Sunderdoss family, for generations, have worn heirloom gold (sometimes even new-fashion jewellery), that the God not forget the merchants that do "give and take" business behind his temple. And so good is our Pandurang, he never forgets his neighbourly worshippers, nor does he forget the owner of Krishnabai, the cow which is fed by the passer-by with a handful of green grass and for an anna. Since the marble cow would not eat the grass this cow will in the name of the Lord, many an office-goer-husband returning from his toils would beat his cheeks before the deity, and offer the cow her anna worth of graze. And at festival times of course, you had more worshippers, and the grasscutters had a gay time. They too prayed for a son, and some had more than a son given by Pandurang Vithala. Of what worth a woman's womb that does not bear a toddling heir? And some middle-class women in gratitude even bought two head-gears for the child, and hung one at the sanctuary, while the other was taken home for the coming baby. And every baby who wore this grew to be intelligent and wise, and often won the first prize at the Anglo-Marathi High School, off the Gowalia Tank. Sometimes, a kind father coming back from his office remembers his baby's first birthday would be the next Friday or Tuesday, and he just enters the Sunderdoss shop (under the new signboard, encrusted with silver and in Marathi, Gujarati and English characters, right over the door: Sunderdoss & Sons, High Class Jewellers. Shop Founded in 1799) to buy something for this coming celebration. And one of Sunderdoss' brothers, Bhagavandoss, the Elder, Ramadoss the Younger, or Ranchoddoss the In-Between (all clad in muslin dhotis, their little caps still in velvet and filigree), would take you in, and seating you on the pillowed seats, show you every type of silver waistband – those with a serpent's hood, those with the lionman's head, or those with just in-turning screws. You could now buy the little silver tumblers or milk-feeders for the baby, also in silver, and in addition, a ruby nose-ring for your wife if you were so tempted. And around the first of the month the Sunderdosses took in one of their cousins, Madandoss, to help them – such the crowd.

Ranchoddoss was not really very different from any other member of
the family. He was hard-working, devoutly honest (a lie on earth costs a
kingdom in Vaikuntha – heaven, his mother used to say) and was a genteel
husband. He had two elder sons, one nineteen and the other fourteen,
and a daughter called Sudha. The boys were good at school, and so was
the girl, though she went to Saint Mary's Convent School,
off Peddar Road. The bus took her to school and brought her safely back.
Sudha was always the pet of Ramaben, her mother, and, "Sudha do this"
and "Sudha do that" ran like a thread amidst the noises of the household,
for all the brothers lived together, and their children as well, but Sudha
was the most loved of all. She was also the youngest. They
say on the day she was born suddenly a peacock, wings outstretched and
keening, strutted past the courtyard (the mother had gone to Kathiawar,
to her own mother, for the childbirth) and everybody said: "Well, this girl,
she will bring in holy riches." However no gold-lotuses rose in the backyard
fountain on Girgaum Road, but money came in more and more – the
Maharaja of Bhavnagar sent his own Dewan for the nephew's marriage,
and since the purchases went over a lakh of rupees (and those were the
true old days when the rupee was still worth its weight in solid silver) and
the honesty of Ranchoddoss impressed the Dewan so greatly, the Rajas of
Gwalior and Indore came along, and even that American wife of the old
Indore Maharaja. Sudha brought prosperity no doubt, but Sudha who
was so full of song and fun, suddenly grew serious, as the women's
things on her chest arose, and she would hide her face behind pillars,
even when her uncles and cousins passed by, or on her bed lie covered
up with a light white sheet, all day. She hated talk, and she began to go
less and less to school – but who cares? – a girl is meant for marriage as
a wheel is destined for the cart. You don't use a wheel for a ladder or for
hanging your clothes on, do you? The wheel is meant for a chariot, a
bullock cart, or even for a brougham, like those wheels rotting at the
housedoor as there is no spring or axle to wheel the box. And all that
European talk of women going to become politicians or professors is so
much like making the river run backwards back. Of course you can
make the river run backwards through canals, etc. But when the floods

come, the dam and the sluices and the canals are washed away as so many cold weather leaves – so too the woman.

Yes, Sudha was very much a girl – a woman, in fact, for she was fourteen years of age, and she hated marriage. For her marriage (and all the girls at St Mary's Convent School, only talked of boys and marriages) was something stupid, no, more than stupid – sinful. "Why touch a man?" was her problem. Men seemed to her (all except her father, her uncles, her brothers) either awkward or evil. One never understood from where she got this idea – some said later it's the way the Christian girls talked of boys, or it's after she started going to films, and it's the European films that did it. Sudha, however, sat for hours on end in the family sanctuary, repeating the Name of the Lord. "Rama, Sri Rama," she said and went on naming His Name a thousand times, and little by little three thousand times, a day. She even started on fasts and days of silence, and sometimes took a vow to name the Name-of-Rama a lakh of times in ten days. She grew pale but beautiful. The family did not worry – she was after all only fifteen.

But one night, however, a few years later she had a real vision. In three days, it revealed, a Sadhu would come to initiate her, and she would then become a true devotee of the Lord. Indeed, as foretold (and she had told no member of her family of this vision, except it be to her father, whom she revered), a handsome looking Sadhu, hardly thirty five years of age, came into the house. He was a man from the South, and was, so he explained, on his way to Badrinath and Kedarnath in the Himalayas, and then finally he would come down and go, he would, to the holy city of Benares. "Passing by this street, Mother," he said to Ramaben, "I could *see* some sincere soul was living here. Is there anyone living in this house who's deeply devoted to the Lord?" Sudha, who was inside, knew this was the saint whose arrival she was anticipating, and throwing away her bedsheet, and coming out, fell prostrate at his sacred feet. "Too long have I waited for you," said the Sadhu. "Where have you been?" – "You, Lord, know more than I do," she whispered back in reply. The Mother could not understand. But Sudha suddenly remembered, so she explained later, all of her past life. A large house somewhere in Kathiawar, or was it elsewhere? They spoke a strange tongue. She was forty or forty five years of age and had raised four or five children. And they were gay and prosperous, horses in the stables and elephants in the yard – some men went to the wars, others played cards or roamed with women, but her husband suddenly died and she then knew she loved him more than she

did God Himself. Her husband was, though a prince and real Rajput, the worshipper of a great Guru. For every sneeze and scratch he would run to the ashram of his Guru which was on the marble cliffs of our beautiful Narbada. She did not care for God. But once her husband had departed, her one thought was he, and her union with him. How noble it was in the old virtuous days: you could be burnt with your spouse, your Lord. It's a pity the British came and stopped it all. She went back to the same ashram on the Narbada. But the Guru had, by now, given up his body. His disciple who had succeeded him gave her a secret mantra. She repeated the mantra again and again, and vowed she would find God now that she had no husband. She died however without seeing God and not even having an intimation of His Holy Presence. She died beautifully though (she could now see her own funeral procession) – people throwing flowers on her bright, elderly, saintly figure.

And she was then born to Ranchoddoss, and when the time came, the past life returned too, if not tell me why this hatred of marriage? Her Lord of one life was the Lord of all lives. And there he was. He knew. She *saw*. And he stayed on in the house, and in a way the whole house became a roundabout for him – the elders said even the business was suffering because of this Sadhu. After three months, on an auspicious day Sadhu Sunderanandaji (for that was his name) initiated her with the full consent of Ranchoddoss and Ramaben, to sanyas. She put on the white sari, and a few days later with her Sadhu, she departed for the Himalayas. Her family did not weep – they were too grave to weep (except the mother, who said, "Lucky I am to have borne you, my daughter, but Lord give me peace of mind. I cannot live one day without my daughter"). However the household moved on as before except that Ranchoddoss began to look more and more like his daughter, talk like his daughter, and he also began to fast and festivate for this and that. The business nevertheless prospered. His two sons Govinddoss and Vithaldoss were honest, devout and money-minded. Now and again when the business was not too bright, he would open the Vishnu Purana or the Bhagavatham, and read chapter after chapter of one of these sacred texts.

One day it would be about the Krishna and the gopis, from the Bhagavatham, or of the Goddess Laxmi, rising out of the milky ocean, on a stalk of blue lotus, and this from the Vishnu Purana. But the story he loved most of all was of that king, who having lost interest in his splendorous world, suddenly comes upon a deer with its young in the forest, and he brought the little one home, petted her and fed her, but when he died he was, of course born a deer, for remember, you are reborn as your last thought be. And again, as a deer he was so wise and sparse of need, for he well remembered his past life, as king, but was born again as a man, and a Brahmin this time, a Brahmin fat and big, uncouth and repulsive, saliva dripping down his cheeks, and destiny made him, though a Brahmin by birth, a palanquin bearer of King Suvera. But so indifferent was he to everything, and bore the palanquin so unequally paced the other palanquin bearers shouted at him again and again, when finally the king himself jumps out of his palanquin, and asks in royal ire, "Who are you? And why do you do this to me?" To which the palanquin bearer Brahmin replied: "Look, sire, I am fat and strong, uncouth, saliva running down my face. Look, look at me but tell me, King, am I my face, my limbs, my nose that drips this snot, am I, I? Tell me truly, who am I?" Then he told the king of his past lives, which he remembered so well, and of the king who loved the little deer so, and of the deer he was born as, and again of the Brahmin he is now. "Who indeed am I?" And boldly asked of King Suvera: "And how shall I denominate you, sire? Are you your body? Who are you, king? And, what, pray is a king? Tell me, please, what is an object? Is this a palanquin? Of what wood however is it made? Do you know its name, and whence it came, and where sawed out, fixed, and made into a palanquin?" And the Brahmin finally said, "just as the universally distributed air, going through the holes of a flute, makes for the variegated melodies, with sariga, sariga notes and all that, yet all this is but one piece of bamboo. There is no I, there is no you." And so saying, suddenly saw within himself

177

then and there as if jumping out of his person, – thus, he was forever freed from birth and rebirth. And so too did the king. Ranchoddoss told this story again and again to himself. He related this story to his wife Ramaben. "The truth is just that, Rama." But she could find no satisfaction in such legendary talks. After all she was a mother. And how can a man, any man understand that?

Some years went this way. However Ramaben could never console herself for the loss of Sudha. When sorrow grows it can grow big as a fruit in the belly, and even pushes out thorns as a cactus does. She suffered as no one had seen people suffer. The doctors gave her radium treatment, but she died one morning, however, very peacefully. She would at least have a better life next time, decided Ranchoddoss, wiping his tears when he came back, with his brothers and sons, from the cremation grounds. One has only to get there, where there is neither birth nor evil death. Is that not so, Sudha?

And now that the two boys – Govinddoss and Vithaldoss – were married, and the elder brother and younger, Bhagavandoss and Ramadoss were both alive and prosperous, Ranchoddoss left home to seek his daughter. And he found her without difficulty in Benares. You can ask any Brahmin in Benares, where anyone else is, and somehow they will tell you, or take you to another who will tell you, all you want to know, where your daughter is, or your uncle. And he will even tell you, not only of all your ancestors, father, grandfather, and great-grandfather, their names all written down in their family documents, but also of your jewellery shop on Girgaum Road, and of Panduranga Vithala, who appeared to Rukmabai, because she could not go to Pandharpur, in addition to the flute, white cow and peacock crown. All, all we know. Such indeed be the Brahmins of Benares. For, remember, what you find not bad and good in Benares, you know you will see no such truths any elsewhere on earth. Here, in this most sacred city, I can tell you, whoever wants to hear that in final wisdom, there is neither virtue nor vice, for both burn like those pyres on the ghats, equally – to ash. Don't you understand this? Even the curs here know it.

So, led by his Gujarati Brahmin guide, Ranchoddoss found Sudha in a little brick and mortar hall off Hanuman Ghat, where she read the Vasistha

Ramayana to widows and ascetics and to a few retired judges and ex-Congress ministers, and in fact to anyone who wanted to hear this great advaitic text. And as it should happen, Sudha, on that afternoon when Ranchoddoss beheld his daughter, – she was reading the story of Utpala the King. She just smiled, lifting her head, when she saw him entering the hall, right at the door, yet went on steadily reading the text. You remember the story, don't you, of how Utpala was a great king, a good and moral king, following all the eight rules of reigning a kingdom, that is – to be generous to Brahmins, to be just, be wholly devoted to his subjects, slept little, kept all the castes under the holy laws, strict with women, kindly to children, and a great worshipper of the sages. And once when he was asleep, in his Hall of Slumber, he had this strange, strange dream. He had gone off on a hunt and had wandered far, leaving all his retinue behind, and how it happened, he could not remember, but that he was lost in the depths of a forest. He came across a hut where an untouchable was curing the carcass of a bull, outside in the courtyard. When surprised to see himself there, he was on the edge of asking the untouchable, in which province or hamlet he found himself now, when he espied a maiden fair. On course he immediately fell in love with her, and married her, and in good time she bore him a son. The years passed, years on years passed, and one day, the Prime Minister appeared, and asking said: Your Highness, we have searched for you all these times. We have searched this whole vast forest. But grace be to Shiva, we have at last discovered you, and when he was, the king was, returning back to his kingdom, he woke up and found himself on his bed in the palace. It was a dream after all. But it was deeply real. He was fully awake in his dream, just as he now was. Who was he, the king in the dream? And the untouchable and the beautiful wife and the son? Who is to decide, which is real, asked Sudha lifting up her head, smiling: Who indeed? The story implies only this: Those years after all were but a few hours of one night. Life is just that. Behind both is the absolute reality, Brahman. It takes but the time a thorn takes to pierce through a lotus leaf to know the truth, – so Vasistha, the guru, declares it to Sri Rama, understand! It is beyond Kala, time, and Desa, space. That Reality, Sri Rama, is you, is I, said Vasistha, the great sage. And of course Sri Rama understood and immediately too for he was, Sri Rama was, is the Ultimate Reality itself. The waking state and the dream state are both states equally wakeful. What is beyond that, continued Sudha, is no state: It is the I, the I, she repeated. Ranchoddoss thinking of the king and the deer, and the Brahmin and the king again, yes, that is it, she is right, he said to himself. Sudha seemed indeed to Ranchoddoss, learned and very, very wise.

And as they walked through the busy lanes of Benares, finding a room for her father, she told her own story. Her Sadhu had passed away a few weeks earlier, she almost whispered with swelling tears in her eyes, and he had been asked by his own Guru in Badrinath, that she, Sudha, should carry on the reading of Vasistha Ramayana. She was happy, she said, of her early morning baths at the Ganga, and her visit to the Shiva temple, off Harischandra Ghat, where she sat, under the ancient pipal tree behind the shrine, first saying her beads and then in meditation for four hours in rapt solitude. And then she went home to the Dashashwamedh Ghat, where in a three storeyed house by the river, she had a large room. At her door, she explained, her followers always left vegetables, rice and firewood. She would cook her food, eat and come after a brief siesta, to the hall of the holy-readings. An oleograph picture of Shiva as Pashupathi, hung on the wall, in the middle (as Ranchoddoss had just seen) with the sacred-seat, garlands and oil-lamps and all. Under the picture of Shiva, she would spread out her volume of Yoga Vasistha, and after a brief bhajan, she would begin her readings, fixed for the day, adding her own humble commentaries on the text. She was no scholar, she explained, but she understood, because of the Grace of her Guru, the nature of what people say is the most difficult of all things in philosophy – Sankara's theory of Mayavada. "Father," she said, looking at the flowing Ganga before her, "Father, I think I have just a chink to the door of Knowledge – to Jnana." And then she went up to her room, laid her book and beads on the sacred table, before her Guru's picture, and offering her deep salutations to him, came down, and gently said: "Father I have not heard of the news from home. Is everybody well? I forget all about them here. But what is there to remember, anyway, and what to forget?" She looked at her father, and in the falling evening, she saw a tear on her father's face. A street lamp revealed it. And she understood.

Her father took a room next to hers, it was at Vishal Nivas, on the sacred Ganga of course, and by the Dashashwamedh Ghat, and he too began his meditations. She gave him just a few hints, because she was no Guru, and then one day a few months later, he and the daughter went up to Badrinath, to see her Guru (that is Sadhu Sunderanandji's Sat-Guru) and the Guru after many words of praise for the daughter, gave initiation toRanchoddoss. He asked Sudha's father to read Sri Sankara's Upadesha Sahasriyam, and come back to him again, and in a year. Life flows as you see, like the Ganga herself, simple and abundant, carrying princes and dancing girls, fishes and carcasses, the pyres burning on her side, reminding you that the Truth is but one indivisible flow. What is dream and which reality, then?

So that Ranchoddoss now lives in Benares, and I assure you, you cannot miss him: always as neatly dressed as in his shop, with his muslin shirt, and his dhoti falling in precise folds, sandal paste on his brow, courteous to passers-by (and Benares is not known for courtesy, as any grandmother will tell you, especially by the ghat sides). And each dawn he will wake, and saying his beads he will go down the ghat to the River. There, like Sudha, he bathes and sits on the steps for meditation, and returns to his room to cook. Once in a while the postman will have thrown in a letter from his family, or some Maharaja he'd known in Bombay will seek him out, asking him silly questions of philosophy. What does Ranchoddoss know? He knows nothing. Only Sudha knows. But Sudha will not help a Maharaja become more virile (she knows of no such miraculous mantras or triturations) nor will she bless them that they get back their kingdom – they made such an ugly performance of it all when they had their ancient thrones, some indeed which had come down from the time of Sri Rama. Once in a while a Bombay professor or Kathiawari aristocrat will come and ask  Sudha real and earnest questions. She will answer them all, even about the serpent and the rope, or the dream and waking states. And some even in that obscure nature of the deep sleep state. Sudha is happy. Ranchoddoss as you see is proud, and happy.

Raja Rao

You can still see him sit on the bank of the Ganges, as the evening begins to fall, and, as the temple lamps begin to leap from tower after tower, and the gongs begin to extone, clapping his hands gently, he will sing Sankara's,

> *mano nivrittih paramopa shantihi*
> *sa tirtha varya manikarnika cha*
> *jnana pravaha vimaladi ganga*
> *sa kashikaham nijabodharupaha.*

The cessation of all mental activities is the supreme peace – that is the holiest of all holy places of pilgrimage, the Manikarnika (in me); the ever-flowing stream of knowledge is the pure primeval Ganges (in me); (thus) I am the Kashika, of the form of pure Consciousness of Self.

# On Understanding

There are, it seems to me, only two possible perspectives on human understanding: the horizontal and (or) the vertical. They could also be named the anthropomorphic and the abhuman. The vertical movement is the sheer upward thrust toward the unnameable, the unutterable, the very source of wholeness. The horizontal is the human condition expressing itself, in terms of, concern for man as one's neighbour – biological and social, the predicament of one who knows how to say, I and you.

The vertical rises slowly, desperately, to move from the I to the non-I, as nondual Vedanta would say – the move towards the impersonal, the universal (though there is no universe there, so to say) reaching out to ultimate *being* – when there is just being there are no two entities, no I, and, you. The I then is not even all, for there is none other to say I to. It is the nobility of Nirvana, of zero, of light.

The horizontal again, on its long, arduous and confused pathways will reach the same ultimacy by divesting the I of its many vestments through

From *The Meaning of India* (1997), this essay was originally written for a discussion group of scientists and humanists at the University of Texas at Austin, USA.

concern for the other, by compassion for the other, and will yet leap into Sakka's flame, as gift, as sacrifice, like the Bodhisattva hare did, and reach the heart of "coolness" in the heaped up fire.

The vertical then is the inherent reality *in* the horizontal: the I and you, the I and I, so no I but "I," and never I again. You can and must go beyond yourself, but you cannot go beyond the self, the "I."

## II

Putting it in other terms (as my friend Denis de Rougemont might say) in the symbolism of the Cross, the vertical is the impersonal personal, the horizontal the neighbour, the human universe. Hence it is the vertical, that is the longer, de Rougemont would say, the *person* (from *persona*) being the ultimate entity. Human experience then is the point of this intersection – man, at every moment, is expressing the crucifixion: the instance of love: the altar of the cathedral, the cathedral itself according to tradition, being shaped in the form of the natural person. Excruciation then is the nature of the holy human condition, the Christian way.

> *No, Raja, I must start from where I am*
> *I am those monsters which visit my dreams,*
> *And reveal to me my hidden essence.*
> *No help, Raja, my part is agony,*
> *struggle, abjection, self-love and self-hate,*
> *prayer for the Kingdom*
> *and reading Pascal.*

## III

Lao Tse said: To go very far you stay where you are. The point of intersection of the here and there – is the no-where, the no-when, the Truth.

In the horizontal, the geometrical Vedic hearth is shaped as a woman, that is, the world, from which Agni, the fire god, the masculine principle, goes vertically upward, shining. He illumines everything, vertically burning it all up: Holy Ash, is Truth.

Raja Rao

All I have been trying to say is: One must rise from epistemology to
ontology – from Aristotle to Plato, as the wise Heisenberg has said. And,
may I add, move on from Plato to Parmenides – and beyond to Nirvana,
to Truth.

> *As It is the Self of everything, not different from*
> *anything, and not an object like a thing separate*
> *from It, the Self cannot be*
> *accepted or rejected.*

Words of Acceptance

I am a man of silence. And words emerge from that silence with light, of light, and light is sacred. One wonders that there is the word at all – Sabda – and one asks oneself, where did it come from? How does it arise? I have asked this question for many, many years. I've asked it of linguists, I've asked it of poets, I've asked it of scholars. The word seems to come first as an impulsion from the nowhere, and then as a prehension, and it becomes less and less esoteric – till it begins to be concrete. And the concrete becoming ever more earthy, and the earthy communicated, as the common word, alas, seems to possess least of that original light.

The writer or the poet is he who seeks back the common word to its origin of silence, that the manifested word become light. There was a great poet of the West, the Austrian poet, Rainer Maria Rilke. He said objects come to you to be named. One of the ideas that has involved me deeply these many years is: where does the word dissolve and become meaning? Meaning itself, of course, is beyond the sound of the word, which comes to

This was Raja Rao's acceptance speech when the Neustadt Prize was presented to him on June 4, 1988. This essay was subsequently published in *The Meaning of India* (1997).

one only as an image in the brain, but *that* which sees the image in the brain (says our great sage of the eighth century, Sri Sankara) nobody has ever seen. Thus the word coming of light is seen eventually by light. That is, every word-image is seen by light, and that is its meaning. Therefore the effort of the writer, if he's sincere, is to forget himself in the process and go back to the light from which words come. Go back where? That is, those who read or those who hear must reach back to their own light. And that light, I think is the hearth of prayer.

My ancestors and, yes, the ancestors of some of you, or of most of you, who speak the English tongue, came from the same part of the world, thousands of years ago. Was it from the Caucasus or the North Pole, one is not certain yet. They spoke a language close to my own language, and close to your language. There is in America a remarkable dictionary called the *Heritage Dictionary*. It gives you almost a hundred pages (at the very end) of the Indo-European roots of many of our words. Most of you are of European origin. At least your thinking has been conditioned by European thought. There's thus a common way of thinking, an Indo-European way of thinking, between us, so that we are not so far from each other as we often think we are. And beyond the Indo-European way of thinking, in Asia, Africa, Polynesia, is *that* same human light, by which all words become meaning. Finally, there's only one meaning, not for every word, but for all words *where* the word, any word, from any language, dissolves into knowledge. It's only there at the dissolution of the sound of the word, or of the image of the word, that you say, you understand. And *here* there's neither you nor I. That is what I have been trying to achieve. That I become no one, that no one shine but It.

Many good things have been said by distinguished speakers – about me – this evening. But I want to say to you in utter honesty: I would like to be completely nameless, and just be that reality which is beyond all of us who hear me – that reality which evokes in me you, and I in each one listening to me this evening, that there be no one there but light. And it is of that reality the sages have spoken. The sage is

Raja Rao

One, someone beyond the saint. He is no one. He's the real seer. In fact, we are all sages, but we don't recognize it. That is what the Indian tradition says. In the act of seeing – that is, of the seer, the seen, and the seeing – in seeing alone is there pure light. Where does this come from, nobody can name.

I once asked Dr Oppenheimer, the scientist, who told me his hands were soiled by the atom bomb. Have you ever seen an object? And he made answer: Never. If a scientist like Dr Oppenheimer said he has never seen an object – that is of seeing the unseeable, as the seen – it is that level of knowledge I would like desperately to reach, from where I could truly write. It is to that root of writing I pay homage. The Neustadt Prize is thus not given to me, but to That which is far beyond me, but in me – because I alone know I am incapable of writing what people say I have written.

# The Silence of
# Mahatma Gandhi

I n the mid-middle of India, the earth is hot, hot. During even the early summer, the foot touches the land as if one walks on pulsing human limbs. And the vast silence that covers the midday air seems an awake sleep. Only the eagles fly – high, and round and around. And there are many, many crows, of course. There could be no India without crows. In Sevagram now every object lies quiet – the dusty pathways, the bucket and pulley over the well, the bare neem tree by the kitchen – the latrine constructs far out, and composting. Nobody is asleep. Yet nobody man or woman is really awake. It's the time when Gandhiji spins his charkha.

I have come to see him in his lone mud hut. My sister was getting married soon. I had to go and tell Gandhiji, I must leave the next day for this wedding. The wedding was to be in Hyderabad. He knew all about it.

At every footstep my breath was deep and slow – with awe. How to face him? The midday quiet was awesome too. The earth around Gandhiji belongs to India. He is India. How can one walk into this India. One does not walk to India in India. One cannot. One circumambulates a sanctuary.

First published in *The Meaning of India* (1997).

One cannot here. But I must enter his hut, when there is nobody anywhere. The sun seems to chant, to hum. I have no beads between my fingers. Yet I feel my fingers moving.

I enter the hut. Gandhiji is seated, on the floor, his eyes shut, his big ears awake, his one hand turning the wheel, his left hand holding the cotton bole. He did something doing nothing. I stood in front of him, hands folded. He opens his eyes. He beckons me to sit down. I sit down.

Then there is a wide space in silence.

"Gandhiji, I am going to my sister's marriage."

"Yes. I remember." His lips trembled and lisped, as he spoke. He seemed too civilized for man. Yet he was such a manly man.

He was silent again. Then he caught himself up.

"Give her my blessings," says Gandhiji, closes his eyes, and begins to spin, once more.

I sit there watching him. He is not a man. He is no god. He seemed the breathful earth, spinning round and around empty space, spinning away. One can almost feel the earth underneath. It spins. It spins around, you know.

I sit thus watching him.

I must not stay too long. How can one stay with such resilient silence. Silence spinning silence seems the round of love. How then disturb a sanctuary.

Yet every devotee knows, when you have burnt the camphor before the deity, you must ring the bell above – once, twice, thrice – and take leave of your God or Goddess, the sanctified coconut and flowers in hand and leave, carrying your sacredness back home.

I sit for five minutes, ten minutes, twelve, seventeen, twenty minutes. It is time for me to go. How make any movement? How disturb the spinning of spinning. The eyes are closed. Gandhiji goes on doing the *something* doing nothing, nothing. An actionless act, as it were. It moves by itself. Who is there? *No one.*

Ultimately I must take courage in my heart. One must not tarry. It is inauspicious to steal time that is not yours. You cannot move. Yet, must you rise and go: fold your hands in namaskar. And go.

You finally give courage to your limbs, and move your left big toe

193

first. Instantly the spinning stops. Nothing happens. However nothing ever happens. "Happening happens to happening," as the texts say. The earth seems to stand still. Does it? No. You feel the earth underneath you, move. When everything spins, nothing truly spins. You go round and around – and you are free.

Gandhiji opens his eyes. "Beta," he seems to say, in a warm whisper, as if he were speaking to himself. His dialogue was always with himself. "Son, give your sister Saroja, my grandfatherly blessings. Could I permit myself to say that? May this be a blessed marriage."

Gandhiji closes his eyes. His spinning wheel seems to move again.

How to rise now? How move. You would burst into tears. But you cannot. The feet do not want to move. Yet must you rise, and leave. How will you cross the threshold. And where will you go, now?

I was one of the hundreds and thousands of people Gandhiji knew. He knew every one, and everyone's family: five brothers and two sisters, the father dead, and the mother paralysed, in Lahore, Punjab; one son left at home, and the others at the War in Europe. But here so many, many young men, in political prisons, some fasting, yet others spinning. He could almost hear the women cry. And all the daughters were Saroja to him. Just as I was his Beta, son – like any other son. And he was Bapuji, our father.

Outside under the beating sun, there is before me fold after fold of untilled land. Thistle and mustard green grow between the folds. There is a lone babul tree, somewhere far away. And maybe some yellowed grass, beyond, on the edge. The eagles still fly. The earth is hotter.

# Chronology

1908 November 8: Raja Rao is born in Hassan, Mysore, India.

1912 Mother, Gauramma, passes away.

1915 Raja Rao enters Madarsa-i-Aliya, a famous school, in Hyderabad.

1925 He graduates from the Madarsa.

1926 He studies English with Eric Dickinson and French with Jack Hill at the Aligarh Muslim University, Aligarh, United Provinces.

1927 Raja Rao studies at Nizam's College, Hyderabad .

1929 He graduates with a Bachelor of Arts Degree in English and History and is invited by Sir Patrick Geddes to the College des Ecossais, Montpellier. He receives the Asiatic Scholarship for study abroad awarded by the government of Hyderabad. Travels to France to begin studies in French language and literature at the University of Montpellier.

1931 He begins writing, in Kannada, for the Periodical *Jaya Karnataka* (Dharwar). He goes on to research at Sorbonne for the next three years on the Indian influence on Irish literature under the supervision of Louis Cazamian.

1932 He is appointed to the editorial board of *Mercure de France* (Paris), a position he holds until 1937.

1933 Raja Rao returns to India to live in Pandit Taranath's ashram in Tungabhadra, Madras Presidency. He publishes his first stories: the French versions of "Javni" in *Europe* (Paris) and of "Akkayya" in *Cahiers du Sud* (Paris). He subsequently publishes "Javni" in *Asia* (New York).

1934 He publishes the French version of "A Client" in *Mercure de France* (Paris), and "In Khandesh" in *Adelphi* (London).

1935 He publishes "The True story of Kanakapala: Protector of Gold" in *Asia.*

1937 He publishes the French version of "The Little Gram Shop" in *Vendredi* (Paris).

---

This Chronology is based on R Parthasarathy's compilation in *World Literature Today.*

| 1938 | Raja Rao publishes his first novel *Kanthapura* in London and "The Cow of the Barricades" in *Asia*. |
| 1939 | He meets the Mother in Sri Aurobindo Ashram, Pondicherry, and then lives in Ramana Maharishi's ashram in Tiruvannamalai, Madras Presidency. In the same year he edits with Ahmed Ali, the periodical *Tomorrow* (Bombay) until 1940. |
| 1940 | Raja Rao's father, H V Krishnaswami, passes away. |
| 1942 | He lives for six months in Mahatma Gandhi's ashram in Sevagram, Central Provinces, and becomes active in an underground movement against the British. |
| 1943 | He meets Sri Atmananda Guru in Trivandrum, Travancore. |
| 1944 | He publishes "Narsiga" in *Horizon* (Bombay). |
| 1947 | He publishes *The Cow of the Barricade and Other Stories* and the Indian edition of *Kanthapura* in Madras. |
| 1948 | Raja Rao returns to France. |
| 1950 | He visits the United States. |
| 1953 | His short story "India – A Story" is published in *Encounter* (London). |
| 1958 | He travels in India with Andre Malraux, de Gaulle's emissary to Nehru. |
| 1959 | His story "The Cat" is published in the *Chelsea Review* (New York). |
| 1960 | Raja Rao publishes a second novel, *The Serpent and the Rope*, in London. |
| 1963 | He publishes "Nimka" and "The Policeman and the Rose" in *The Illustrated Weekly of India* (Bombay). He visits Yaddo in Saratoga Springs, New York, and publishes the US editions of *Kanthapura* and *The Serpent and the Rope* in New York. |
| 1964 | He receives the Sahitya Akademi Award from the government of India for *The Serpent and the Rope*. |
| 1965 | His third novel *The Cat and Shakespeare: A Tale of Modern India* is published in New York along with the French version of *Comrade Kirillov* in Paris. |
| 1966 | Raja Rao begins teaching Indian Philosophy each fall semester at the University of Texas in Austin. |

| | |
|---|---|
| 1968 | He publishes the Indian edition of *The Serpent and the Rope* in New Delhi. |
| 1969 | He is awarded the Padma Bhushan by the Government of India. |
| 1971 | His novel *The Cat and Shakespeare* is published in an Indian edition in New Delhi. |
| 1972 | He is named a Fellow of the Woodrow Wilson International Centre, Washington DC. |
| 1976 | He publishes *Comrade Kirillov* in English in New Delhi. |
| 1978 | Raja Rao's collection of short stories, *The Policeman and the Rose*, is published in New Delhi. |
| 1980 | He retires from his post as Professor Emeritus of Philosophy from the University of Texas in Austin. The Malayalam version of *The Cat and Shakespeare*, the only novel of his translated into an Indian language, is published. |
| 1984 | He is elected Honorary Fellow of the Modern Language Association of America. In the same year he visits Japan. |
| 1988 | The first part of his trilogy *The Chessmaster and His Moves* is published in New Delhi. He is named the Tenth Laureate of the Neustadt International Prize for Literature. He receives the Neustadt Prize in a formal public ceremony at the University of Oklahoma in June. The Autumn issue of *World Literature Today* is dedicated to Raja Rao's work. |
| 1989 | He publishes *On the Ganga Ghat*, a collection of stories, with Vision Books, New Delhi. |
| 1997 | His collection of essays, *The Meaning of India*, is published by Vision Books, New Delhi. |
| 1997 | Raja Rao is elected a Fellow of the Sahitya Akademi. |
| 1997 | A symposium, *Word as Mantra: The Art of Raja Rao*, is conducted by the University of Texas, Austin. |
| 1998 | His biography on the life of the Mahatma, *The Great Indian Way: A Life of Mahatma Gandhi*, is published by Vision Books, New Delhi. |

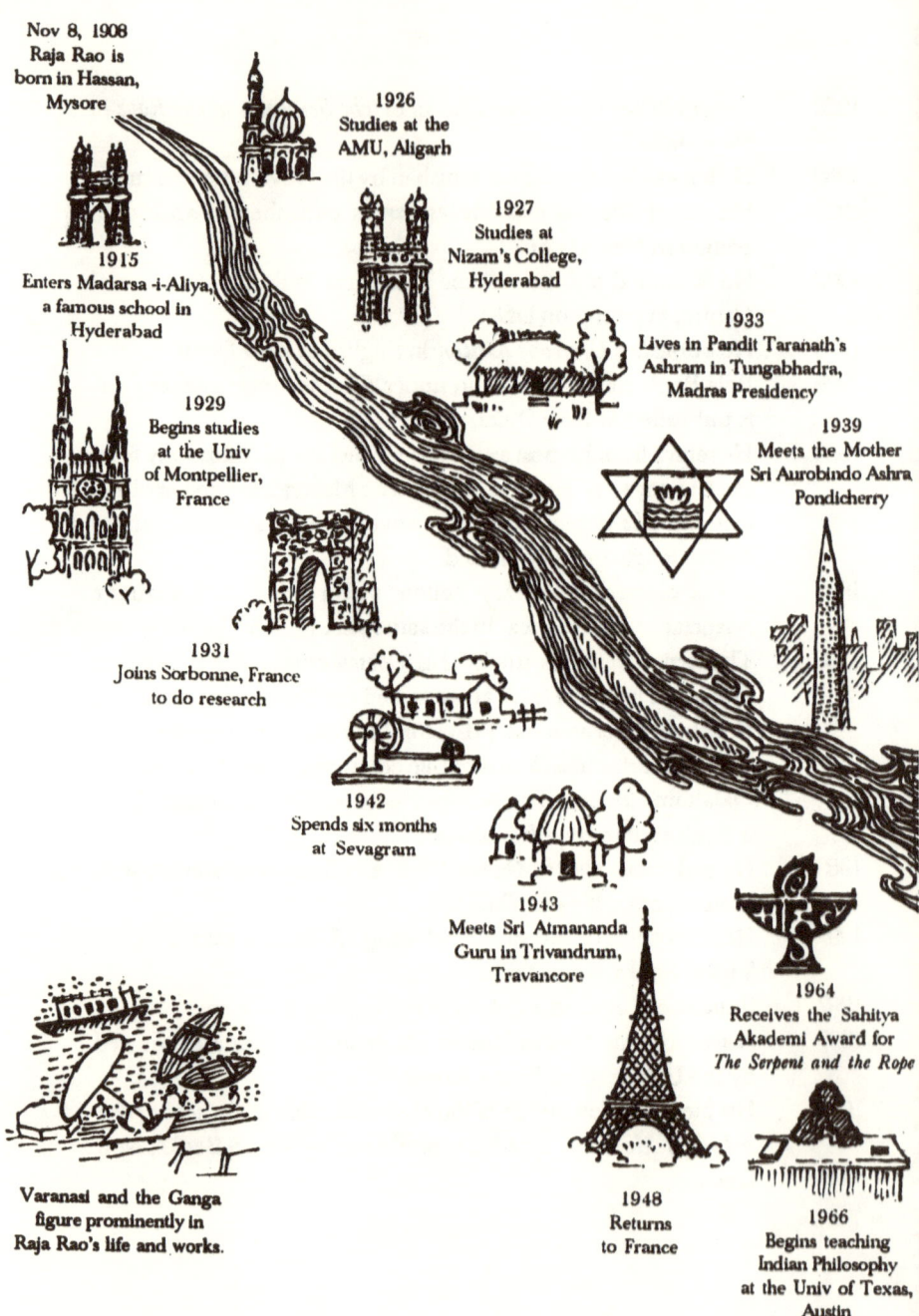

Nov 8, 1908
Raja Rao is
born in Hassan,
Mysore

1926
Studies at the
AMU, Aligarh

1927
Studies at
Nizam's College,
Hyderabad

1915
Enters Madarsa-i-Aliya,
a famous school in
Hyderabad

1933
Lives in Pandit Taranath's
Ashram in Tungabhadra,
Madras Presidency

1929
Begins studies
at the Univ
of Montpellier,
France

1939
Meets the Mother
Sri Aurobindo Ashra
Pondicherry

1931
Joins Sorbonne, France
to do research

1942
Spends six months
at Sevagram

1943
Meets Sri Atmananda
Guru in Trivandrum,
Travancore

1964
Receives the Sahitya
Akademi Award for
*The Serpent and the Rope*

Varanasi and the Ganga
figure prominently in
Raja Rao's life and works.

1948
Returns
to France

1966
Begins teaching
Indian Philosophy
at the Univ of Texas,
Austin

# Why not just flow with the Ganga ...
### – RAJA RAO

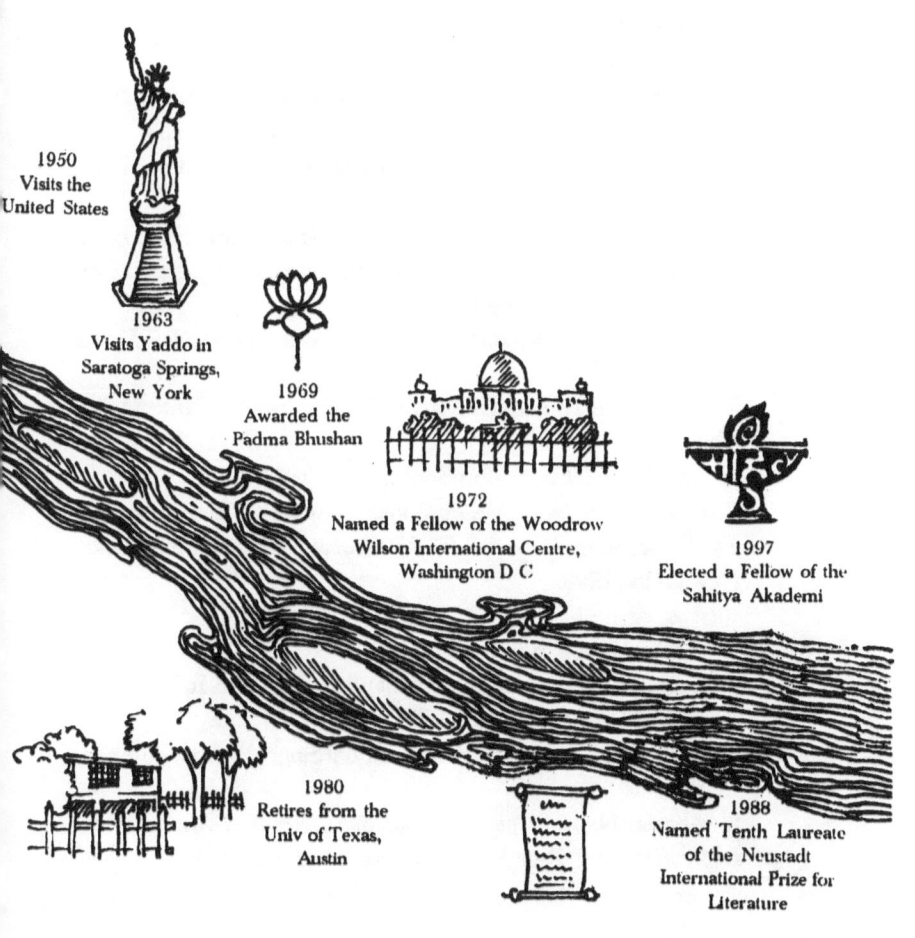

1950
Visits the
United States

1963
Visits Yaddo in
Saratoga Springs,
New York

1969
Awarded the
Padma Bhushan

1972
Named a Fellow of the Woodrow
Wilson International Centre,
Washington D C

1997
Elected a Fellow of the
Sahitya Akademi

1980
Retires from the
Univ of Texas,
Austin

1988
Named Tenth Laureate
of the Neustadt
International Prize for
Literature

# Bibliography

## Books by Raja Rao

1. *Kanthapura*, George Allen and Unwin, London, 1938; Indian ed, Oxford University Press, Champak Library, Bombay, 1947; US ed, New Direction, New York, 1963.

2. *The Cow of the Barricades and Other Stories*, Oxford University Press, Champak Library, Bombay, 1947.

3. *The Serpent and the Rope*, John Murray, London, 1960; Indian ed, Hind Pocket Books, Delhi, 1968; US ed, Pantheon Books, New York, 1965.

4. *The Cat and Shakespeare: A Tale of Modern India,* Macmillan, New York, 1965; Indian ed, Hind Pocket Books, Delhi, 1971. (First published as "The Cat," in *Chelsea Review,* New York, Summer, 1959.)

5. *Comrade Kirillov*, Orient Paperbacks, New Delhi, 1976. (First published in French as *La Comrade Kirillov*, trans Georges Fradier, Calman-Levy, Paris, 1966.)

6. *The Policeman and the Rose*, Oxford University Press, New Delhi, 1978.

7. *The Chessmaster and His Moves*, Vision Books, New Delhi, 1988.

8. *On the Ganga Ghat*, Vision Books, New Delhi, 1989.

9. *The Meaning of India*, Vision Books, New Delhi, 1997.

10. *The Great Indian Way: A Life of Mahatma Gandhi*, Vision Books, New Delhi, 1998.

## Books Edited by Raja Rao

1. *Changing India: An Anthology*, (eds) Raja Rao and Iqbal Singh, Allen and Unwin, London, 1939.

2. *Whither India?*, (eds) Raja Rao and Iqbal Singh, Padma, Bombay, 1948.

3. Jawaharlal Nehru, *Soviet Russia: Some Random Sketches and Impressions,* (ed) Raja Rao, Chetana, Bombay, 1949.

## Raja Rao's Contributions to Books

1. "Recollections of E M Forster," in *E M Forster: A Tribute with Selections from His Writings on India,* (ed) K Natwar Singh, Harcourt, Brace and World, New York, 1964, pp 15-32.
2. "The Meaning of India," in *The First Writers Workshop Literary Reader,* (ed) P Lal, Writers Workshop, Calcutta, 1972, page numbers not available.
3. "The Caste of English," in *Awakened Conscience: Studies in Commonwealth Literature,* (ed) C D Narasimhaiah, Sterling Publishers (P) Ltd, New Delhi, 1978, pp 420-22.
4. "The Cave and the Conch," in *The Eye of the Beholder: Indian Writing in English,* (ed) Maggie Butcher, Commonwealth Institute, London, 1983, pp 44-45.

## Books on Raja Rao

1. *Raja Rao,* M K Naik, Twayne, New York, 1972.
2. *Raja Rao: A Critical Study of His Work,* C D Narasimhaiah, Arnold Heinemann, New Delhi, 1972.
3. *Truth Within Fiction: A Study of Raja Rao's The Serpent and the Rope,* Alaister Niven, Writers Workshop, Calcutta, 1978.
4. *Perspectives on Raja Rao,* (ed) K K Sharma, Vimal Prakashan, Ghaziabad, 1980.
5. *Raja Rao and Cultural Tradition,* Paul Sharrad, Sterling Publishers (P) Ltd, New Delhi, 1987.
6. *Raja Rao: The Man and His Works,* Shyamala A Narayan, Sterling Publishers (P) Ltd, New Delhi, 1988.
7. *World Literature Today,* Special Issue on Raja Rao, University of Oklahoma, Autumn, 1988.
8. *The Novels of Raja Rao,* Esha Dey, Prestige Publishers, New Delhi, 1992.

## Additional Bibliography

"Raja Rao: A Selected Checklist of Primary and Secondary Material," S R Jamkhandi, *Journal of Commonwealth Literature,* XVI (1), 1981, p 132.

I am a man of silence. And words emerge from that silence with light, of light, and light is sacred. One wonders that there is the word at all – sabda – and one asks oneself, where did it come from? How did it arise? I have asked this question for many, many years. I've asked it of linguists. I have asked it of poets, I've asked it of scholars. The word seems to come first as an impulsion from the nowhere, and then as a prehension, and it becomes here & there esoteric – till it begins to be concrete. And the concrete becoming even more & earthy, and the earthy communicated, on the common word also, seems to possess less of that original light.

The writer or the poet is he who seeks back the common word to its origin of silence, that the manifested word become light. There was a poet of the West, the Austrian poet, Rainer Maria Rilke. He said objects come to be named. One of the ideas that has involved me deeply these many years is: where does the word dissolve & become meaning? Meaning itself is beyond the sound of the word.

———
The 1988 Neustadt Prize acceptance speech handwritten by Raja Rao. This was originally published in *World Literature Today*, 62:4 1988, and has been reproduced here with the permission of the writer and the *WLT* editor.

# About the Editor

**Makarand Paranjape** is currently an Associate Professor in the Department of Humanities and Social Sciences at the Indian Institute of Technology, New Delhi. He studied at, and received his Masters and Doctorate degrees from, the University of Illinois, USA.

A poet, novelist, critic and columnist, he is the author of *The Serene Flame* and *Playing the Dark God* (poetry); *This Time I Promise It'll Be Different: Short Stories* and *The Narrator: A Novel* (fiction); *Mysticism in Indian English Poetry* and *Decolonization and Development: Hind Swaraj Revisioned* (criticism). He has also edited six books, published several academic papers, and is a well-known literary journalist. He travels extensively, participating in both academic and non-academic gatherings, engaging in issues of culture, criticism, spirituality and society.

## ABOUT KATHA

Katha, a registered nonprofit organization set up in September 1989, works in the areas of education, publishing and community development and endeavours to spread the joy of reading, knowing and living amongst adults and children. Our main objective is **to enhance the pleasures of reading for children and adults**, for experienced readers as well as for those who are just beginning to read. Our attempt is also to stimulate an interest in lifelong learning that will help the child grow into a confident, self-reliant, responsible and responsive adult, as also to help break down gender, cultural and social stereotypes, encourage and foster excellence, applaud quality literature and translations in and between the various Indian languages and work towards community revitalization and economic resurgence. The two wings of Katha are **Katha Vilasam** and **Kalpavriksham**

**KATHA VILASAM,** the Story Research and Resource Centre, was set up to foster and applaud quality Indian literature and take these to a wider audience through quality translations and related activities like **Katha Books, Academic Publishing**, the **Katha Awards** for fiction, translation and editing, **Kathakaar** – the Centre for Children's Literature, **Katha Barani** – the Translation Resource Centre, the **Katha Translation Exchange Programme, Translation Contests. Kanchi** – the Katha National Institute of Translation promotes translation through **Katha Academic Centres** in various Indian universities, **Faculty Enhancement Programmes** through Workshops, seminars and discussions, **Sishya** – Katha Clubs in colleges, **Storytellers Unlimited** – the art and craft of storytelling and **KathaRasa** – performances, art fusion and other events at the Katha Centre.

**KALPAVRIKSHAM,** the Centre for Sustainable Learning, was set up to foster quality education that is relevant and fun for children from nonliterate families, and to promote community revitalization and economic resurgence work. These goals crystallized in the development of the following areas of activities. **Katha Khazana** which includes **Katha Student Support Centre, Katha Public School, Katha School of Entrepreneurship, KITES** – the Katha Information Technology and eCommerce School, **Iccha Ghar – The Intel Computer Clubhouse @ Katha, Hamara Gaon** and **The Mandals** – Maa, Bapu, Balika, Balak and Danadini, **Shakti Khazana** was set up for skills upgradation and income generation activities comprising the Khazana Coop. **Kalpana Vilasam** is the cell for regular research and development of teaching/learning materials, curricula, syllabi, content comprising **Teacher Training, TaQeEd — The Teachers Alliance for Quality eEducation. Tamasha's World!** comprises **Tamasha! the Children's magazine,** *Dhammakdhum! www.tamasha.org* **and ANU – Animals, Nature and YOU!**

# BE A FRIEND OF KATHA!

If you feel strongly about Indian literature, you belong with us! KathaNet, an invaluable network of our friends, is the mainstay of all our translation-related activities. We are happy to invite you to join this ever-widening circle of translation activists. Katha, with limited financial resources, is propped up by the unqualified enthusiasm and the indispensable support of nearly 5000 dedicated women and men.

We are constantly on the lookout for people who can spare the time to find stories for us, and to translate them. Katha has been able to access mainly the literature of the major Indian languages. Our efforts to locate resource people who could make the lesser-known literatures available to us have not yielded satisfactory results. We are specially eager to find Friends who could introduce us to Bhojpuri, Dogri, Kashmiri, Maithili, Manipuri, Nepali, Rajasthani and Sindhi fiction.

Do write to us with details about yourself, your language skills, the ways in which you can help us, and any material that you already have and feel might be publishable under a Katha programme. All this would be a labour of love, of course! But we do offer a discount of 20% on all our publications to Friends of Katha.

Write to us at –
Katha
A-3 Sarvodaya Enclave
Sri Aurobindo Marg
New Delhi   110 017

Call us at: 652 4350, 652 4511
or E-mail us at: info@katha.org

# OUR RECENT TITLES

A celebration of the Indian experience in all its diversity.
*The Express Magazine*

## FORSAKING PARADISE: STORIES FROM LADAKH
### BY ABDUL GHANI SHEIKH
Translated and Edited by Ravina Aggarwal

The first ever collection of Urdu stories from Ladakh, in English
translation, showcasing Ladakhi society today.

## HOME AND AWAY
A COLLECTION OF KANNADA SHORT STORIES
BY RAMACHANDRA SHARMA
Translated by Padma and Ramachandra Sharma

Fifteen engrossing stories by one of the leading writers of the Navodaya
Movement in the Kannada literary scene, reflecting the preoccupations
of a writer in his own country and abroad.

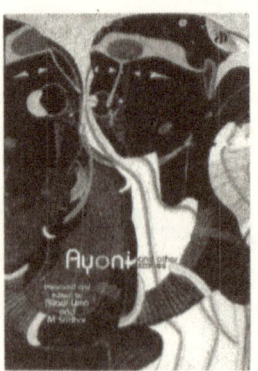

## AYONI AND OTHER STORIES
A COLLECTION OF TELUGU SHORT STORIES
Translated and edited by Alladi Uma and M Sridhar

Outstanding stories by men and women writers, spanning a centur
portraying the pain, struggle and triumph of womanhood with
compassion, sensitivity and integrity.

# The best of India translated.
*– India Today*

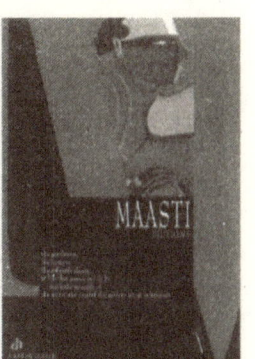

## MAASTI
ED BY RAMACHANDRA SHARMA

Simple stories of ordinary men and women pulsate with life at Masti's masterly hand.
*– The Indian Express*

... immensely readable, gentle ...
*– The Pioneer*

## MOUNI
ED BY LAKSHMI HOLMSTRÖM

The most sensitively edited and translated Indian book ... a dazzling collaboration of love.
*– Indian Review of Books*

... brilliant translations.
*– The Book Review*

## BASHEER
ED BY VANAJAM RAVINDRAN

The aesthetically designed, and almost flawlessly printed book is a must for all those who are lovers of the exquisite and the brilliant in Indian literature.
*– The Hindustan Times*

... A celebration of the Indian experience in all its diversity.
*– The Express Magazine*

Katha's collection of short stories are a treasure, once again.
*– The Week*

Katha's work is of tremendous significance in building a new India.
*– Business Standard*

www.ingramcontent.com/pod-product-compliance
Lightning Source LLC
Chambersburg PA
CBHW030536030726
47495CB00004B/1015